The
BROKEN
Road

The Broken Road Series, Book 1

MELISSA HUIE

ISBN-10: 0-9980511-0-1

ISBN-13: 978-0-9980511-0-9

Editorial provided by Swift Ink Editorial Services, BookIvy Word Studio http://bookivyediting.com.

Proofing provided by Ultra Editing
www.ultraeditingco.com
Formatting Provided by Cassy Roop, Pink Ink Designs
http://www.pinkinkdesigns.com/
Cover Design by Robin Harper, Wicked by Design
www.wickedbydesigncovers.com
Model – William Scott
www.facebook.com/WilliamScott55555
Model Photography by James Sasser
www.facebook.com/sasserfrazphotography
Author Photography by Cassy Roop, Pink Ink Designs
http://www.pinkinkdesigns.com/

To my wonderful and amazing children—
Always reach for the stars. I know you can do
anything you set your mind to.
I love you.

To my amazing husband—
Without your love and support, this wouldn't have
been possible.
Thank you. I love you.

This book is dedicated to the memory of my mother.
You always knew I would put my imagination to good
use. You always believed in me.
I love you and miss you every day.

Jayme—
Thanks for purchasing
the books. I hope you
love them!
miss you guys!
Melissa Huie

THE
BROKEN
Road

CHAPTER 1

I SHOULD HAVE STAYED IN BED. I really should have just stayed in bed.

The mantra repeated in my mind as I watched the police officer approach my car with his trusty ticket book in hand. After my day from hell, this was the last thing I needed.

"Ma'am, I clocked you at 66 in a 55 mile per hour zone. License and registration please."

I smiled and flipped open my pink leather wallet and found the empty space where my driver's license should have been. My heart sank. My mind retraced where I'd had it last. Was it at home? At the office? I scrambled through the contents of my black messenger bag, tossing makeup, tissues, change, and other items onto the passenger seat.

"Excuse me, miss. Is there a problem?" he asked, peering at me.

No doubt he would rather have been in his warm car instead of on the side of the parkway in the bone-chilling weather. I gave him my most brilliant "I'm cute, please don't be mad at me" smile.

"I'm sorry. I am not normally this disorganized. It's here somewhere."

Apparently, it didn't work because he sighed and looked away. My stomach dropped when all I found at the bottom of the bag was a crinkled receipt and a lint covered mint. At my wit's end, I finally felt around the pocket of my pea coat and exhaled in relief when my fingers wrapped around hard plastic. I handed over my paperwork and with a huff, the officer headed to the warmth of his car.

I heaved a heavy sigh. This day had been the pits, doomed before the sun came up. I didn't hear my alarm clock. It took my lab mix, Penny, practically licking my hand off before I raised my head off the pillow and realized the time. In jumping out of bed, I barely missed her brown paw and ended up crashing into my dresser. Somehow, I managed to shower and dress without any major issues, but then I spilled hot coffee on my hand and left my lunch sitting on the kitchen counter.

Going to work wasn't the best idea either. I tore a nail, spilled even more coffee on my brand-new shirt, and a junior partner yelled at me because he forgot to put back his file in its proper place. And to top it all off, my period started two days early. I was hungry, tired, and mentally drained. This day needed to end.

A knock on my window interrupted my pity party.

"Ms. Connors, here is your paperwork. You have the right to protest this ticket by appearing in court on March 3rd. Please watch your speed." He handed me my documents and returned to his car. I glanced at the ticket. One hundred dollars. Great. One more thing to subtract from my meager budget.

***

IT TOOK LONGER THAN usual to get home, thanks to going the speed limit. Two tickets in one day would have sent me beyond my breaking point. My Volvo was on autopilot and pulled onto Hazelnut Court and into the carport of my half of a 1980's red brick duplex in the town of Crofton, Maryland. It was small with a backyard barely big enough for Penny, but it suited us just fine. I unlocked the door to the mudroom and forced my way in as Penny tried to rush out.

"Whoa, Penny! Whoa!"

Whistling for her, I opened the back door to the fenced-in yard and she scampered through. We usually went on a nice long walk after work, but with the chill in the air and how crappy the day had been, that was the last thing I wanted to do. While Penny ran around outside, I added food to her bowl and checked the contents of the fridge for myself. My New Year's resolution was the same as everyone's—to eat healthier and get into better shape. Unfortunately, the workouts had stopped before they even started, so I really had to make an effort with the eating part. However, everything in the fridge required actual cooking. *Heck no*, I thought. My stomach rumbled, and I didn't feel like slaving over the stove. I opened up the back door and whistled for Penny. She bounded over, a slobbery ball in her mouth.

"Aw, Penny. It's too cold out. Get inside. Come on, baby girl! Where's your woobie? Let's get your woobie!"

The fake enthusiasm worked. Penny dropped her ball and barreled inside. I headed upstairs while she scrounged around in her toy box for her favorite toy. As the old water pipes heated up, I studied myself in the mirror.

I hadn't gone on a date since I'd broken up with my fiancé, Tommy Greene, a year ago. Since then, not much had changed. At twenty-six, I was a size twelve with curves. Not overweight, but not going to win any fitness contests, that's for sure. I could look good when I wanted to, but lately, the effort had been minimal. Up until recently, work had been so hectic that there wasn't time to meet anyone new. And, well, nor did I really want to. I'd only been in love twice and both relationships ended with being "just friends".

Just friends...with no benefits.

After the shower and feeling a million times better, I threw on a pair of sweats, pulled my dark brown hair into a messy ponytail, and padded down to the kitchen to address the food issue. Penny was at her food bowl, searching for scraps.

"Oh, my piglet Penny, what am I going to do with you?"

She greedily took the butcher's beef bone I offered her into the living room while I pulled out the takeout menus. I was contemplating the menu for Hunan Express when the phone rang.

"Hello?"

"Hey, Megan. What's going on?"

The husky voice sent my heart racing. Shane Turner. We'd been really good friends for the last nine years. Well, he thought that we were just friends. I had been, and pretty much still was, completely in love with him. Not that he knew, of course. We were constantly together, whether it was hanging out with our other friends or closing down the bars. But he always caught the eye of the prettier, skinnier girls and I was the insecure idiot. Our relationship cooled after I found him at a restaurant with a strange girl and I treated her rudely. It was pure jealousy; I acted as if I had a claim to him when I really didn't. After calming down, it mortified me to learn that the girl was an old family friend. He accepted my apology, but our friendship became awkward and strained. The death of my father slowly mended it, but it was never the same. "Just friends" seemed to be where our paths would lead. No matter how many lies I told myself, our friendship was too important. And it didn't matter anyway. Shane was dating someone else and that someone was not me.

"Hey, Shane. We're just hanging out. What's up?"

"What are you doing later? I'm thinking about swinging by there and picking up that movie I left last week."

"Yeah, that's fine. I'm home now, about to order Chinese, so come by whenever. Do you want me to order you something?" *Please?* I silently begged.

"No, I'm good. I'm meeting Allison for dinner." I mentally groaned at the mention of his new girlfriend. Shane and Allison had been dating for the last few months and it seemed to be going well. She appeared nice enough, but I wasn't one hundred percent sold on her. She wasn't good enough for him. Hell, nobody is good enough for him.

"Oh. Okay. That's fine. I'm in for the night, so whenever."

I tried to play it cool, but inwardly I hoped he would come over alone. Being the third wheel with Shane and his girlfriend? Yeah, no thanks. I'd rather pass.

"Sounds good," he replied, sounding rushed. "Hey, I need to go." And before I realized what had happened, he'd hung up.

"Stupid Allison," I grumbled to Penny.

I shouldn't get mad at Allison. After all, no one—except for my best friend Jen—had any idea that my feelings for Shane were this strong. Even when Tommy and I were together, Shane always had a piece of my heart, but I had given up on the idea of "us". We had both grown up and, sadly, apart. It was when I moved back home that we became close again. But no matter how much time passed, Shane always made my heart jump whenever he came near me.

I threw myself on the oversized brown couch, covered up with a burgundy fleece blanket, and called the restaurant for delivery. My gaze landed on the game console and all the fitness games gathering dust. Some games had never been opened. A twinge of guilt gnawed at me for the money I'd spent and the lack of effort that I'd put forth. I shook away the guilt from my head and stuck out my tongue at the offensive console. I didn't need a game system to tell me how much weight I'd gained. Not today.

Penny came over, laid her head on my leg, and immediately put me at ease.

"That's my good girl," I murmured, rubbing her silky ears.

I rescued Penny right after I moved back to Crofton, saving her from a shelter. In turn, she helped me get through a tough time. The breakup was a total life changer for me. I went from living with someone and planning a life with him to being on my own. Tommy and I were together for three years. We bought a condo in Virginia and were going to get married. As a rising star in the FBI, Tommy's dream assignment was New York City, which was hard for me to accept. Virginia was close enough to my mom and brother that I didn't panic, but far enough away that we had our space. For a while, he understood. However, he never stopped chasing his dream. Once it started to become more of a reality, our relationship went downhill.

Tommy changed; his job became more important than our relationship. Tension began to build. We fought about the everyday mundane things like chores and bills; then the fighting escalated to the lack of trust and the future of us. Then, he decided one day that he was done. He was through with the fighting and he wasn't happy anymore. A good thing in hindsight; I wasn't ready to get married. At least not then and not to him, not when we were either fighting or not speaking to each other. We had lost what was important. So, eight months ago we sold our condo in Virginia. He went to New York and I came back to my hometown. We still occasionally exchanged texts, the cordial "hellos" and "how are yous?" I thought about him occasionally but I knew it was for the best. His career was his first priority and I was not willing to leave my family to accommodate it.

The doorbell interrupted my train of thought and Penny started her happy wiggle. I quickly put her in the mudroom so she wouldn't charge the delivery guy and grabbed some money from my purse. I was startled when I opened the door. Standing on my front porch was Shane holding my dinner.

"Trying to steal my dinner? Don't make me sic Penny on you!" I joked as I let him in.

As always, he looked gorgeous. Dressed in his usual attire of baggy jeans, a black long sleeve shirt, and motorcycle jacket, my heart hurled into my throat at the sight of him.

"Oh, what? Death by pooch?" he shot back, following me into the kitchen.

He shook his head when I offered him money for the dinner. His six-foot-three, 230-pound hockey player frame filled my small kitchen. Shane had this presence about him that always made me feel safe and secure. That same presence made me want to fold myself into his muscular arms. Shane gave fantastic hugs.

"I thought you were meeting Allison for dinner," I said, taking the food out of the bag.

Shane shrugged out of his leather jacket and hung it on the back of the chair then opened the door for Penny.

"Yeah, we were supposed to meet her brother later on, but she said that she didn't feel well."

He poked his head in my fridge.

"What's up with the rabbit food in here?" he asked, taking out a beer and sitting at the table.

"You know my New Year's resolution." I smacked his hand as he inched toward my egg roll. "I'm trying to be healthier."

Shane took a swig of beer and laughed. "Right. That's why you have Chinese food for dinner, beer in your fridge, and a bag full of candy up in the cabinet."

"Whatever. That's my emergency stash. Every woman needs to have her emergency stash," I said with an indignant huff. "Besides, you can't complain about the beer, especially since you drink it. Here. You might as well eat this since you can't find anything else."

I tried so hard to not act like a total idiot, but the goofy smile couldn't be helped as I handed him a plate. Penny's tail thumped on the wood floor as she looked expectantly at the food. We ate for a few minutes in silence. My heart raced a mile a minute; every time I looked up, his hazel eyes stared straight back at me. It was as if he could hear my heart skipping.

"So what's going on tonight?" I dumped my leftover rice into Penny's bowl and put the plate in the sink.

Shane tiredly rubbed his face and goatee. His brown hair looked like it had been weeks since it had last seen the barber. He stretched his long legs out in front him and yawned.

"I'm not sure. I'm beat. Adrian has had me working all night on this special project and then I was running around all morning. I feel like I haven't sat down all day."

"That sucks. So why aren't you at home sleeping?" I replied, putting away the food.

Shane stood up and silently washed the dishes. As he dried his hands on the dishtowel, he turned and looked at me.

"Honestly, that's the main reason I'm here. You remember that Ben is getting married to Paige, right?" he asked, mentioning his roommate. "Well, Ben has accepted a job in Baltimore near Paige's condo. So he's moving in with her next week. The lease on the apartment is up anyway, and since I'm practically broke I need a place to crash," he said, his eyes boring holes into mine.

It took a beat before I fully grasped what he was saying. *Holy shit, he wants to move in with me,* I thought. The romantic, wishful part of me started doing a happy dance in my head, until the smarter, more realistic side smacked the other one down and told it to shut up.

"So, you're asking to move in." Caution filled my voice as I walked into the living room and sat on the couch.

Shane sat down at the opposite end facing me. *So, that's why he's here. I should have known.* The word "sucker" must've been stamped on my forehead. I could never say no to him and he knew that.

"It will only be for a little while, until I can get my own place. Please?" He gave me a pleading grin.

I chuckled and then became curious.

"What happened? How did things get so screwed up?" I asked casually.

"It's been building for a while. I lost my job at the dealership two years ago. At that point, I couldn't find anything substantial, except for side jobs working with Adrian. I couldn't keep up with the rent at the old place, so I was evicted and moved in with Ben. Credit cards were maxed out and I depleted my savings. But things are looking up. I'm paying off my debt a little bit at a time and I managed to get a full-time spot at the shop. I'm trying to clean up my act, but I really can't get a place of my own quite yet," he said quietly, almost as if he was ashamed.

I never knew about these problems, but then again, Tommy had kept me removed from most of my friends when we lived in Virginia. My best friend Jen was practically Shane's sister. She had told me a few times that he was having some issues, and that he was just being a regular pain in the ass, but she never went into detail. I felt a swell of pride for him; it took a lot for him to say that to me.

"I'm sorry to hear that. What about Allison? Why don't you move in with her?" I replied, playing with the string on my sock. I wasn't sure if I wanted to hear the answer to the question.

Shane gave a dry chuckle. "Yeah, we're not on that page yet. Plus, her two roommates don't really like me."

Relief settled over me. Then some slight apprehension. Could I block out these feelings? Yes, I had to. Besides, he had a girlfriend. We could be just friends...I hoped.

"Yeah, sure, you can move your stuff in," I said with a smile. "But only until you can find something on your own."

I pushed aside the doubt that had been looming. We were just friends. What could go wrong?

"Thanks Megs. You're so great to me."

He surprised me by wrapping me up in a hug. I quietly inhaled his cologne and closed my eyes. This was going to be harder than I thought.

I let out a fake chuckle and pulled back. "So, when are you bringing over your stuff?" I hope that I had a few days to prepare.

"Well, I figured you wouldn't leave me out in the cold, so I brought over what I could fit in the truck." He practically bounced off the couch and gave me a knowing smile.

I swatted him in the leg. "You arrogant jerk! What made you think I would say yes? I could have said no!"

"Aw, come on. You can never say no to me. Don't try to lie," he said, calling my bluff as he walked out the front door.

I sat on the couch for a minute, shocked at what had just happened. He had pulled a fast one on me. He was moving in and I didn't think I could have said no. I chuckled. He hadn't changed one bit. Still used his charm and smile to get what he wanted.

While Shane brought in his pillows and trash bags of clothes, I made up his bed in the guest room. He added his toiletries to the bathroom and a pang of nervousness hit my gut. This was going to be interesting. There was only one shower in the house and my fantasies about the two of us in the shower flooded back. My face flushed and I quickly turned my attention to an invisible speck on the comforter.

"So, is Allison going to be okay with you living with me?"

He paused while he hung up a white polo shirt and winked. "She's just someone I like to have fun with. We're not serious, so she's cool with it."

"Ah. Okay. Good. I just wanted to make sure there weren't going to be any issues," I mumbled as I headed back down the stairs to cool off. These feelings would need to be separated if this was going to work. I quickly pulled on my shoes and winter coat for Penny's last walk of the night.

The temperature had dropped and the smell of snow lingered in the air. Penny and I quickly walked down the treelined street. I hoped she would hurry up and go already, but she took her sweet time. Twenty minutes later, we returned home to find Shane's black Ford F150 gone and the lights off. It was none of my business where he went. It was none of my concern. *Remember that, Megan!*

I shucked off my snow boots and coat, locked the

doors, set the alarm, and headed upstairs with Penny in tow. After peeling off my clothes, I paused. Normal sleepwear included underwear and nothing else. That had to change since Shane was living here. It would be awkward if he peeked in and saw me in nothing but my Victoria Secret panties. I slipped on a tank top shirt and cotton boxers and climbed underneath the cloud-soft down comforter. Penny climbed onto her large dog bed and did her usual routine of turning around until she got comfortable. This had been one hell of a day, and the last thought I had was, *Will Shane come home alone?*

CHAPTER 2

THE HYPNOTIC VOICE OF Bob Marley woke me up. I reached over to turn up the volume then quickly remembered that another person lived in my house. Shane had lived with me for the past week and I still wasn't used to having a roommate. So far, it hadn't been bad. He was barely around, so I sometimes forgot that he had a bed at my house.

Since Shane moved in, my morning routine had been completely out of whack. Instead of showering with the door open and my iPod blaring, I now started each morning by peeking out of my bedroom to see if he was around before darting across the hallway to the bathroom.

After a quick shower, I dried my hair and gathered

my pajamas in my arms. Clutching the bathrobe tightly, I tried to sneak back to my room. I thought I was safe until I heard a cough behind me.

"Do you always get up this early?"

His deep voice laced with sleep stopped me in my tracks. Shane stood in the doorway to his room blurry-eyed and wearing only green and white stripped boxers. I looked away, averting my eyes to anything but his broad shoulders and muscular arms that sent shivers down my spine.

"I'm sorry. I didn't mean to wake you up," I said with a sheepish grin.

Shane returned a sleepy smile of his own. "It's okay. I just got to bed an hour or so ago."

My mouth fell open. "What the heck were you doing until five thirty this morning?" Then I shook my head. "Never mind. I don't think I want to know. I forgot that you're such a night owl."

Shane chuckled. "Yeah, and you always go to bed early. When we were younger, I tried to get you to sneak out after midnight but you were always fast asleep. I remember that. I remember a lot actually. Have a good day at work." He gave me a wink and then closed the door behind him.

I didn't realize I had been holding my breath until I exhaled. *Damn, that man is beautiful.* I reminded myself to breathe. I shook my head and dove into my closet. I dressed in a knee-length wool black skirt, a ruffled button-down pink top, and black knee-high boots. With Penny at my heels, I quietly headed down the stairs to let her outside.

I had just let Penny back inside when I spied a paper sack on the table. To my delight, there were two of my favorite pumpernickel bagels. My heart swelled. He remembered. Shane's caring nature shouldn't have surprised me. He remembered the little things and never asked for anything in return. When my father died five years ago from a heart attack, Shane was my rock. He was the only person to see me fall apart, after trying to be strong for my mother and brother. He made sure that my mom's house was stocked with groceries. He ran our errands and did our laundry for a week. Shane's bad boy image suited him. He had a passion for fast bikes, large trucks, and causing mischief. Unfortunately, Shane had a wild streak and he used to run with a bad crowd. He had been arrested several times for bar brawls, drug possession, trespassing, and one time for indecent exposure. Thankfully, Shane grew up. Despite the baggy jeans, the tattoos, and the piercings, he was a sweetheart. Shane would give a stranger the shirt off his back and his last dollar if that person needed it. He had such a good heart and believed the best in people.

I left a note of thanks next to the bag, threw one of the bagels into my lunch bag, and headed out to the car. Halfway to work, my cell phone rang

"Hello?"

"Hey. Are we still meeting at the pub tonight?" Jen Walsh asked. We had been best friends since we were sophomores in high school. Our birthdays were a month apart. We grew up in the same neighborhood and had the same interests. Jen was the person who introduced me to Shane with the hopes that we'd end up as a couple, but to her dismay I started dating Tommy. After Tommy and I got engaged, she tried to talk me out of it. Jen said that Tommy wasn't good enough for me, that he was too focused on his career. I should have listened to her.

"Hey. Yeah, the pub's fine. What time again?" I asked, shifting into fourth gear.

"Let's make it eight. I have to drop Lauren off with my mom," Jen replied, naming her darling three-year-old daughter.

Jen was a nurse at the county hospital where she met her husband, Matt, a pediatrician. They married young, had a child a year later, and were happier than any other couple I knew. I often felt like I was living a child's life compared to theirs. To be twenty-six years old and already know what you were doing with your life, to have it already laid out in front of you—I couldn't wrap my head around it. I didn't even know what I was doing tomorrow.

"Yeah, that's fine. That will give me time to take Penny on her walk. Oh, by the way, did you hear? I have a new roommate," I joked.

Jen laughed. "Yeah, I heard. He sent me a text last week. I meant to call you. Is it weird? I mean, given your feelings and all?"

I hesitated as I pulled to a stop light. "It's okay. I haven't seen him around much. I'm sure there will be some awkward moments, but we're both adults now. I'm sure we can deal with any past issues."

"I bet." I heard a thump followed by a cry in the background. Jen cursed under her breath. "That was Lauren. I'll see you tonight."

I laughed as I pressed the END button. Lauren was the most daredevil child I had ever met. There wasn't a couch or playground set that she couldn't conquer.

***

I PULLED INTO THE office parking lot with a minute to spare. My Uncle Bob had hired me as an office manager right after I moved back to the area. While I suspected the offer was out of familial obligation, I liked to think that my degree in business management made it happen.

I walked into the outdated industrial office building, which totally contrasted to the firm's modern office suite. I stowed my bags underneath the desk, hung up my coat, and had started checking the voice mail when Paul Jenkins, a junior partner, came up to my desk.

"Good morning, Megan. I see you managed to find your alarm clock," he said snidely. Paul demanded the respect of a senior partner even though he was only a junior. He was on a very high horse and on more than one occasion, I had to knock him off of it.

"Yes, Paul. I was able to get out on time this morning, just like every other morning this week. Is there something I can help you with?" I didn't want to help him as much as I wanted to flick a rubber band directly between his beady rat eyes, but I refrained, begrudgingly.

"I need the Anderson file. Do you have it?" Paul demanded. His god-awful toupee slid slightly to the right of his dome-shaped head.

I checked the file log-out sheet. "I spoke to you and the other partners about this on Wednesday. We need to make sure that every file is signed in and out. According to this sheet, you signed it out on Monday. I suggest you speak with Miranda, your paralegal, about this." I always felt like I had to speak to Paul the same way I spoke to three-year-old Lauren—slowly, deliberately, and carefully avoiding big words.

Apparently, Paul didn't like that suggestion, as he turned up his large nose and walked off in a huff. He always treated me like his personal secretary and was a sexist, pigheaded jerk to boot. It was a golden rule that the front desk personnel were treated with the utmost respect. We had the ultimate control in the office. We decided if there would be regular or decaf coffee in the morning, and if that new pain-in-the-ass client would be settled in your office to your surprise or if you would just call him back later. And if you pissed us off enough, we would put your butt in the economy section in the middle seat close to the bathroom when we made your travel arrangements. We were the foundation of any firm and had the power to make or break your day.

I dialed Miranda's internal number. It was only fair to give her a heads up that Mr. Stick-Up-My-Butt Paul was on his way to her office.

"This is Miranda," her African accent trilled. Miranda Reinhardt was from South Africa and I just adored her. She was a beautiful, talented paralegal. We became fast friends when she joined the firm the previous year.

"Hey Mir. Just a warning. Paul is on the warpath. He's on his way back to your office," I hurriedly whispered, watching Paul as he stomped down the hall.

"Lovely. Thanks for the warning." She quickly

hung up and I could hear him down the hall loudly demanding the file.

I sighed and logged into my computer.

***

THE MORNING WENT by quickly. When lunchtime rolled around, I took my meager lunch and walked into the break room just in time to see Uncle Bob sneak some chips out of the vending machine. "Ahem," I said with a smile. "You know, if Aunt Karen knew that you're eating chips, she'd be highly upset."

Bob laughed. His big belly jiggled like Santa Claus. "Your Aunt Karen won't find out. This diet has me going crazy. Did you know she packed me a grapefruit and turkey sandwich today? That's all! How am I supposed to survive on that?"

I joined him at the table. "Aunt Karen doesn't want you to go through what Dad went through."

Uncle Bob grumbled. "Yeah, well. I'll die of starvation before that happens."

I laughed, handing him half my bagel. He gratefully took it.

"So, how are your mom and Kyle doing?" he asked, smearing cream cheese on his bagel. He closed his eyes in happiness after the first bite of carbohydrates.

"They're doing well. Kyle loves his job. He transferred to the station in Edgewater. Mom is happy that he'll be close to home and he's happy that he can mooch off her for dinner."

Bob nodded. "It's great to see Kyle come around. He was a bit of a hellion after your father died."

My younger brother had only been eighteen when my father died. He took it extremely hard. Kyle rebelled and acted as if he were invincible. Mom pleaded and begged him to straighten himself out, but it took getting arrested for vandalism and destruction of property for him to change his ways. Thanks to Uncle Bob, he was sentenced to community service and avoided time behind bars. Now Kyle was with the Anne Arundel County Police Department and doing a lot better.

"Good, Bob, I'm glad to see you're still here," Paul called as he walked into the room.

"Afternoon, Paul. What can I help you with?" asked Bob wearily. Paul had an affinity for being obnoxious, a trait not lost on Bob.

"Megan, I need to speak with Bob alone," Paul insisted arrogantly.

I rolled my eyes and kissed my uncle on the cheek. I left the room, but not before I gave Paul an evil glare. If it was so important, he should have taken it to the office. Bits of the conversation wafted up the hall.

"It's a high profile case, Bob. We should talk about assisting the district attorney on this one. Think of all the potential clients," Paul insisted.

"This is a federal case, Paul. My hands are tied. Besides, there could be a conflict of interest..." Bob's voice trailed off and I couldn't hear what he said next.

That's interesting. Uncle Bob is normally all about the high-profile cases, so why is he hedging about this particular one? I brushed the thought out of my mind. *It's not my concern*, I told myself.

Before I knew it, it was five o'clock. I had just logged off the computer when my phone rang.

"Connors, Piper, and Dobbins. This is Megan. How can I assist you?"

"Hey, Megs." I practically melted at the sound of his voice. *God, get a grip. I should not be acting this way.*

"Hey, Shane. What's going on?"

"Are you going to the pub tonight?" he asked. I heard traffic in the background so I figured he was on his bike.

"Yeah, I'm meeting Jen around eight. Are you gracing us with your presence?" I teased.

Shane laughed. "Yeah, I think Allison and I might join you. Is that cool with you?"

I silently groaned. *Seriously? Yes, I mind, you fool.*

"No, that's cool. We'll get a booth," I replied, hoping

he hadn't noticed the sarcasm in my voice.

"Okay, good. I'll see you at Artie's." And with that, he hung up.

I sighed. *Really?* Did he have to bring Allison with him? I sucked it up because I knew that if I wanted to hang out with him I'd have to deal with her tagging along.

***

SHANE'S TRUCK WAS parked on the street when I got home. I brought my bags inside and was greeted by an eager Penny. I went upstairs to trade my dress clothes for a pair of sweats and track shoes and clipped a leash to her collar.

"Come on, Pen. Let's go."

We took off down the street and made it a good mile and a half before turning around. By then my cheeks were freezing and my nose was running. I turned the corner and noticed a green Expedition pulling up to the house. Oddly enough, it stopped in the middle of the road and then drove away. I watched the taillights fade. *I wonder what that was all about,* I thought.

I deactivated the alarm in the house with a push of a button on my key ring and let Penny in. I quickly turned the alarm back on and locked the doors. I didn't know who they were, but I didn't want to advertise that I was home. My parents' rule on home safety echoed in my head: always lock your doors as soon as you're inside. I fed Penny and ran upstairs to take a shower before I left to meet everyone. It was six thirty and I was late.

CHAPTER 3

AN HOUR AND HALF LATER, I arrived at Artie's Pub and Grill. The noise was deafening and the pub was full of familiar faces. The old neighborhood hangout had always been the place to be on Friday nights. It took a while, but I finally saw Jen through the crowd and made my way over to her table.

"Hey, girl," Jen gave me a big hug. She was about three inches taller than I was, with long curly hair and deep green eyes. Her white cowl-neck sweater and dark jeans set off her tan from last month's Aruba trip nicely.

"Hi. It's crazy in here," I shouted. I could barely hear her above the din of the crowd.

"Yeah, it's nuts. It's too cold to do anything else. What better way to get rid of the wintertime blues than to come and drink?" Jen laughed.

I joined in. It felt so good to see her again. Even though we only lived twenty minutes apart, life just kept getting in the way.

"How are Matt and Lauren?" I motioned for the waiter and asked for a beer.

Jen sipped her wine. "They're great. Matt's working the late shift tonight at the hospital and Lauren's going through the terrible threes. How are you? How's work going?"

I launched into a tirade about the way Paul was treating everyone. I took a breather to sip my beer and felt a hand on my shoulder.

"Feel like moving over?" said a low voice. I looked up to see Shane and Allison standing next to me.

"Sure thing." I smiled weakly and shifted over next to Jen.

Shane sat down across from me. "Guess you couldn't get a booth, huh?" he joked, putting an arm around Allison's petite shoulder.

It felt like I had been punched in the heart. She was beautiful, with long black hair, very small frame, and stunning blue eyes. *He's hers, not mine,* I mentally chastised myself. I hoped I wasn't turning green with envy.

Jen gestured around. "Shoot. What do you think? I

had to practically bribe someone to get this table. You're lucky you're not sitting on the floor."

We all laughed. Memories of old times came flooding back. The four of us—Jen, Matt, Shane, and I—used to come here once a week and close down the bar. It was so easy back then. We didn't have the stresses that we had now—bills, mortgages, kids; they didn't exist to us.

But then times changed. I met Tommy three years ago here at Artie's, as a matter of fact. He had just graduated from the FBI academy in Quantico and was helping the Annapolis police with a case. He came in for a break and everything changed. We went out on a first date soon after and were inseparable from that point on. Not to say it wasn't without its period of awkwardness. Tommy never belonged to our group; he just never clicked. Shane, Matt, and Jen were always nice to him, but Tommy had grown up differently from the rest of us. He grew up with money, a private school education, and a trust fund. The rest of the group had blue-collar parents that struggled to send us to college. The fact that he was on the good side of the law hadn't given Shane warm and fuzzies either.

Most newcomers didn't last long. Allison definitely didn't belong with our group. Jen, who was the go-getter and tried to include everyone, even admitted that there was something off about her. Allison had never offered anything about herself except that she grew up in New Jersey. She didn't give off the vibe that she cared to get to know us. While we chatted, Alison stayed quiet and looked around as if we bored her. My big mouth opened to say something to that effect when she leaned into Shane and whispered something in his ear. Shane looked up and, I swear, a quick glance of nervousness crossed his face. It disappeared as quickly as it came so I brushed it off as a figment of my imagination.

"Hey, we need to go talk to someone. We'll be back later. Go ahead and order without us." He grabbed Allison's hand and disappeared into the crowd. I moved into her vacated seat.

"What the hell was that about?" A hint of annoyance came through in my voice. Jen gave me a sympathetic smile.

"You are still not over him, are you?" she asked gently.

I hesitated, then frowned and shook my head. As my best friend, she knew me better than I knew myself.

"I'm not, but I'm going to have to be. That's all there is to it." I took a long drink of my beer. "Are we ordering food? Screw my resolution. I need something with grease."

Jen handed me the menu. "You should get back out there. You need to meet someone."

I ignored her and perused the menu, settling on a cheeseburger and fries. Artie made the best burgers. "I know, I know. I don't feel like it. Does that make sense?"

Jen smacked my menu. "No, it doesn't. Look Megs, it's been eight months. You've got to be in need of some company by now," she said, scanning the room. "There, at the bar. See that guy with the navy blue polo? He's looking this way. Why not go and talk to him?"

I glanced in the general direction of where she was talking. I didn't want to be obvious, but the guy in the polo was pretty cute. Slim, tall, nicely dressed with beautiful Asian eyes, and drinking a beer. I blushed when he looked at me and I ducked my head.

"Jen, I'm not looking for a one-night stand. That is something I don't need. I want something more substantial. Like what you and Matt have."

Jen raised her eyebrow. "What? You want marriage and a baby? I think you're missing a step. You need to meet a man first."

I rolled my eyes. "No, dingdong. I want the connection that you guys feel for each other. Remember when you first met Matt? You knew he was the one for you from the moment you first saw him."

Jen sighed. "I know. I saw him in the elevator and it was instant. I had the goose bumps and butterflies. But sometimes it's not like that. Sometimes you have to really get to know the person first. You can't be scared to talk to someone just because you're not one hundred percent sure of the connection. Sometimes it takes time to build up to that. And how do you know you don't have that spark unless you go and try to meet someone?"

She was right and I hated it. Whenever we went out and guys would approach us, I'd give off the not-so-subtle signal that I wasn't interested. It wasn't like the guys were rude or obnoxious, or ugly even. The connection just wasn't there. I felt that instant attraction with both Shane and Tommy. Tommy's compassion and dry humor drew me in. He was a genuine, wonderful man. If we didn't have his career issue, I'd like to think that we might have stayed together. But at the same time, there was Shane. Even though we were just friends all those years ago, we seemed to be always touching. Play fighting, tickling, giving back rubs—all in the guise of friendship, but for me there was more to it. When we were in the same room, a magnetic force pulled us together. I knew why I wasn't actively dating. It would be very hard to top the feelings I had for Shane or Tommy.

I sheepishly hid behind my menu. "I know. This sounds so dumb, but I hate the idea of having to go up to a guy just to see if we have a little bit of a connection. I don't want to waste my time with a one-night stand. I

want to be able to look across the room and see fireworks.
I want that instant chemistry. I want the goose bumps
and the butterflies and the 'oh my God' feeling. I want
the magic spark." I winced at the outpouring of fairytale
nonsense. "Whatever. Can we please change the subject?
Let's just order," I pleaded.

Jen rolled her eyes and appeased me. She dropped
it, although I suspected we'd get back to my lack of a
love life sooner rather than later. We shifted gears and
talked about life in general; how Matt was opening
up his own practice, my mom's latest date, and Kyle's
transfer. Our food came and went, and still no sign of
Shane and Allison.

"I guess someone decided they were too good to
join us." I pulled on my jacket after paying the tab.
Jen shrugged. She knew Shane better than most. Only
someone special could lure him away from us.

"I don't know. She's very distant. Maybe she's just
insecure. We've been tight for so long; maybe she feels
like she's intruding. We should try to include her more.
If we want Shane to hang out with us we have to accept
that she'll be with him. We need to get used to that. It
wouldn't kill us to be friends with her," she said as we
left Artie's. Jen always tried to make the best of any
situation.

"I guess." I hit the button to unlock the Volvo and

started the engine. I was thankful that I had thought to get an automatic start installed.

"Well, talk to Shane about it. Maybe he has some suggestions. But I need to get home. It's the first time I've had the night to myself in so long and I plan to do some serious sleeping." I had to laugh. Lauren constantly crawled into bed with her parents and Jen always complained of lack of sleep. We hugged, promised to do something together again soon, and went our separate ways.

***

I GOT INTO THE Volvo and headed toward home. I was halfway there, singing along to Aerosmith, when my phone rang.

"Hello?" I checked the caller ID but didn't recognize the number.

"Hey, big sister. What's shaking?"

"Hey Kyle. What's going on? Is this your new cell?" It had been a while since I'd heard from my brother. The department was working him to the bone. My mom complained that she rarely got a call from him. I talked to his girlfriend, Sarah, more than I talked to him.

"Nothing much. Just checking in. How are things?"

"Things are great, Kyle. But really, what's going on?

You never call to see how I'm doing. What's wrong?"
My big sister alert radar went up a couple of notches.

"Nothing is wrong. I promise. I…" he hedged,
raising my concern even more. "I decided that I'm going
to propose to Sarah on Valentine's Day."

My concern turned into exhilaration. "OH MY GOD,
Kyle! That's amazing. I'm thrilled! Is she coming down
from Boston or are you going up there?" I inquired.

In all my excitement, I could barely pay attention
to the road. Sarah and I were college roommates and
practically sisters. I was thrilled when they started
dating two years ago. Now at Boston University
working on her master's degree, I couldn't wait until
she came home. She was going to be part of my family.

Kyle laughed. "I'm surprising her at her place. I'm
going to show up while she's in class and set everything
up. I got the ring from the safe last week and I'm ready.
I love her, Megs."

"I'm so happy for you. I really am. Did you ask her
dad? Did you tell Mom yet?"

My mom was notorious for not being able to keep
secrets, so I really hoped that Sarah didn't talk to her
until after he proposed.

"Yes and no. I went up to Philly on Saturday and
asked her dad. It went better than I expected. And I'm
not telling Mom, not until after. She sucks at keeping

surprises. So please, don't tell her. I mean, she knows that it will happen at some point but she doesn't know when, and I don't want her stressing Sarah out over wedding details. We'll think about all that after she graduates in May."

His plan impressed me. "I cross my heart. I won't tell Mom. I promise. You know I can keep a secret. At least from her. Can I tell Jen?"

Kyle chuckled. "Just try and hold it in. We've got about a week until Valentine's Day. Can you wait that long?"

I let out a dramatic sigh. "Fine. I'll wait. But if I spontaneously combust while holding this secret in, it's on your conscience."

"I think I can deal with that. I love you, Sis. I'll call you when it happens. Okay?"

"Bye, baby brother." I couldn't help it. A tear escaped from my eye. My baby brother was growing up.

I was in such a good mood when I got home, until I saw Shane's truck still parked outside. His motorcycle sat in the carport; I assumed they had taken Allison's Lexus. I didn't want to think about what they could be doing. Annoyed, I slammed the door a little too hard and winced, waiting for Penny to start her welcome home serenade. Nothing happened. Walking around to the mudroom with my keys in hand, I was startled to see the door partially open. Shane must have forgotten to lock the door and somehow Penny got out, I thought irritably. The annoyance quickly vanished when it dawned on me what had happened.

CHAPTER 4

I FROZE WHILE I QUICKLY debated in my head. *Should I call the cops right now or get Penny?* My semi-maternal instinct overcame my rational side and I pushed the door open a bit with the toe of my boot.

"Penny! Come here, Pen. Pen! Come here!" I whispered fruitlessly. Penny usually heard my car from down the street; she should have been able to hear me whispering. Dread overtook me and I feared the worst. I pushed the door open further and ventured into the house. My stomach dropped at the sight of my kitchen. With a shaky breath, I looked for Penny amid the knocked over chairs and broken glasses. Drawers were pulled out, papers thrown on the floor, items from my cabinets and pantry were smashed and ruined. I peered been oblivious to the outside temperatures and hadn't realized it was so cold until I got into the warm car.

"I just have a few more questions and I promise they will be quick. I know you're anxious to check over your house. Now, just to forewarn you, there is a big mess inside. As far as we can tell, there is no damage to the house itself besides the door. But before we go into that, we'll start with the questions," he said emphatically. "Now, do you know of anyone who would cause you any harm or do something this destructive?"

"No," I said quietly as I looked out the window for Shane. I couldn't see him anywhere. "I'm pretty friendly with everyone. I don't have any enemies."

"Okay. Have you noticed anything strange in the area? People that don't belong in the neighborhood, perhaps?"

I shook my head again and then reconsidered. "There was a green Expedition that came by earlier this evening. I didn't pay much attention. It stopped at the house for a quick second and then drove away." I put my arms around myself and shivered in the warm car.

"Did you catch the plate number or see the driver?" Officer Vaughn quizzed, his blue eyes narrowing.

"No. I was coming up the street walking Penny. The truck literally drove up, stopped for two seconds, and then drove away," I recalled. I searched my memory, trying to remember something—anything—that could be useful, but nothing came up.

Officer Vaughn made a few notes. "The gentleman you were with a few moments ago? What is his name? Does he live with you?"

I frowned. "Shane Turner. He just moved in. Why?"

"Just checking. We're going to have to ask him a few questions as well. It looks like they are ready for the walk through so I'll talk to Mr. Turner in a minute."

I got out of the car and was hit with a blast of chilly air. I looked around for Shane and saw him talking to an officer. Our eyes met and he walked over to me with the officer in tow.

"They want us to walk them through the house."

Shane nodded and followed me inside. We walked into the living room through the front door, taking pictures with our cell phones to record the damage. The couch was in disarray but not damaged. DVDs and CDs littered the floor, plants were overturned, and pictures were lopsided on the walls. The only items missing were the gaming console and all the video games. While everything in the room was upturned, the only damage was in the form of a smashed blown glass vase that I had gotten from the Renaissance festival. I glanced over into the reading area. It broke my heart to see my favorite room of the house destroyed. I hurried over to the shelf and frantically searched for my father's prized pocket watch. It was my favorite memento. I let out a sigh of relief when I found it on the floor underneath a pile of books. The kitchen didn't fare much better. The broken wine glasses in the kitchen mixed with the spilled flour and spices from the pantry. Bills and mail littered the ground like confetti, and the bastards had gone through my fridge and taken the beer.

We headed upstairs and into my bedroom. It seemed fine with the exception of my mattress turned on its side and my jewelry box rifled through. Luckily, my most priceless possessions were tucked in a box underneath a floorboard in my closet along with all my important documents that needed safekeeping. The box had not been touched.

We walked into Shane's room and it contrasted dramatically to mine. His bed was torn apart, ripped to shreds. Clothes covered the carpet. The drawers were pulled out of the dresser and the curtains were torn from their rods. Shane didn't have much in the way of valuables so it was quite alarming to see such destruction in his room. He quickly checked the contents of his closet and looked around. Nothing had been taken. The hard look in his eyes told me how furious he was.

The officer glanced at his notes. "With the lack of theft, I am led to believe this is a random break-in. It was probably just a bunch of teenagers. I'll turn in the list for the gaming console and games, but I doubt you'll get that back. You can report it to your homeowner's insurance when you call them about your mudroom door. I suggest you call a twenty-four-hour locksmith to have them add a lock to the inner door."

Shane spoke up before I could. "No, that's okay. I'll go to the hardware store right now and install it myself."

I checked my watch. It was eleven thirty. I knew that the hardware store closed at midnight so he'd have to hurry. When I opened my mouth to say something, he gave me a quick smile. "I'll make it, don't worry. Are you guys going to be here for a while?" he asked. He took a hooded jacket out of the closet and shrugged it on.

Officer Vaughn replied, "I can stay until you get back if you'd like." Shane nodded in appreciation. I followed him downstairs and out the front door, stopping at his truck. He pulled me into a hug, knowing that was what I needed. I felt so cold, and not because of the weather.

"Just be careful. No need for any more police activity tonight. Okay?" I said quietly, knowing his need for speed. Shane chuckled. His beautiful hazel eyes softened.

"Don't worry. I'll be fine. Go get Penny and I'll be back soon. Do you want me to call Ben? He could stay if you want," he asked as he climbed into his truck. I shook my head.

"No, thanks. We're fine. I need to get cleaning anyway."

I crossed the street as he drove away and couldn't help but shiver. The fact that someone had been in my house and pawed through my belongings had left me shaken. *What could possibly possess someone to do this*? Mrs. Sanders threw open the door before I could raise my hand to knock and gestured me in. I knew she was waiting for the real dirt.

"What did the police say? Do they know who did it?" Mrs. Sanders quizzed.

I shook my head. "They think it was teenagers. All they took was my video game system and my beer, and left a big mess to clean up." I clipped Penny's leash to her collar. She was anxious to leave. Mrs. Sanders' orange cat, Cuddles, did not like dogs and Penny wanted to get away from the cat's hateful glare.

"Hmm. I'll have to make sure that Ronald sets the alarm tonight." She patted my arm and smiled at me kindly. "Penny was a welcome addition and we were glad to have her over. Weren't we Cuddle-wuddles," she said in a high-pitched voice, picking up the bowling ball of a cat. Cuddle-wuddles didn't look so happy and swiped at Penny's nose. Penny whined to leave and started to pull on her leash so I quickly thanked Mrs. Sanders and headed back to the house.

I let myself into the house through the front door and left my coat and the leash on the sofa. Officer Vaughn was sitting at the kitchen table, making notes.

"Is it alright if I put stuff away?" I asked. The urge to clean strongly took over any thought of sleep. I couldn't go to bed knowing that someone had been in my home. I felt violated. Returning my house to its normal state would ease some of my anxiety. He nodded absent-mindedly while he wrote. Once I started putting away items and sweeping up the mess, I felt more in control.

***

By THE TIME SHANE returned home with the new deadbolts I had put the reading area and the living room back to order. I slowly made my way upstairs and set about straightening my room. I vaguely wondered where Shane would sleep. With his bed in shambles, he had few options. I figured that he'd make do on the couch or at Allison's. *Or he could sleep with me,* my inner Shane worshiper whispered. I rolled my eyes as I put on new sheets, the slate blue ones that were the exact same color as my walls.

I washed my face, brushed my teeth, and put on

a pair of boxers and a T-shirt. I was physically and mentally exhausted, but too jumpy to sleep. I let Penny climb into bed with me, a rarity since she liked to kick while dreaming. Shane or no Shane, I needed some company. I climbed under my comforter and looked for mindless entertainment on TV, anything to keep me distracted.

I jumped when a shadow crossed my threshold. I looked up to see Shane leaning on the doorframe.

"How are you doing?" he asked in a low voice. His brown hair glistened from the shower. He wore gray boxers, a white T-shirt, and his rimless glasses, the kind he only wore when he was ready for bed.

"I'm okay, I guess. How are you?" I asked with a half-smile. What did he expect me to say? *It sucks that I was robbed, but, oh gee, you can sleep in my bed.*

"I'm beat. Scoot over. I'm crashing in here tonight," he said, his pillow in hand. My pulse raced and I turned beet red.

"That's fine. Just don't snore," I shot back. Penny looked up at Shane and thumped her tail. She was happy too.

Shane took the remote out of my hand as he settled down next to me.

"We're not watching Oprah reruns," he scoffed, turning the channel to the hockey game.

"Thanks for coming back. I'm sorry to have interrupted your evening," I said quietly as I looked at my hands. They were shaking. He looked over at me and put his arms around my shoulders.

"Hey. I'm glad you called. You know that you should call anytime you need me. How are you really holding up? Don't lie. Are you okay?" he asked softly, looking me in the eyes. The fear of the evening, the fatigue, the anxiety of him staying with me, melted away when I looked into those hazel eyes. I wanted to kiss him right then and God only knows how I restrained myself.

I gave him a weak smile. "I'm exhausted. That's all."

Shane rubbed my shoulder. "Yeah, it sucks. I'm just glad that you and Penny are okay. The rest we can deal with. Why don't you try and get some sleep?" His eyes turned dark and he looked like he wanted to say something more. "Don't worry. The alarm is on, Penny is in here with us, and I'll be here. So try to sleep. Okay?" Shane moved his arm and put it behind his head as he lay down next to me. I sighed and nodded, then kissed his cheek.

"Thanks, Shane," I whispered. I rolled over on my side. I hugged my pillow and closed my eyes. I had nearly drifted off to the sound of sports highlights when I thought I felt a feather of a kiss on my cheek.

CHAPTER 5

I WOKE UP SLOWLY AS reality set in. The previous night's events weighed heavily on my mind. I slept horribly and woke up several times thanks to nightmares. I didn't see how Shane could have fared any better because I knew I woke him up as well. *Coffee. Must have coffee.* I knew that copious amounts of caffeine would have to be consumed. I quickly put on my bathrobe and slippers and hurried down the hall to the stairs where I heard Shane talking. My heart stopped when I heard what he said.

"She's like a sister to me. That's all. She's cool. I can trust her."

A sister? All I am to him is a sister? Disappointment washed over me. *What the hell did I expect?* I went into the bathroom and splashed cold water on my face to clear my head. I didn't know what the heck I was thinking. There was no reason to get upset, no reason whatsoever. I should have been pissed off about the robbery and the fact that my home was violated, not some kiss that I imagined. *Get a freaking grip.* Angry at myself for being such an irrational love-struck teenager and knowing full well that last night's events were causing me to stress, I took a deep breath to compose myself. I padded downstairs and walked into the kitchen. I stopped cold when I saw who Shane was talking with. Sitting at my kitchen table, drinking out of my favorite large coffee mug, was Allison. I mentally rolled my eyes and plastered a bright smile on my face. "Good morning."

"Good morning, Megan. Shane's telling me about last night. It must have been awful," she said. *Oh yeah, which part? Feeling something for Shane when I shouldn't? Or the fact that some jackass decided that breaking into my house was a great way to get some free beer?* I bit my tongue to keep the nasty comments from flying out. Regardless of my feelings toward the ice princess, she didn't deserve my bitchiness.

"Yeah, it sucks. I have to make some calls today to get an estimate on the door frame," I said as I poured coffee into another mug. Yeah, it was the same coffee but, dammit, it was different drinking out of a mug that was for guests. I reached for the creamer, which was empty. *Seriously? Should I just go back to bed and start over?* I contemplated the notion while I threw the bottle into the recycling bin. I added regular milk and then sat at the table with a huff. Shane and Allison just stared at me.

"Didn't get much sleep did we?" Shane teased. *What the hell do you think?* I couldn't help it. My bad attitude boiled over.

"No, Shane. I didn't. I had a pretty crappy night last night, if you remember. I'm exhausted. I'm out of creamer and I need to go to the grocery store. Penny has a vet appointment. I have a laundry list of things to do today on top of making sure that someone comes and fixes my damn door. Plus, Mom is expecting me over tonight for dinner. So excuse me while I feel a little out of sorts," I snapped. The look in their eyes told me exactly how much of a bitch I was being. I took a deep breath. "I'm sorry. Forget I said anything. I need to get going. Tell me what you need and I'll pick it up," I said, sipping my coffee and making a face. My coffee wasn't the same without hazelnut creamer, for God's sake.

"I don't need anything. I already took Penny for a walk. We have things to do, so we'll see you later." Shane put their coffee mugs in the sink and headed out of the kitchen.

"I really am sorry for what happened. Take care," Allison said softly with a gentle smile.

I smiled back. "Thanks, Allison. I appreciate it." She followed Shane out the door. I looked at the coffee in disgust. *Looks like it's a Starbucks kind of morning.* I rinsed out the cup and put it in the dishwasher, called Penny in, and headed upstairs. I had a lot to do and the lack of coffee was going to hamper my productivity. After my shower, I threw on a hooded cable-knit sweater and jeans. As I applied my makeup, Shane's comments kept running through my mind. *This is ridiculous. Maybe Jen's right and I need to actually make an effort to move on.* I needed to do something, because the whole "unrequited love" situation had gotten to be a bitch.

I headed back downstairs and started the car from my key fob while I put on my jacket and gloves. As I locked the house, I received a text message. "Heard what happened. Call me later. Jen." Ah, Jen. My best friend always knew when I really needed to talk to her. She would understand my frustration.

***

I PUT IN MY EARPIECE and called Jen back once I was on the road. She answered on the first ring. "Hey, Megs. I heard what happened. Are you guys okay?"

"Yeah, we're fine. They let Penny go and I thought she was gone. Since the jerks took my beer and video games, the police think teenagers are behind it. Wait a minute. How did you know?" I asked. She was supposed to be sleeping in.

"Shane sent me a text this morning," she replied.

I should have figured. Jen's parents had taken Shane in eight years ago after his parents died. Shane and Jen were so close that they were practically related. When something happened to one of them, the other was the first person called.

"Yeah, well it sucks," I said quietly.

"That's crazy. Did anyone call your brother?" she asked.

I sighed. My brother had been very concerned about my safety when I bought my house. He didn't like the idea of me living alone. Since my father passed, Kyle had been the man of the family and was overprotective. He was the one who insisted I have an alarm installed. *A lot of good that did me.*

"No and don't say anything about it either. He would worry and he doesn't need to. This was totally random, and I highly doubt anyone will do it again."

"That's up to you. So, to change the subject, has Allison been over yet?" Jen asked.

I groaned. "Yeah, this morning. They left about an

hour ago. I wasn't awake when she came in so I'm not sure how long she was over. And I don't even want to think about what they were doing. But you know what? I'm done with that. I've been thinking about what you said yesterday. You're right. I'm stupid to even be thinking of him. I need to get back out there and find someone new."

Jen chuckled. "I know it's going to be rough, but you're twenty-six years old. There are a million guys out there. It doesn't hurt to look. It's not like you're rushing to get married or something. Just take your time. You'll find someone."

"Yeah, well. We'll see. I gotta go. I have a bunch of things to do today and caffeine is number one on my list," I said as I pulled into Starbucks.

We hung up and I walked into the store. As usual, it was crowded. I stood behind a lady with an adorable baby and passed the time making googly eyes at the kid. I loved kids. So innocent and sweet. After placing my order, I started scrolling through my Blackberry while waiting for my caramel latte. Engrossed in an email from Sarah, I thought I heard my order called. Not paying attention, I reached for my drink and grazed another hand at the same time.

"Oh!" I said with surprise. The hand was attached to a gorgeous superhunk, with caramel skin and sexy gray eyes. He obviously worked out and had great style; he was dressed in a navy sweater and fitted jeans. He grinned, showing his perfectly straight teeth.

"Sorry. I think this is yours," I muttered, stepping back. Superhunk chuckled.

"No, no. You can have it," he drawled. *Good Lord, a Southern accent.* I was a sucker for accents.

The barista then put a larger drink down. My drink. I quickly apologized to Superhunk, grabbed my coffee, and headed for the door. I chirped the button to my car and noticed Superhunk climbing into a sleek Porsche Turbo. I turned green with envy. Puppies, babies, and fast cars were my ultimate weaknesses.

"Nice car," I called out and added under my breath, "Nice Ass."

"Thanks. My pride and joy," he said with another perfect smile. For some strange reason shyness came over me. I felt so awkward. It had been a long time since I had done any sort of flirting.

I gave Superhunk a quick smile as I got into my car and let him pull out first. I put the Volvo into reverse and started to back out. Suddenly, a black Lexus coupe came to a complete stop right behind me. I slammed on the brakes so I wouldn't crash into it. The last thing I needed was my insurance going up because of some stupid jerk that couldn't drive.

I waited a few beats for the Lexus to move before I gave the universal sign for "What the fuck?" by throwing my hands in the air. I honked the horn but the Lexus didn't budge. *What the hell is this?* I threw open my car door and stalked over to the Lexus, "What the hell do you think you're doing? I'm trying to leave. Did you want me to hit you?"

The darkly tinted windows came down and a familiar laugh billowed out. I peeked inside. Shane was in the driver's seat holding his sides and laughing hysterically. Allison was in the passenger seat trying to hold it in.

"You should have seen your face!" he managed to say between breaths. I stomped over to the driver's side and reached in to smack him. He dodged my hand.

"You stupid jerk! Why are you such an ass? Argh!" I said with exasperation. I looked at Allison, who was also laughing. "And you! How do you put up with this?"

Allison muffled her laughter with a cough. "Sorry, Megan. You know you can't control the man once he's behind the wheel."

"Whatever. Can you please move so I can leave? I have a lot to do today and you're not helping," I said as I folded my arms across my chest. I gave the best evil eye I could muster. It failed.

Shane covered his laugh with a cough. "Yeah, yeah,

yeah. Keep your clothes on. I'm moving. But I forgot to tell you this morning that I'm running up to Trenton for the next couple of days. I'm helping Adrian with his brother's bike. I've ordered a new mattress and box springs. It should be here either today or tomorrow. If you're not home, they'll leave it in the carport."

He was leaving. Good. I didn't need him around stirring up old feelings. I guess I should have been grateful. Part of me didn't want him to leave, not after what had happened last night. I didn't want to be that girl, though; the girl who needs someone to protect her. I gave him my most evil Megan stare just to show him that he wasn't off the hook yet. Yeah, it didn't work.

I finally said, "Okay, sure. Thanks for letting me know."

"No problem." Shane gave me a wink and set off.

I walked back to my car in a huff. I wanted to say I was mad about that little shenanigan that he pulled, but deep down, *way* deep down, I was sad that he was leaving so soon. I ignored the little voice in my head that wondered if Allison was going with him to Trenton. *I'm not going to think about him. I'm not going to think about him.*

When I got home, I quickly put the groceries away. Penny's vet appointment was in half an hour and she would fight me every step of the way. I grabbed some of her favorite treats and her leash, and headed up the stairs. I found her on my bed and when I walked in the room, she looked scared.

"Come on, Penny. Let's go for a car ride," I said, with as much sweetness as I could muster. It didn't fool her. With her tail between her legs, she gave me the saddest look I'd ever seen.

"Oh, Penny. Don't be such a baby. You'll be fine," I said as I clipped on her leash and led her down the stairs. She tried to balk at the car door, but realized that resistance was futile.

***

WE MADE IT TO DR. Collins's office with a minute to spare. Penny didn't care very much for Dr. Collins, but he was a good vet and within my budget. His bedside manner wasn't the best, but hey, we can't have everything.

I practically dragged Penny into the office, giving her treats every third step or so. Penny looked so pathetic that it was hard not to laugh. When she was finally called, Penny dug her back paws in, but seeing as how we were on laminate flooring it didn't stop her from joining me in the exam room.

"Dr. Collins will be right in," the nurse said, trying hard not to laugh.

I chuckled. The big baby whined and immediately tried to climb into my lap

"Isn't she a bit big to be a lap dog?" asked a voice behind me. I turned around and was taken aback to see Superhunk from earlier that morning. Embarrassed, I tried to put her down. The stubborn dog whimpered and strained to stay on the bench. I was struggling with her weight on me when this new Dr. Collins gently lifted her down to the ground. I sighed with exasperation. What a great first impression.

"Yeah, she's not fond of going to the vet. I'm Megan Connors. This is Penny," I said as I reached out my hand to him.

"Dr. Collins. Alex Collins. Nice to meet you," he said, flashing those perfect teeth as he shook my hand. He started to read Penny's file. I felt like I had to say something. Anything.

"You're not the Dr. Collins I was expecting," I said as I tried to get Penny to calm down. My heart jumped nervously. He squatted down to Penny's level, right next to me. Dr. Collins took her face in his hands and started rubbing her ears. Penny immediately became at ease.

"Yeah, this is my grandfather's practice. I just moved here from North Carolina to help him out. He's retiring at the end of the summer. You can call me Alex," he said as he checked Penny's teeth. Amazingly, there wasn't a growl or snarl to be heard.

"That's really nice of you, Alex," I said lamely. I couldn't think of what else to say. The man had me dumbfounded.

Mr. Superhunk smiled while he checked Penny's hips and limbs. "She seems to be in good health. Not overly big, but she could stand to lose a few pounds. Maybe cutting back on the treats would help," he said with a grin. I sheepishly grinned back and put the rest of her treats back into my purse. *This guy is gorgeous.* I discretely checked for a ring on his left hand. Nope, no ring. Jen's voice rang in my head. *Talk to him you fool*, it urged.

"Penny seems to like you. This is the most relaxed I've seen her at the vet's," I said shyly.

"Yeah, lucky for me, dogs like me. I don't have any dogs of my own right now, but the place where I'm staying has some," he said, listening to Penny's heart. Penny was cool as a cucumber.

"Oh really? Your girlfriend's dog or something?" I inquired nonchalantly. I had to ask.

Alex chuckled and gave me a crooked grin. "No. I'm renting the guesthouse at Copper Ridge Farm over in Davidsonville. They have a bunch of dogs over there along with every other farm animal."

Good. No girlfriend. Obviously likes animals. Sexy as sin. Seems like he has a good head on his shoulders. Time to put on my big girl undies and go for it.

"Copper Ridge? I used to ride there when I was younger," I said in hopes of prolonging the conversation.

"It's a nice place. Bill and Mary Patterson are great people. Aside from the discount in rent, I'm able to take out some of the horses for exercise. That's a major plus since I had to leave my old gelding back in North Carolina. Do you still ride?" he asked. *Do I ride?* Of course, my sex-deprived mind went straight for the gutter.

"Not lately. It's been awhile. Eventually, when I have the time, I'd like to get back into it," I said lightly.

"You should come up to the farm. I'm sure Mary and Bill would love to see you," he said absentmindedly as he jotted down notes on Penny's chart. "Well, her shots are up-to-date and she seems to be in perfect health," Alex stated, handing me the appointment summary sheet. *Now's my chance. Do it!* I cheered myself on. *Good Lord.* I sucked in my breath and said, "Thanks Dr. Collins. It was nice meeting you."

The daredevil in me was calling out horrible names, such as chicken shit, fucking coward, wimp, and some other expletives. *I can't do it. I really can't do it.* As I left the clinic, I was kicking myself in the ass when I heard, "Ms.

Connors, wait." *Oh! It's him!* I quickly turned around with a big smile on my face.

"You forgot this," he said, handing me my cell phone. Thoroughly embarrassed, I smiled tightly and thanked him. I tended to lose my phone quite frequently.

"Thanks," I said, gathering up my courage before I lost my nerve again. "If you're not busy tomorrow morning, would you like to get together for coffee? Say around nine?" I blurted out. I almost clamped my hand over my mouth in utter shock. I couldn't believe I did it. How humiliating.

Alex looked taken aback as well. "Wow. Um. Nine? I think that will work. Same Starbucks?" he said, a gleam in his eye.

"Yeah, same one," I said, trying to hide my shock that he had said yes.

"Sounds great. I'll see you there." Alex chuckled and headed back into the office. I quickly walked to the car and as soon as I was out of earshot I squealed in excitement. *I can't believe it. I did it! I actually did it!* Penny looked at me like I had lost my mind. *This is AWESOME!* I tried desperately not to look like an idiot, but I couldn't help myself and did a happy dance next to the car. Was this considered a date? God, it had been so long since I'd been on one, I couldn't tell.

***

ONCE WE WERE HOME, I quickly let Penny inside and dialed Sarah's number.

"Hey Sarah! How are things going?" I asked as she answered the phone.

"Hey Megan. It's going great. I was just talking to your brother. He can't wait for his break next week," Sarah said excitedly. She and Kyle had been trading weekends here and there, but with him on the force, there was so little time for them to see each other.

"You mean he can't wait to see you?" I teased. I was so glad I introduced them. They were such a great couple. We chatted for a few minutes, before I told her about Shane. Sarah knew all the Shane stories. After Jen, Sarah was my closest friend.

"I can't believe that he said that you were like his sister," Sarah said quietly. "That must have hurt."

"I have to say that it did. But you know what? It was needed. It's been almost a year since Tommy and I split, and obviously I need to get over Shane too. Hearing that this morning reaffirmed what Jen said. We were talking last night and she said that I needed to get back out there. I'm twenty-six years old; I should be having the time of my life, not wasting time being depressed and sitting around in my pajamas all day."

"So do you have anyone in mind?" she asked.

"Well..." I hedged a bit. "I met a guy today. He's Penny's new vet. He's sexy as sin, single, gray eyes. Sarah, he's beautiful. And he's really nice too. We're meeting for coffee tomorrow."

"That's a start. Coffee is always a great start. That's how I got your brother hooked," she giggled.

"Right. And here I always thought it was your good looks," I laughed. Sarah had modeled for a couple of campus calendars while we were in school. She was so gorgeous, with long black hair, her father's Asian brown eyes, and her mother's French nose. I had been totally intimidated when I first met her.

Sarah had to get off the phone. Apparently, class was more important than our phone call, but she threatened to not bring me my favorite Boston potato chips if I didn't give her all the details of my date. I did a few loads of laundry and then the doorbell rang. It was the mattress that Shane had ordered. I directed the deliverymen upstairs and they hauled away his old one. Being the good friend, I made his bed. I put on some white cotton sheets and a new comforter. His cologne still lingered in the air and I paused as I walked out the door.

"No. No more of this," I said to myself, pushing out the old feelings. "We're purely platonic. We're practically family. No romantic feelings whatsoever."

My calendar tone rang on my phone to remind me that mom was cooking me dinner. I whistled for Penny and hustled down the stairs. Penny gazed at me forlornly as I clipped her leash to her collar, as if pleading for no more doctor's visits.

"Oh shush. We're going to Grandmas," I said as I pushed her into the back seat. My mother demanded an audience of her children once a month at the very minimum. We always followed Kyle's schedule and today just happened to be the day.

***

MOM STILL LIVED IN my childhood home in Davidsonville just twenty minutes away. When I looked for a home, I looked for one close to my mom. I was so glad when I found one so close to her. When we arrived, I let myself into the house and Penny ran ahead of me into the kitchen. The aroma of Mom's baked chicken and sweet potato fries greeted me.

"Hi, baby doll," she said, coming around the corner. Dressed in jeans and a sweatshirt, she was the older version of me. Long dark brown hair, dark brown eyes, and a slightly heavier frame. We looked exactly alike. I gave her a huge hug. I missed living with my mom. The house always smelled like apple turnovers, vanilla, and chicken.

"Hi, Mom. Dinner smells good," I said as I hung my jacket on the hook. I wandered into the kitchen, and Penny was already there sniffing for scraps.

"Penny! Here you go!" my mom called as she put down a bowl of chopped chicken and rice.

"Mom, Dr. Collins said that Penny needs to lose some weight. So no more table scraps," I admonished.

My mom waved me away. Her fourteen-year-old bichon came hobbling down the hall, sniffing for food. Micki was nearly blind, partially deaf (although my mom called it selective hearing), and just very elderly. Penny let Micki get into the food bowl and backed off. She knew who ruled this house.

I sat at the old oak table, the same one my father bought for Mom on their ten-year anniversary. "What time is Kyle coming over?" I asked as I watched her take the fries out of the oven.

She checked the country clock on the wall. "He should be here shortly. He can smell dinner from a mile away so I doubt we'll have to wait very long for him."

I nodded. Kyle was a food magnet. He enjoyed cooking almost as much as he loved eating. I drummed my fingers on the table with mock impatience.

"So what's new, Megs?" she asked, taking the chicken out of the oven.

"Nothing much. Shane moved in," I mumbled. She was going to find out anyway so I figured I might as well tell her now.

Mom paused and raised an eyebrow. I gave the same look when I found the truth hard to believe. "Shane? Shane Turner?" she asked as she stirred the gravy.

I sighed. "Yes, Mom. Shane Turner. Don't worry. We're just friends. He has his own room. Plus, he's still dating that girl Allison."

"Hmmm." She knew better than to not press me about Shane. She always had her suspicions about my feelings for him. Mom knew me better than I knew myself sometimes. I rolled my eyes. I didn't have to ask her what she was thinking because I knew what she would say. Luckily, the dogs' barking saved me from answering any questions. Kyle walked in and threw his book bag on the sofa.

"Hey guys," he said as he kissed mom on the cheek. I raised my cheek for my kiss but got a raspberry instead.

"Ugh. You're so gross!" I cried, wiping the spit off my cheek. Kyle just laughed.

"So, Kyle, how's Sarah doing?" Mom asked as she pulled out the plates and handing them to me. I set the table and shook my head slightly at Kyle when he widened his eyes at me, as if to say, "No baby brother, I didn't tell her." I wanted his proposal to be a surprise just as much as he did.

Kyle coughed. "She's good. I'm going up there next weekend. She has a break and I'm able to get some time off." He brought over the water pitcher and sat down. Mom and I followed suit.

We ate in companionable silence, enjoying the best food we'd had in a long time. I learned my cooking skills from both my parents, but even with their simplest recipes, it wasn't the same. It didn't take long for my mother to ask the question that I knew she was dying to ask.

"So Kyle, what's going on with you and Sarah?" she said as she passed around the broccoli. I kept my eyes down, quickly took a serving, and passed the bowl to Kyle. I was a horrible liar. Kyle was only slightly better than I was.

"Um. Things are really good. She's doing great in school. We're going to try to take a vacation after she gets back from Boston. Not sure where, but some place nice," he quickly stuttered.

Mom gave him a raised eyebrow. Quickly taking the bullet, I interrupted. "That's right. I think a bunch of us were talking about going down to Myrtle Beach for Memorial Day weekend."

Kyle gave me a grateful look and I stored that in my brownie points file. You never knew when you might need a police officer to owe you a favor. Especially if that police officer was your younger brother and you just got a speeding ticket.

After dinner, Kyle and I did the dishes while Mom put the leftovers into bags for us. She always worried about us eating well and made enough for a couple dinners.

"I heard about your house," Kyle said under his breath. He checked over his shoulder to see where Mom was. He was supposed to be drying the dishes, not checking up on me. I groaned.

"Well, nothing much we can do about it now. It was just some random thing," I muttered back. I handed him the last dish and dried my hands on the checkered dishtowel.

He gave me his "who are you kidding?" look. I just rolled my eyes and walked into the living room.

"Megan, would you like me to add some for Shane?" Mom asked, cutting Kyle off from saying what I'm sure would have been a condescending comment about me being careful. I settled on the couch and blew out a breath. I couldn't move. "No, thanks," I called back. No need for Shane to have leftovers if he was going to be away for a while. Full from dinner and feeling all cozy from the roaring fire in the fireplace, my body melted into the folds of the couch. I tucked up my legs and pulled the afghan over me. I could have fallen asleep right there.

"Shane? We're not talking about Shane Turner are we?" Kyle mocked as he fell into the other end of the sofa. Shane and Kyle were friends, although not as close Shane and I were. They had similar interests so their paths crossed frequently. "Does that mean you and Shane are finally hooking up?"

I reached over and punched him in the arm. "Whatever, Kyle. You know it's not like that. We're friends. Two adults of the opposite sex can be friends," I replied hotly. Were my feelings for Shane that obvious? *Sheesh.*

Kyle laughed. "Yes. Two adults of the opposite sex can be friends, but we're talking about you and Shane. Before Tommy, you and Shane were inseparable. Ever since you met him, you've been crushing on him. It's written all over your face!"

My cheeks flamed as my temper rose. He had a point, but did he have to be so freaking blunt about it? I did what any big sister would have done. I picked up a throw pillow and smacked him upside the head with it.

"I have moved on, thank you, mister pain-in-the-butt. In fact, I'm meeting someone for coffee tomorrow!" I retorted, then quickly clamped my mouth shut. That wasn't supposed to come out. *Crap.* Mom's eyes lit up.

She wanted grandchildren in the worst way, and I was delaying her plans. If she had her wish, I would already be married with three kids.

"Oh really? I'm surprised you didn't mention him earlier. Who is he? Where did you meet?" she pressed.

"It's just coffee, Mom. Not a big deal," I replied with a yawn. I leaned my head back against the sofa and closed my eyes. I knew that if I didn't want to stay the night, I should leave soon.

"Well, what's his name?" My mother knew practically everyone in the area.

"Alex Collins," I mumbled in defeat. I was sure she knew about Dr. Superhunk. Micki went to the same vet.

"Oh, old Dr. Collins's grandson? He's adorable. We met him the other day. I took some cranberry bread over to Mary Patterson and he was there working with the children," she said approvingly.

My heart thumped slightly faster. *He works with kids as well? Is this man not perfect?* I stood up and stretched. "Um, right. Well, Mom, I'll let you know how it turns out. But we have to run. Come on, Pen. Let's get a move on." Penny lazily thumped her tail. With her full belly, Penny didn't want to move. I threw on my jacket, grabbed my purse, and hugged my mom and brother goodbye.

The shock of the frigid air outside woke me up and

I was able to keep my eyes open all the way home. I pulled up to my house and sat there, just watching. It felt odd to see Shane's truck parked on the side of the road. I hoped another car in front of the house would deter any future would-be thugs. Regardless, I was uncomfortable being by myself after the previous night's fiasco. After setting the double locks, alarm, and motion detectors, I brought Penny upstairs to my room and shut the door. I peeled off my clothes, settled underneath the covers, and fell into a dreamless sleep.

CHAPTER 6

I WOKE EARLY THE NEXT morning feeling anxious. I had never asked a total stranger out before. I debated calling and canceling, but then realized that I never got his number. *What am I doing?* I shook my head at my own anxiety. I took a shower and dried my hair, all the while trying to downplay the morning.

"It's just freaking coffee," I muttered as I scanned my closet. I finally decided on jeans, a fitted navy turtleneck, and a white quilted down vest. Casual but not underdressed. I let Penny outside to do her thing while I warmed up the car. Snow had fallen the previous night and it was gorgeous. Luckily, it was only an inch and wouldn't hamper my drive.

I pulled into the parking lot two minutes before nine.

I saw his Porsche sitting in the lot, backed in at an angle. My palms started to sweat and I felt like puking. "Stupid first date jitters. It's just coffee!" I muttered. I stepped out of my car and immediately slipped on a piece of ice. As I oh-so-gracefully fell into the splits, an arm reached out to steady me before I did any real damage.

"Oh, crap. Thanks!" I said, looking up into Alex's beautiful gray eyes. *Good job, Megan. Way to make a complete fool of yourself.* My cheeks flamed with embarrassment.

"No problem. I'm used to women falling over me," he joked. *Ah, a sense of humor.* I chuckled. Still, completely embarrassed, I couldn't think of a witty comeback and just felt like a dope. Alex held the door open for me and gestured inside the warm coffee shop.

"Did you just get here?" I asked, hoping that he hadn't already had a drink. That would have been awkward.

He shrugged off his leather coat revealing a gray and white striped long sleeve polo shirt. The white matched his teeth perfectly. "I pulled up a second before you did. I was waiting in the car talking to a lady about her aging bichon."

Aging bichon? That sounded suspiciously like my mother. But there was no way she would call him. I shook that thought out of my head and got in line.

"What would you like?" I asked when I got to the front. He gave his order and handed over his cash before I could pay. "My treat," he said with a smile. I smiled back; his smile was contagious. We took our drinks over to the circle of oversized chairs. The shop was crowded with adults trying to keep warm and children drinking hot chocolate.

"So, tell me about yourself," he said easily as he settled back into the armchair.

"Not really much to tell. I've lived in this area for most of my life. I graduated from the University of Maryland with a bachelor's in business administration. I work for my Uncle Bob at his law firm. I have a brother and a dog, which you know. That's basically it," I replied with a smile. *This feels slightly like a job interview.*

Alex laughed a sexy, Southern, baritone laugh. "And that's all there is to you?"

"Well, you have to ask the right questions. What about you? I know you love animals, but what else do you like to do in your spare time? What's life in North Carolina like?" I countered back.

"You're right. That was a very generic question. Let's see. I do love animals. I'm also a huge movie buff. I love all things sports. I'm basically your average guy," he said, smiling his beautiful smile.

"Ah, I see. What about life back home? What's that

like?" I replied, grinning. My imagination must have been working overtime because he seemed slightly uncomfortable at the question. Still, he was too cute for words.

"Home. Well. I grew up in Granite Falls, North Carolina. I went to school at Duke and moved to Raleigh about two years ago. I started helping my grandfather up here back in January," he said as he finished off his coffee.

"Were you always interested in being a vet?" I asked, returning to what seemed to be a safer topic.

"Oh yeah, ever since I was a little kid on my grandmother's farm. Sometimes I get more satisfaction out of helping animals than I do humans. Animals never talk back," he joked, seeming more at ease. I wondered what was really going on in his mind. Maybe he had just gotten out of a bad relationship or something. I found him easy to talk with. We had a similar sense of humor, liked some of the same movies, and liked to travel. I was surprised when I looked at my watch and saw that it was nearly lunchtime.

"Oh. It's almost noon. Do you want to grab some lunch?" I asked as my stomach growled. Alex opened his mouth to agree with me, but then his cell phone rang. He quickly checked it and gave me a small smile.

"I wish I could, but I can't. I have to take this. Can you

give me a minute?" he said, standing up and walking a few feet away. I nodded and leaned back into the chair. Alex was really sweet. He seemed genuine in his nature, but had that air of mystery about him. I wanted to get to know him better.

"Sorry about that," he said as he came back toward me. "I should really get going. I promised a friend that I would help him out today with his horse. Can I call you sometime though?"

Well, okay then, I thought as I wrote down my number. *This certainly feels like a brush off.*

I handed him the piece of paper and smiled brightly. "Thanks for the coffee. It was really nice getting to know you."

Alex smiled and, surprisingly, kissed me on my cheek. "Same here. But we're far from done getting through these questions. We'll talk soon."

"Sure," I said and walked out the door. My inner romantic was geeking out, squealing and crowing about a sexy man who had just kissed me. I got into my car and sighed. On the way home I overanalyzed everything I said and did. Alex appeared interested and engaged, but I knew enough to take it slow. On a happier note, I hadn't thought of Shane once.

***

ONCE I GOT HOME, I ate a quick snack and made some beef stew in the slow cooker for dinner. The contractor came out to fix the mudroom doorframe and added a new lock on the door. Penny and I played outside in the snow for a while then came back in a couple hours later, frozen to the bone. The house was filled with the aromas of bay leaves. My mouth watered. I put a loaf of Italian bread in the oven and headed upstairs to take a shower.

I threw on some sweats then started a fire. A ping from my phone indicated I had an email. Uncle Bob had cancelled work for the next day due to the snow. Good thing. I knew the roads would be like glass in the morning. The snow had started to fall again, crystallizing the trees, making the backyard shimmer.

The heat from the kitchen and fire fogged up my windows. As the bread cooled on the counter, I dished some soup into Penny's bowl. I had just made my bowl when my cell phone rang. Curious at the unfamiliar number, I answered it.

"Hello?"

"Hey, Megan. It's Alex. I want to apologize for leaving you like I did this morning." His accent made my toes tingle.

"Hi, Alex. No worries. I totally understand," I replied, as I tried hard not to let him hear the big cheese of a smile that was on my face.

"I appreciate that. I'm wondering if you'd like to meet for dinner tonight. I'm in Annapolis right now, so I can meet you anywhere." Butterflies replaced the growling in my stomach. I wanted to squeal, but kept it cool.

"Actually, Alex, I just made some beef stew. Would you like to join me? I have plenty," I offered, surprising myself. The suggestion just came tumbling out.

"Sure, if you don't mind. I haven't had a good home cooked meal in a long time. And I love beef stew."

I gave him the directions to my house. Barring any traffic issues, he was about twenty minutes away. I stared at the phone for a minute in a daze. Then it hit me: I was a mess!

I tore upstairs and threw on a pair of slimming jeans and a low cut pink shirt. Thinking way out of line, I quickly disrobed and changed into a sexier pair of pink boy shorts and a matching bra then put the outfit back on. I wasn't planning anything in particular, but one should always be prepared.

I went back downstairs, threw the bread back in the oven to keep it warm, straightened up the kitchen, and closed the laundry room door. Act natural, I thought as the doorbell rang. I walked through the living room to the front door.

"Hi," I said brightly, opening the door wide. Thick

snowflakes fell heavily around him. Alex dusted off his boots and shook off his hat. He walked in as he blew into his hands to warm them.

"Hi there," he said, planting a kiss on my cheek. "It's really coming down out there." I took his coat and led him inside.

"It looks nasty out," I replied as I hung his jacket in the closet. "I hope you're hungry. I made enough for an army." I led him to my kitchen.

"You have a beautiful home," Alex said. His gray eyes surveyed the oak floors and wine colored walls. He handed me a bottle of wine. "Oh here. I picked this up. This should go well with the stew."

"Thanks." I looked at the label. It was a brand I had heard of but never tried. I was not a wine connoisseur by any means, but I had my favorites and a budget. This was over my budget. I went over to the cabinets and pulled out some wine glasses.

"If you don't mind opening this up, I'll get everything else on the table," I said as I handed him the corkscrew and glasses. I pulled out the bread and started cutting off thick slices. I set down two cranberry-colored bowls filled with piping hot stew. Alex poured the wine and seconds later, we were digging in.

"This is fantastic," Alex said and took a sip of his wine. The wine was delicious and a great complement to the stew.

"Thanks. It's my mother's recipe," I replied.

"Well, it's your mom's recipe but you made it. It's great," he teased gently, the gray in his eyes shining like silver.

I blushed slightly and smiled. He was flirting with me. He was cute. I was slightly buzzed. Things couldn't be better.

"I'm glad you decided to join me. With all this snow, my car would have never made it home," I joked as I refilled our glasses. Our bowls were practically empty. "Would you like some more?"

Alex stood up and stretched. "Yeah, I'll have some more. I'll get it." He refilled both our bowls and brought the rest of the bread over to the table. "You guys don't get much snow up here do you?"

I shook my head. "We get snow about once or twice a month. Just enough to royally mess up the roads and cause headaches, but nothing substantial. What about you? I am curious if your Porsche handles well in a mess like we have out there."

Alex laughed. "Yeah, I'm surprised she made it here. Roads were horrible, just like you said."

We talked easily about his grandfather's declining health and about how he was moving into an assisted living facility in Edgewater. He told me stories of his grandfather's antics back when he was younger, and I could tell that he was quite fond of his predecessor. I told him about my relationship with Tommy and about Shane moving in. I left out the part about being in love with him. It didn't make much sense to bring that into the conversation when I was technically trying to get over him.

We finished the stew and he helped me with the dishes, then we moved into the family room with our wine. After realizing that we shared a common favorite movie, I put *Super Bad* into the DVD player. We watched the movie, sitting close to each other, but not quite touching. This was a new feeling, the feeling of discovery and getting to know someone. Once the movie ended, Alex stood up and stretched. An electric shot went through me as I sneaked a peek at his muscular abs. The temptation to touch them was almost too great.

"I really don't think you should be driving in this," I commented as I stood at the window. The snow had stopped, but a good four inches of fresh powder was on the ground. Especially in his small car, the roads would be treacherous.

Alex came up behind me. I could feel his breath on the back of my neck as he looked over my shoulder.

"Yeah, it's not looking pretty. I think I'll be okay." I turned around and ended up being right under his chin.

"But I'll stay, if that makes you feel better," he whispered softly. My heart started racing. I raised my head to his at the same time he lowered his chin. His lips touched mine, hesitantly, and then added a slight bit of pressure. I relaxed and gave in. He wrapped his arms around me as the kiss intensified, the fire burning hotter as I felt his tongue caress mine. I could feel myself going down a road that I wasn't necessarily sure I should go down. The two sides of me were dueling. The starved, ready-for-anything side cheered me on. The sensible side warned me of going too fast, too soon. He slowly broke off the kiss that I was almost sure I didn't want to end.

"Wow," I said, with a staggered breath. Alex tightened his grip around my waist and I didn't object when his hands lightly grazed over my butt.

"Yeah. Wow," he said. His eyes resembled liquid mercury, all shiny and silky. He reached down for another kiss, which I eagerly anticipated when—

RRRRRRRING.

Damnit all to hell. Someone had some serious bad timing. I jumped back in surprise, gave Alex an apologetic smile, and reached for my phone. *Of course it's Shane calling.*

"What's up?" I answered, not bothering with pleasantries.

"Well, hello to you too, Ms. Sunshine. I'm well,

thanks for asking," he quipped back. Sigh. He was such a pain in the butt.

"Hi Shane, how are you?" I muttered, as I took the glasses into the kitchen. I didn't need Alex to hear me banter with Shane.

"Just checking in with my roomie, seeing how things are," Shane said with a laugh.

My irritation lessened. He was such a caring guy underneath that annoyingly sexy exterior. He just had horrible timing.

"Thanks, Shane. Things are going okay. It's snowing down here. We've got at least four inches. You better be careful coming home. Roads are going to be a mess tomorrow," I replied as I watched Alex play with Penny. I started laughing at him. He was on all fours with Penny, trying to take away her woobie. *Fat chance of that pal,* I thought.

"What's going on over there?" Shane asked.

"Alex is over and he's wrestling with Penny," I said vaguely.

"Who's Alex?"

"Dr. Collins's grandson. The vet," I replied. I purposely answered in the most nonchalant way I could.

"Uh, okay. Well, anyway. Did they deliver my new bed?" Shane dismissed my news and changed the subject. Apparently, the jealousy that I was hoping for was not there.

I sighed. "Yes, they delivered your bed yesterday. It's all ready for you."

"Good. I'm not sure how long we'll be up here. Allison's family's up here so we may take a side trip on the way home." *Really? Is he trying to make jealous?* I brushed aside the ridiculous notion. *He has no idea how I feel, and it's going to stay that way.*

"That's fine. Just be safe," I replied, blushing furiously. I couldn't help feeling a pang of jealousy.

"I will. Hey, Megs?" he said softly.

"Yeah?"

"Just be careful. Okay?" Shane's voice was suddenly thick with worry.

"Yeah, Shane. I will. You too. Tell Allison I said hi," I replied. Might as well heed Jen's advice and try to include her.

I disconnected and stood for a moment. I knew that my affection or feelings for Shane wouldn't dissolve instantaneously. I guess I hadn't factored in how hard it would actually be. I pocketed my phone just as Alex came into the kitchen.

"Everything okay?" he asked as he put his arm around my waist. "You look, I don't know, annoyed."

I had to chuckle at his perceptiveness. "Yeah, I am slightly. Just a friend causing trouble again, that's all.

Nothing big."

"Good." Alex leaned in for another kiss. I raised my lips to his and then gently pressed my hand to his chest.

"Alex, I'm relatively new at this whole dating thing. And, honestly, I want to go slow. Okay?" I said as I looked into his eyes. No point in playing games; I was through with all that nonsense.

Alex looked surprised. "I completely agree." He kissed my lips softly again. "Just tell me where I can sleep tonight. It's getting late and I've had a long day." I smiled and led him into the laundry room where I kept the spare pillows and blankets.

I offered up Shane's sweats, but he actually came prepared.

"I always keep an overnight bag in my car in case I have to spend the night in a barn waiting for a mare to foal," he replied before he braved the short distance to his car. *A gentleman, a boy scout, a great kisser—wow, I can get used to this.* I made up the couch with fresh linens and a heavy comforter. Alex changed in the bathroom and came out in a pair of jersey shorts and a long sleeve gray T-shirt. The man had beautiful legs and I had to shake my head to clear the clouds.

"Thanks for a wonderful dinner," Alex said, giving me a good night hug. He brushed his lips against mine.

"Good night, Alex. Sleep tight," I said softly.

His cologne stayed with me as I went upstairs with Penny trailing behind me. I debated if I should lock my door, but figured if I couldn't be safe with a vet in my house, who could I be safe with. I changed into what had now come to be my standard bedtime uniform of boxers and a T-shirt and climbed into bed. As I drifted off to sleep, I heard the muffled ring of a cell phone.

CHAPTER 7

Jimmy Buffett's "Margaritaville" jolted me awake, sending my heart into a panic. I almost jumped out of bed when I remembered that I had the day off. Groaning, I turned my alarm clock off and rubbed the sleep from my eyes. I knew I needed to get out of bed, but I hesitated. I wasn't sure how to act after last night. I mean, I liked Alex. I liked being around him and I definitely liked kissing him, but this feeling of waking up with someone I didn't know very well downstairs was almost akin to doing the walk of shame in the aftermath of a drunken one-night stand. I dragged myself out of bed anyway. I pulled on my discarded sweats from last night and followed Penny down the stairs where she headed straight to the kitchen. I sniffed the air and breathed in the delicious aroma of coffee brewing and something else. *Nutmeg?* I wandered into the kitchen and my mouth dropped open in utter disbelief. What used to be a clean and orderly kitchen was a disaster zone. Spices covered the counters, the sink was filled with dirty dishes, and a busy Alex was clanging away on the pans. *Is that egg on my tile?*

"Good morning," I said cautiously.

"Good morning," Alex said, giving me a sheepish grin. "Um. I hope you don't mind, but I figured I'd, you know, make breakfast since you made such a great dinner last night and all."

I let Penny outside and laughed. "Can I help you with anything?" I said as I wiped up some of the nutmeg from the counter.

Alex hurriedly took away the sponge and led me to the kitchen table. "Nope. Here's your coffee. I wasn't sure how you took it, but I got out the creamer. Just relax. I got this." He quickly leaned over and brushed my lips with his. I glanced around him and realized that he was making French toast. I loved French toast.

I ignored the mess and sat down at the table. "So, do you normally cook like this?" I teased.

He chuckled. "I'm normally a quick bagel or breakfast burrito type of guy. My mornings are hectic, so I don't get a chance to go all out like this. But when the weekends come around, it's my time to shine."

I thought he told me that he lived alone. I tried to remember if he'd had a roommate or family living with him back in North Carolina, but I couldn't. "I bet your housemates appreciate that."

He paused for the slightest beat and chuckled again. "I didn't have any housemates back home. I lived with my parents, helped them out for a while. I tried the roommate thing but that didn't work out. I always ended up being the one to clean up."

Okay, that makes sense, I thought. I got the plates out of the cabinet and set the table. Alex brought a large stack of golden slices of French toast, the carton of orange juice, and the syrup.

"This looks great. I'm normally a small breakfast kind of girl myself. You can't make a lot of food like this when you live alone," I said as I handed him the syrup. With his mouth full, he nodded. The food tasted amazing.

The familiar drone of the snowplow cut through our conversation as we finished breakfast. It was the unspoken cue that it was time for him to go home. After all, going slow meant giving each other space, not being in each other's faces right off the bat.

Alex got up to change into his warmer clothes. I pulled on my winter gear and we shoveled our way from the carport to the street along with the front walkway and the sidewalk. Without a word, he continued shoveling to my next-door neighbor's front door, clearing the steps as well. When I gave him a quizzical look, he just chuckled.

"There was an old guy sitting on the front porch smoking his pipe when I drove up last night. He reminded me of my Dad."

Seriously? The guy was a saint to animals, was a decent cook, had a hot body, and was thoughtful toward the elderly. *Is he for real?* His compassion and sincerity amazed me. *Maybe I've found a good one after all,* I thought.

After a quick trip inside to grab his bag, it was time for him to leave. "Thanks for letting me crash here and for a wonderful dinner. I'm really glad you asked me over. It feels good to talk to you," Alex said as we walked to his car.

"Yeah, same here."

Alex leaned in and gave me a slow, lingering, syrupy kiss. I reluctantly pulled myself away. I didn't want to show him too much too soon.

"Drive safely," I murmured against his lips.

"Of course. I'll give you a call later," he said softly. With a grin, he got into his Porsche and drove away.

I walked into the mudroom, locked the door behind me, and did the happy dance. Alex was a great guy. Not what I had expected and far better than had I dreamed.

***

PENNY AND I LAY around the house for most of the day cleaning and doing laundry, only venturing outside for a quick walk around the block. We ate Mom's leftovers for dinner and, by the time I switched on a rerun of "Glee", I still hadn't heard from Alex. It's not like I was a clingy person—I was very much about space and personal freedom—but I was a worrier. It was in my genes. The temperature had dropped and who knew where he had gone after he left here. For all I knew he was dead in a ditch somewhere. I figured a quick text wouldn't hurt and it would relive my anxiety. He said that he would call me later that night so I was just making the first move.

"Hope you got home safely."

There. Short and simple. I'm such a dork, I thought. I heard tires crunching on the packed snow. Out of the window, I saw a green SUV creep down the street and my nerves went on high alert. My stomach dropped. There was something strange about this SUV. Especially since it seemed to slow down even more once it got to my house. It was the same Expedition I had seen three days ago. If it had been any other car, I would have attributed the slowness to the driver being careful on the icy roads and wouldn't think anything more about it. I quickly locked both mudroom doors, set the motion detector and the alarm, and hustled Penny into my room. I couldn't stand being so afraid, so paranoid. There was probably a very logical reason behind that Expedition's slow crawl. It was probably someone new to the area or a visitor. Nothing to freak out about. A quick thought passed through my mind about sending a text to Shane, but I nixed that idea. He was up in Trenton, and it wasn't like he could get home in twenty minutes like usual. *No, I can do this. I'm not some wimpy girl who is going to be scared of her freaking shadow.* I patted the mattress for Penny to join me. I waited for sleep to take hold and after looking out of the window at nothing for the umpteenth time, it finally did.

CHAPTER 8

I WOKE UP TO A TEXT from Alex telling me that he had gotten home fine but his phone had died. He also said that he had a great time and that we should do it again. I was relieved to hear from him; the endless possibilities of things we could do together were running through my mind. I pushed my dirty thoughts aside so I could focus on getting ready for work. I let Penny outside while the coffee brewed and pulled on my snow boots. The boots looked ridiculous with my brown suede skirt, but I didn't care. Heels and ice were never a good combination and I was klutzy enough that I didn't need another reason to fall.

The next few days went by in a blur and before I knew it, it was Thursday. The federal case that Uncle

Bob was reluctant to take on actually came to fruition. A major player in a drug cartel had been arrested and the Assistant U.S. Attorney requested my uncle's firm to help. This case became the firm's highest priority, and most of the partners and paralegals were assigned to it. Everyone picked up the slack, including me. It entailed late nights and working meals. Because of the late nights, I didn't get to see Alex. We texted and emailed, but that was the extent of our communication. I hoped I could see him at some point during the weekend. Friday was going to be Valentine's Day and I wondered if he would be my "valentine". I could do without the lingerie, dying flowers and boxed candy. However, being a sentimental romantic dingdong, I couldn't help but get wrapped up in the romance of the holiday.

I also couldn't wait to hear Sarah squeal in my ear after Kyle's proposal on Friday. I was happy for both of them, but couldn't help but feel slightly jealous. Alex had potential, but there was that small pang of bitterness that always creeped up when I was smacked with the realization that I was the last in our group to have a relationship. It was pathetic really.

Friday came and no word from Alex. I wasn't surprised, just slightly disappointed. I kept telling myself that I was exhausted anyway and really should just go home and sleep. Most of the preliminary legwork on the case had been completed and Uncle Bob let everyone out at a normal hour. Of course, I believed that our being able to go home on time also had something to do with Aunt Karen coming into the office and giving Uncle Bob the look. The "we had plans, don't you DARE change them again or you will not make it out of here alive" look. I didn't argue and hightailed it out of the office. The week had been draining and it felt so good to leave work before eight o'clock. I headed to my mom's house, looking forward to a home-cooked meal after a week of nothing but pizza, deli sandwiches, and Chinese food. I would be happy if I never had to see another cardboard container again.

***

MOM DIDN'T FAIL ME and had meatloaf waiting. She'd been watching Penny, who greeted me at the door with a new woobie clenched in her jaw. "Hi Penny! Grandma is already spoiling you, huh?" I said to my wiggly fur-child.

"I'm not spoiling her. She didn't have any toys here. I couldn't let her be bored could I?" Mom asked, as she kissed my cheek.

I headed into the small kitchen where Mom was making a pot of mashed potatoes. "Apparently, your brother is up in Boston. Do you know anything about that?"

I gave Mom the wide-eyed innocent look. "He told you that he was going up there. It's Valentine's weekend, after all." I grabbed the plates from the cabinet and busied myself with setting the table.

"You forget, Megan; I know you. I know when you're hiding something," she retorted as she put the pot on the table. She hated being kept out of the loop and I hated keeping secrets from her, but I knew that Kyle wanted the proposal to be a surprise. I struggled between good and evil for a quick second and was saved by my phone ringing. I checked the caller ID and saw my long lost roommate's number. I hadn't seen him since the day after the burglary.

"What's up, Shane?" I answered. I brought over the corn and green beans from the counter while Mom filled the water glasses.

"Nothing much, I'm back in town and there's nothing in the fridge. What's for dinner?" Shane replied. The assumption that I would feed him and make sure the fridge was fully stocked annoyed me. He's a big boy; he could go grocery shopping. I rolled my eyes.

"I'm having dinner at Mom's. I've been working late and haven't had time to shop. There are some chicken nuggets in the freezer," I offered, as I shooed away

Mom's gestures. I knew she was offering to have him over but, truth be told, I didn't want him there. I didn't want to hear about his trip with Allison or think about what they did. I reminded myself I didn't care but, of course, a small piece of me did. Mom, on the other hand, did not like to hear about anyone being hungry. She grabbed the phone from my ear.

"Shane, it's Mom. Come on over. We have plenty." She ignored my looks of protest while she chatted with Shane. Shane and my mom had always gotten along. They had a similar sarcastic sense of humor and he always sided with her during our many debates. I sat down at the table with a huff as Mom hung up the phone.

"Don't act like that. He's practically family," she chided me. She placed another plate at the table, across from mine. She was right. I was acting childish. But I'd had a long week at work and was cranky. I deserved some spoiling from my own mother.

Ten minutes later I heard the truck in the driveway. Shane let himself in and greeted my mom with a big hug. My heart skipped a beat as usual, but it wasn't as difficult having him around as I thought. It also wasn't easy to look away; faded jeans hung on his hips and his green shirt played off the green in his eyes. He looked gorgeous. As usual, Mom fretted and fussed over him like he was her son or something. *Whatever*, I thought, as I gave him a small smile. *Where was my love and fuss?*

"Shane, you don't look like you feel well," Mom said, putting a soda in front of him.

Shane nodded. "It's been a tough couple of weeks. I'm drained." He took a small helping of meatloaf and started eating. She was right; Shane looked like he was coming down with something but maybe he was just tired. I scooted my chair slightly; I didn't want his cooties. I had big plans for the weekend. Okay, maybe not, but I was hoping.

"How was Jersey?" I asked. I wasn't curious. Much. I didn't want to hear details of whatever they had done. I was just trying to make conversation.

"Jersey was good. Busy." Simple answers. Par for the course with Shane. He wasn't one for details and obviously nothing exciting had gone on. I was grateful, until my mother started digging deeper.

"Why did you go to Jersey?"

"Oh. I had to work on Adrian's brother's bike. Then a couple other bikes came in, so I helped him with those."

"That's such a long drive for just you. Did Adrian go with you?" My mom knew damn well that he went with Allison. *What is she doing?* I shot her a look of annoyance.

"No, Allison went with me. We stopped by her folks' place on the way home and had a visit with them. We had a good time. She ended up staying there this weekend. Her brother will drive her back Sunday," Shane replied nonchalantly. He helped himself to more potatoes. I tried to ignore their conversation about Allison and her family. Not that I was jealous, mind you. It was just that I was more concerned with my own life. I didn't need to hear what I was missing or lacking.

Finally, the conversation and dinner came to an end. I declined dessert, not wanting to stay longer than necessary. I was exhausted and couldn't wait to take Penny home, take a hot shower, and watch mind-numbing TV. I gathered up my coat and Penny's overnight bag and gave Mom a hug.

"Thanks for everything, Mom," I said, kissing her on the cheek.

"Anytime, baby. Shane, wait a minute. You look really bad. Come here." She went over to Shane and did the whole cheek-to-forehead routine. Shane was a good foot taller than she was, so she made him bend over. Shane did look bad. His cheeks were flushed and his eyes were glassy.

"Yep. You feel hot. Megs, go get the thermometer." With an internal groan, I set my bags down. I knew it was selfish, but I just wanted to go home. I grabbed the digital reader and brought it back into the kitchen. I felt bad for him; he looked like garbage, and I cheerfully

body, but Shane had spent his entire youth as a jock. He had lifted weights every afternoon, played hockey, football, and lacrosse every year in high school and it was obvious that he had kept up with the workouts. Ten minutes later, Shane slowly emerged from the bathroom in just the pants. *Good gracious, this man is beautiful.* I pulled back the covers on the bed and handed him the Advil and juice.

"Take this. You'll feel better soon."

"Thanks, Megs. I knew I loved you for a reason," he mumbled, as he climbed into bed. *Loved me? Right. As a sister.* I ignored the wistful angst that suddenly surfaced in me as I pulled the blankets over him.

"Go to sleep. Feel better in the morning," I muttered, as I turned out the lights. I grabbed my pajamas from the bedroom and took a long shower myself. Mentally and physically drained, I thought about having a glass of wine but decided to have tea instead. I took some vitamin C to help fight off whatever Shane had brought home, and took my phone and tea upstairs. After some debate, I sent a quick message to Alex.

"Happy Valentine's day." *Maybe that will jog his memory*, I thought.

I had turned on a repeat of *Gone with the Wind* when my phone startled me. *It's eleven at night. Who in the hell is calling me at this hour?*

"Hello?"

"EEEEEEEEEEEEK!" A shrill squeal came through. *What in the world?* Then I recognized the squeal as Sarah.

"Hi, Sarah!" I exclaimed. I so desperately wanted to congratulate her, but I wanted her to tell me first. I didn't want to ruin anything if Kyle had a big elaborate proposal planned. I didn't have to wait long.

"WE'RE GETTING MARRIED!"

I burst out laughing. "Oh good! He did it! Congratulations! How did he do it?"

Gushing, Sarah told me how Kyle had surprised her when she got home with flowers and candles everywhere. She described the ring in perfect detail. I had known that Kyle had given Sarah my Great Aunt Nancy's engagement ring. Their marriage was the perfect symbol of love— sixty years of wedded bliss. My mother was all about preserving family heirlooms. In fact, Kyle would wear my father's wedding band, just as I would wear Mom's if or when that happy event happened for me.

"You do realize that as soon as the wedding is over Mom's going to expect some babies, right?" I teased.

Sarah laughed. "I figured as much. But it won't happen for a while. We have so much to plan. We're thinking October. The weather is still nice and the fall leaves will make a beautiful backdrop. And of course, you're my maid of honor."

"Perfect!" I replied. "I'm so excited! I can't wait to help you."

Sarah gave another squeal. We made plans to get together when she got back from school. Once we got off the phone, I smiled. After everything that Kyle had been through, Sarah was his guiding light. She had seen him through his juvenile delinquent stage, his angst about my dad. She had made my brother so happy. I was ecstatic for them. I wished for the same happiness for myself. Someone to come home to at night, someone to share the future with. Alex had potential, but I felt like he was holding back. Anytime I asked him a question about his home or his family, he got an uneasy expression on his face. Almost as if he didn't want to talk about it. Whatever. I pushed the thoughts out of my mind and clicked off the TV. Like Scarlett O'Hara, I decided I'd think about it tomorrow.

CHAPTER 9

PENNY WOKE ME UP early the next morning by licking my hand and whining. I looked at the clock with barely an eye open; it was only seven thirty. I glared at her.

"We have to get you off Mom's schedule," I grumbled, unhappy about getting up so early on a Saturday. I dragged myself downstairs and let her out, then checked on Shane. Still hot and flushed, I made sure he was still breathing. I brought him up some more juice and gently forced him to take another Advil. I felt bad for him. He was overworked and exhausted; no wonder this bug had hit him so hard.

I let Penny in and made breakfast. I checked my phone and realized Alex had texted me during the night.

"Had to go out of town for a day or so. Hope to get back tomorrow. Happy V-Day."

Well, that's good, I guess. He hasn't forgotten about me totally, I thought as I put away the dishes. Even though the sun was out, the temperature hovered around freezing and I didn't feel like venturing out. I spent the rest of the day bringing Shane juice and Mom's soup, and just hanging out with Penny. After the week I'd had, it felt good to sit and relax.

At a quarter to four, I got another text from Alex. "Will you be my valentine? I want to take you out to dinner tonight."

My heart did a little dance. He wanted to meet tonight! I started typing "sure", but hesitated. I really wanted to meet up with Alex but I didn't want to leave Shane alone. Granted, he wasn't my boyfriend and I wasn't responsible for him, but he was my friend. I couldn't leave him on his death bed. I felt conflicted. Deciding honesty was the best policy, I replied to Alex. "Would love to, but Shane's sick and I don't want to leave him."

Immediately, I received a response. "I understand. I'll see you soon then."

Well that blew it. No guy wanted to date a woman who would choose to take care of their sick roommate over them. I sighed as I tossed my phone on the couch and headed upstairs. Shane was snoring softly. Poor buddy, I thought, as I gently checked his forehead. His temperature seemed to have gone down, but he was still slightly warm. I closed his door and took a long shower. I was oddly tired for just having lain around the house.

After throwing on some yoga pants and a T-shirt, I wandered downstairs and checked the fridge hoping that by some luck we had something for dinner. Nope, no such luck. Mom's leftovers were gone, so it looked like takeout for us. I grabbed a bunch of menus and brought them up to Shane.

"How are you feeling?" I asked, standing in his doorway. There were dark shadows under his eyes. He looked exhausted.

"Feeling better than yesterday, I guess. What time is it?" he asked, sitting up in bed.

"It's five. Are you hungry? I'll even be nice and run to the store for you."

"Nah, not right now. I may order something later," he said, sinking back into the pillows.

I shrugged. "Okay. Do you want anything else? Some more juice?"

"Megs, I'll get it. I'm feeling okay enough to walk. I'm not a kid, you know," he teased.

"Whatever. You're such a baby when you're sick," I teased back. "Let me know if you need anything. I'll be downstairs."

I padded back downstairs and let Penny in. I was mentally debating what I could eat that wouldn't kill my diet when the doorbell rang. Hoping it was my mother with groceries, I dropped the menus on the table and rushed to the door.

"Hi Mom—oh!" I said with a start. Apparently, I had a knack for attracting good-looking men with food because Alex stood on my doorstep with a pizza from Ledo's, a box of chocolates, and a bouquet of roses.

"Hi! What are you doing here? Come in!" I said, standing back. He looked absolutely gorgeous in a gray ribbed sweater that matched his beautiful silver eyes.

"Hi, beautiful. Surprise. I knew you couldn't get out so I decided to come to you. Is that okay?" he said sweetly, kissing me on the cheek. I smiled like a goofball. What an amazing guy.

"Absolutely. I'm glad you came by," I replied, taking the pizza in one hand and his hand in the other. I led him into the kitchen where Penny was anxiously anticipating her slice. I gave him some plates and busied myself with the flowers. *Yeah, he's good.* I grabbed a slice and sat down next to him.

"So where did you have to go in such a rush?" I asked, trying to make conversation. I hoped I didn't sound nosy.

"I had to go to Virginia where my buddy Sean had a mare that was having a hard time foaling. It turned out okay though. She's fine. The filly was born with no issues," Alex said, gulping down his soda.

We had a good casual conversation and then headed into the living room to watch a movie. I turned on the latest *Pirates of the Caribbean* sequel and nestled in next to him. The moment I sat down Alex leaned in and gave me the softest kiss.

"I missed you. I really didn't mean to leave you hanging on Valentine's Day," he murmured.

"I missed you too. I'm glad you're here," I whispered, losing myself in his eyes. I lifted my lips to his and kissed him harder. Alex pressed me to him, wrapping his arms around my waist and pulling me onto his lap. His soft hands roamed the inside of my shirt, shooting electric sparks all the way down to my toes. I could feel him about to lift off my shirt when I heard a low cough.

"Oh, sorry guys. Didn't mean to interrupt."

I broke off mid-kiss and looked over at Shane. Fresh out of the shower and wearing nothing but low-cut sweats that left nothing to the imagination as to what was underneath. He had a serious issue with bad timing.

"What are you doing out of bed?" I asked, slightly out of breath. I felt a tinge of embarrassment and at the same time a bit smug. I knew it was juvenile, but

I wanted to prove to myself that I was over him. He apparently didn't care what he almost interrupted, because he came over and sat down on the couch next to us. He opened the box of chocolates sitting on the coffee table and popped one his mouth.

"I'm starving. Did you end up getting something for dinner?" he said pathetically. I sighed. I knew I shouldn't be mad at him. After all, he was sick. I looked over at Alex with the question on my face.

Alex gave a resigned sigh and said, "Hey, man. There's some pizza in the kitchen. Help yourself."

Shane slapped his shoulder and heaved himself off the couch. "Thanks, bro. I appreciate that."

"Thank you," I whispered to Alex, leaning in to kiss him. He gave me a beautiful smile.

"Maybe he'll take that pizza upstairs with him," he said with a wicked gleam in his eye. I giggled, but then gave a low groan when Shane plopped himself next to us again. I didn't have to look at Alex to know the frustration he was feeling.

"Why don't you go back to bed? You still look like crap," I urged, hoping he'd get the hint.

He shrugged. "Megs, I feel lousy, I'm just tired of being in bed. Plus, I miss Penny," he replied, handing Penny his crust. Out of habit and my mother's internal nagging, I reached over and felt his forehead.

"You're not terribly hot, but you should take some Advil—which is upstairs, by the way—just in case." Shane ignored me. With a sigh, I got off Alex's lap and stomped upstairs. I grabbed the Advil off Shane's nightstand and started back down to the living room. I stopped when I heard them talking, their voices low. I felt like a teenage spy, but I couldn't help myself from eavesdropping.

"I know you're feeling ill, but why don't you give Megan some space. You're a grown man; you don't need her to be your nursemaid," I heard Alex say quietly.

"I know I don't need her to be my nursemaid. She does it because she's my friend," was Shane's dry reply.

"Yeah, I guess. But why doesn't your girl come over and take care of you? Let me and Megan have some quality time," Alex asked. I couldn't see what he was doing but I was surprised at Shane's tone.

"Really? I believe my girl is taking care of me. She is my girl, dude. I have her best interests at heart. Which is more than I can say for you," Shane sniped back.

"What's that supposed to mean?" Alex shot back.

"What kind of man leaves a woman like Megan alone on Valentine's Day? What the hell was so important that you had to totally ignore her?"

Silence.

"I don't have to answer to you." Alex's voice

sounded pissed.

"Actually, yes you do. Because if you hurt her or upset her, I'll make sure it's the last thing you do," Shane said.

Oh shit, I thought. This wasn't good. I hurried downstairs and found Alex and Shane standing up, facing each other.

"Hey guys, what's going on?" I asked. The air was thick with testosterone. *What is this? Some sort of my-dick-is-bigger-than-yours contest?*

Alex was the first to break the stare-off. "You know what, it's late and I'm beat. I'm going to head out. Happy Valentine's Day." He gave me a quick peck and walked out the door.

I stared after him then spun around to Shane. "What the hell did you do that for?"

Shane looked indifferent. "He's a jerk, Megs. He's playing you."

My temper, as well as a lack of good sleep, got the best of me. "What the hell do you mean, he's playing me? How the hell do you know that? You don't know him at all! I would have liked to spend a night with the man I'm interested in. But no! Not even on Valentine's weekend. Seriously, Shane. What the fuck is your problem?"

He looked contrite, but that quickly changed when

he opened his mouth. "Look. Whether you find out now or later, I can just tell that he's a jerk. He's a player. I know guys like him and they are only after one thing. And where the hell was he yesterday? Certainly not spending Valentines Day with *you*."

The tiny seed of doubt grew bigger at Shane's words. He said out loud what the tiny voice in my head had been saying all along. But I pushed back. *Screw this. Shane has no idea what he's talking about.*

"So what! Who cares what he's after? Maybe I want the same thing! You don't know that! You don't get to decide who I see. Next time let me handle my own business. Stay out of it," I retorted. I grabbed a bottle of water and headed upstairs. My temper flared, but I wasn't sure who I was more pissed at. Antagonizing Alex like that was a purely selfish move on Shane's part, but Shane's accusation echoed in my head. Is Alex really a player? *Shut up!* It didn't matter if he was seeing someone else. We never said we were exclusive. I climbed into bed and sent a quick message to Alex. "Sorry Shane ruined our night. We'll get together soon."

And with that, I shut my phone off and closed my eyes. I knew Alex wouldn't be angry with me so I wasn't worried about a return text. I just wished I knew what had gotten Shane worked up.

CHAPTER 10

THE NEXT MORNING, I WOKE UP and Shane was gone. "Apparently, the sickly is unsick," I said to Penny. It irked me that he could get up without apologizing. But his priorities were evident. Then I remembered that it was Sunday: Allison was due home. I banished all negative thoughts. Especially about Shane. Shane and Alex were going to have to get along if Alex and I were going to continue to see each other.

I made myself get dressed and sent a quick message to Jen. "Let's do breakfast."

Jen agreed and we made plans to meet at the diner down the street for some pancakes and coffee. I started to head up the street when I got a message from Alex. "We WILL get together soon. Don't you worry about it.

I'll call you later."

I let out a sigh. I knew he wouldn't be mad at me; I had done nothing wrong. Nevertheless, the fact that he still wanted to get together was promising. And I knew full well what type of together he wanted and any type of together was fine with me.

***

I walked into the diner and found Jen and Lauren in a corner booth with Lauren's array of distractions spread out in front of her.

"Hi, guys!" I exclaimed, giving them each a kiss on the cheek.

"Hi, Auntie Meg. I'm coloring a picture for you," Lauren said brightly. She was dutifully working on a picture that I was unable to identify. Jen just shrugged.

"So what's going on? How are things going with Alex?" she asked, sipping her coffee.

"Okay, I guess." I proceeded to fill her in on what happened the night before. She was more clued into Shane's mind than I was, so I was hoping she had some insight. Apparently, his behavior baffled Jen as well.

"I don't know what's been going on with him. He's had some issues lately at the shop from what I can gather. Maybe Alex just pressed his buttons," Jen offered, digging into her pancakes.

"You're right, I'm sure." I deftly changed the subject. I pushed the incident out of my mind. I wasn't going to worry about it anymore. He'd been overstressed, and being sick hadn't helped matters. "What's going on with you?"

We sat and talked for the next hour and eating until we were stuffed to the gills. I put Lauren's latest picture in my purse and promised her that I'd put it on my fridge.

***

SHANE WASN'T HOME when I arrived, which I took as a good sign. Whatever his issue was, he needed to chill out. I spent the rest of the day texting with Alex. He was stuck at the emergency vet hospital so we couldn't spend any more time together, and the way my work load was shaping up, it didn't seem like we'd be able to get together any time soon.

Or so I thought. As the weeks went by, I saw Alex quite a bit. Not for long periods of time, but enough to keep up our mutual interest. He came over to the house and we would have dinner, or we'd meet for coffee. Shane always disappeared when Alex came around, which I took to mean that he still didn't like him. Fine by me. I didn't need that drama and Shane's absence helped things progress between Alex and me. I felt like we were getting closer, but it never went beyond kissing. I was holding back, but not entirely sure why. I enjoyed spending time with him though, so I was especially excited when he unexpectedly asked me over to his place for the first time.

I reminisced about my teenage years as I drove down the gravel path toward the farm. Cooper Ridge Farm was only fifteen minutes away from where I lived. It was a beautiful and picturesque farm with a guest and main house on top of a hill. The stables, pastures, and barns were the first things you saw when you came down the driveway. Weather-beaten and a faded blue, the stables were still the way I remembered them. The smell of hay and horses brought me back to when Dad would drop me off at the crack of dawn to feed and water the horses, muck out their stalls, and clean the tack. I did it every weekend to pay for my riding lessons.

"When's the last time you rode?" Alex asked. It was a beautiful, cool day with a light breeze coming from the west.

I glanced at him and listened to our boots crunching the small rocks. "Geez, it has been a while. I think it's been at least two years."

Alex led me down the concrete walkway past the

empty stalls and stopped in front of my favorite old mare. Her dark brown eyes looked deep into mine, maybe seeing the teenager I used to be. I almost started to cry. I wrapped my arms around her and buried my face in her neck.

"Wow. Coffee. She's still here," I said, amazed that she was still around. "I thought her owner had sold her."

Alex gently ran his hand down Coffee's shoulder, patting her lightly. "Mary bought her off of the owner about three months ago. She's a great teacher for the kids."

I brought her out into the barn's hallway, hooked her up to the crossties, and quickly fastened her tack. Alex's bay, Avery, was already saddled and ready to go. We rode up and down the hills, across the pastures, and through the woods. Being outside with Alex made me feel free and at ease. I felt so comfortable with him. The conversation never died. Despite the cool air, we returned to the stable flushed and sweaty. We cooled down the horses by walking them around the indoor ring. I missed this part of my life and welcomed the achiness I knew I would feel in the morning. After we put Coffee and Avery back into their stalls, we walked up the hill, hand in hand, to the cozy guesthouse. The light faded as the sun set; the promise of dinner had my stomach grumbling.

"I can't make any guarantees that you're going to be blown away by my cooking. But I promise that you won't go hungry," he joked, as he opened the door. The cottage had an open area with a bedroom and bathroom and a small galley kitchen. The beautiful brick fireplace was the main source of heat.

Surprisingly, he had done very little to make it into a home. I didn't see any framed pictures on the walls or on the maple side tables, just piles of car magazines, books, and three different gaming consoles. Simple and spartan, it reminded me of a grown-up dorm room. While he tooled away in the kitchen, I wandered over to his couch and perused his books. With the exception of two bestsellers, I had not heard of any of the titles.

"Do you want some wine?" Alex called. "I have red." I was normally not a fan of reds but I was never one to refuse wine. I hoped tonight would be the night we took our relationship to the next level. A little liquid courage couldn't hurt.

"Sure. Are you sure I can't help you with dinner?" I asked, as I wandered over to the kitchen to stand in the archway. He flashed me one of his brilliant smiles and handed me a glass of wine.

"I know you're used to taking the helm in the kitchen, but I have it under control," he said, as he slipped his arm around my waist and gave me a quick kiss. I had to chuckle. For the last month and a half, I had been doing most of the cooking. I enjoyed trying out new recipes and updating old favorites. Alex didn't seem to mind being my guinea pig. And ever since the french toast disaster the first time he came over, I didn't want him near my kitchen. We chatted while Alex cooked, joking and flirting. The wine warmed me from the inside and replaced my nervousness with confidence. My anticipation for dessert heightened every time he smiled at me. *Oh yeah. This is why I shaved my legs!* I thought. Once dinner was ready, Alex called me in to fill my plate. With no table to sit at, we carried our food to the couch in front of the fire.

"Sorry about this. I haven't gotten around to getting furniture," he said sheepishly, taking a sip of his wine.

"It's okay. It just looks like you packed up your dorm and brought it with you," I joked with a knowing glance to the video games. Alex laughed along with me.

"I didn't have much when I came up here. I'm lucky that the place came with furniture. I just brought my TV and clothes."

"Such the typical bachelor," I teased, as I leaned in for a kiss. He tasted like red wine and responded eagerly. I could forget dinner, I thought, as I wrapped my arms around his neck. Alex leaned me back, his arms wrapped around my waist. The kiss was never ending.

I could feel his hands gently gliding underneath my sweater and I loved every minute of it. My pulse raced and my toes curled. The feeling of enjoyment quickly disappeared when a knock came at the door.

"Ignore it," I muttered. Alex obliged and his hands continued roaming my rib cage. The knocking got louder, until I could hear an old man's voice loudly.

"Alexander! Open up, it's your grandpa!"

Suddenly Alex shot up. His eyes grew wide and he looked like a teenager getting caught with a girl in his room. "Shit!" He fixed his shirt and pulled me up into a sitting position.

"Sorry about this. Let me get him out of here." He hurried over to the door. This was so funny, seeing him so worried. *Has he never had a girl over before? Why is he so nervous?* I wondered, as I took a bite of the cooled chicken.

"Hey, Pop. What's up?" Alex said, blocking me from his grandfather's view. It was obvious that he was hiding something.

"Alexander, it's fifty degrees out here. What kind of ungrateful grandson are you to leave an old man outside in the cold? Move aside and let me in. I need to talk with you," Dr. Collins grumbled, brushing past him. With a sigh, Alex opened the door farther to let him in.

"Oh good, you have dinner cooking. I'm starved

and the old fart's place is having creamed chicken. Everything is creamed and mashed for people without teeth. Oh. You have a visitor," he mumbled, barely acknowledging me as he headed into the kitchen. I looked at Alex, puzzled. He just shrugged his shoulders in response.

Dr. Collins brought his plate over to the love seat and began eating without a word. Alex nervously drank his wine and waited for his grandfather to finish his meal. I was eager to get back to where we left off.

"You're Norah Connors's girl right? How's Micki doing?" he asked, not looking up from his food. "Alex, get me a soda will you?"

"Um, yes. I'm Norah's daughter. Micki is doing well. Thank you," I stammered, not sure of what else to say. Alex and I watched his grandfather eat in awkward silence. It was obvious that Dr. Collins took his sweet time and enjoyed the inconvenience that he was bestowing on his grandson.

"I have to say boy, this isn't half bad. Course, not as good as Lenny's cooking, but it should do for you while you're up this way," Dr. Collins said, patting his bulging stomach and leaning back in the chair.

Knowing that Alex had a great relationship with his grandfather and feeling good about where I stood with him, I piped up. "Who's Lenny?" I figured Lenny was a cousin, since Alex had told me he was an only child.

"Alex's wife, of course," Dr. Collins said innocently. My heart dropped into my stomach. *Married? Oh my God, Alex is married? What the hell?* My eyes narrowed as I turned to gape at him. Alex buried his head into his hands. I glanced at Dr. Collins. That was not an innocent comment. Dr. Collins knew exactly what he was doing.

"Oh. That's right. Your wife," I said slowly. I debated throwing my now-cold dinner at his head, but decided against it. I simply picked up my plate and carried it into the kitchen, with Alex following my every step.

"Megan. Wait! Don't go," he whispered, desperation flooding his voice. I ignored him. Too many curses and insults swirled in my head. I couldn't speak. I was in shock.

"Megan, I'm so sorry. Please let me explain," he pleaded. I flew around and poked him in the chest.

"Married? You're fucking married? Are you kidding me? When were you going to tell me? Were you just going to go back to North Carolina and not say anything?" I sputtered.

"Megan, it was never brought up," he said weakly.

"Never brought up? You wanted to get me in bed the first time you came over! It should have been brought up then! I guess kissing another woman is okay as long as you don't bring up your wife!" I spat out. It infuriated me that he was making excuses. What possible excuse could he come up with that would remotely make any sense?

"You would have never told me and would have just kept leading me on. I can't believe I fell for your scam! Is this why Shane got upset? Did he know that you were married?" I demanded. He said nothing, which confirmed my suspicions. I shook my head and tried to rein in my fury. "You son of a bitch. He was right. You're nothing but a lowlife asshole. I can't believe I trusted you. Go to hell. You don't deserve me and I sure as hell don't need a jackass like you. And for that matter, neither does your wife," I said venomously. I squelched the urge to hit him and instead simply turned my back and walked over to Dr. Collins. I wasn't sure if he had heard our exchange, but I didn't care. His grandson was a bastard, and I wasn't going to listen to his excuses.

"Dr. Collins. It's been really enlightening talking to you today. Thank you. Enjoy your retirement," I said as I pulled on my jacket and scarf. I ignored Alex's pleading stares as I walked over to the door. Before I closed it behind me, I heard Dr. Collins tell Alex, "You done screwed up, boy."

I pulled away from the house, my tires spinning on the gravel driveway.

***

I WAS HALFWAY DOWN Central Avenue before the hot angry tears started rolling. I brushed them away furiously. I refused to cry over this bastard, but my emotions had other ideas. As if on autopilot, my car went directly to the Davidsonville Deli. I came out with a carton of Ben and Jerry's and two freshly baked peanut butter cookies. I drove home, let Penny out, and curled up on the couch with my ice cream in hand, only getting up to let her back in. Stupid Alex. I wasn't sure if I should be angrier at him or myself. The late night calls, the fact that he rarely brought up his home life, the odd times he was "out of town". All these things were signs and I just ignored them. Guys just suck, I thought, as I spooned the last of the Chubby Hubby ice cream into my mouth.

And now, because of Alex, I barely saw Shane anymore. We hadn't spoken much lately, only exchanging texts about bills and Penny. The incident between him and Alex had cooled our friendship. Shane rarely came home before the sun came up and, by the time I got home from work, he was gone again. I missed having him around, but I suppose it was for the best. I had been trying to get over him and for the most part I thought I had. Those feelings never truly went away. Alex was a good distraction and it proved that I could move on from Shane.

Speak of the devil. The familiar roar of Shane's motorcycle broke the silence. *I don't want to deal with anyone right now. I'd rather be left alone in my misery.* Apparently, Shane wasn't in the mood to be social either; he just walked through the door and up the stairs with a grunt of hello. I rolled my eyes. He probably had a fight with Allison or something. I hadn't seen her around, but then again, I hadn't been paying attention. I checked my watch. Only eight thirty. I figured I might as well go to bed; I had already disgusted myself by eating an entire container of ice cream.

I let Penny out one last time and, as I waited for her to do her business, I checked my Blackberry. One missed text from Jen inviting me out to our favorite tavern in Edgewater. I thought about telling her no, then shook my head. Why sit here at home and wallow in self-pity? I was better than that. I wasn't going to let some loser bring me down. Cheering myself on, I let Penny inside and headed up the stairs.

I passed by Shane's room. *What the hell,* I thought. *I'll bring him along.* He probably needed to let loose as well. I knocked on his door. He answered me with his phone against his ear and a little gasp escaped. I was completely awestruck. Shane still had on his dirty shop jeans but they hung low on his hips. His chest was completely bare. Absolutely hot. I struggled to remember the reason why I was at his door in the first place.

"Hang on," he mouthed to me and then turned around and sat on his bed. I didn't dare move from the door frame. I waited until he had finished his conversation.

"What's up, stranger?" he asked, as he squeezed me tightly. My mind stopped functioning and my body warmed at his touch. *Good lord, get a grip.*

"I haven't seen you in a while. Just checking in with my roommate," I joked. I pulled myself out of his embrace reluctantly. Rebound or not, I knew this was a path I shouldn't go down again.

"Yeah, I know. Work has been hell," Shane replied, running his hands through his short hair.

"Same here. It's been a hellish week. I need to let loose. Jen and the rest of the crew are meeting up at Double J's later. You and Allison should join us."

"Um. I'll think about it. I'll probably come by later. There are a few things I need to do tonight. But Allison won't be there. We aren't together anymore, or whatever you call it," he said. Shane didn't look too upset about the breakup. I guess he was telling the truth when he said that they were just having fun together.

"Oh yeah? What happened?" I asked, then hurriedly corrected myself. "You don't have to tell me. It's none of my business."

Shane shrugged. "It doesn't matter. We just, you know, decided to go our separate ways. We're still cool though."

I nodded nonchalantly. "Yeah, Alex and I split too. Apparently, he's married. You were right. He was playing me," I blurted out. Shane looked away and I realized he had been holding back. "You knew."

Shane shrugged. "I didn't know he was married, but I knew he was with someone else. The day I left for Trenton, I was behind him at Starbucks. He was talking to someone on his phone, and he mentioned something about being in love for the last four years and how he wished she could be here with him. I didn't realize it was him until he came over. I'm sorry I didn't tell you. I didn't want to be right."

I was stunned. Shane knew all this time and had kept it from me. I didn't know if I should be angry or not. Would I have believed him, I wondered. *Just like you believed Shane when he told you Alex was a player?* the sensible voice in my head said. Probably not.

"Don't sweat it. I've learned my lesson to go with my gut instinct more often," I joked weakly.

Shane lightly punched my arm. "Did you at least kick his ass?"

"I thought about it, but didn't. I wish I had," I

replied. I checked my watch and realized the time. "So about tonight, I'm planning on drinking so I'll call a cab around ten or so. Let me know if you're going to come with me."

"Yeah, maybe."

I turned around and headed to my room. I quickly showered and pulled on my sexiest panties and bra. Who knew? I might decide to bring someone home. Penny's tail thumped as I looked through my closet. I needed to look good, feel confident. I decided on a low-cut, navy blue wrap shirt and my favorite dancing jeans. After drying my hair and running a flat iron through it, I called for a cab and applied my makeup while I waited. I knew Shane had already left. He didn't tell me he was leaving, but a quick check of his room confirmed it. I had no clue where he went off to and pushed aside a pang of disappointment. Shane didn't need to be at the bar for me to have a good time. No more relationships. No more talk of Mr. Right, or sulking and whining. Only thing to do was to have fun with my friends.

***

I GOT TO THE BAR a little before ten thirty. Jen, along with the rest of my friends, had commandeered a corner booth.

"Hey, everyone!" The chorus of hellos could barely be heard over the din of the music. The bass rattled my bones and the music beckoned me to the dance floor.

"Drinks are on the house, Megs," called Josh. Since he was the club's co-owner, our group received special perks.

I gave him a thumb up sign. Thank God I took a taxi. Free drinks were dangerous. I headed for Jason, my favorite bartender, Josh's brother, and the other co-owner of Double J's.

"Hey, girl! Haven't seen you in forever," he said with a big grin. He reached across the bar to give me a big hug. Jason and I have been good friends since high school. It was easy for me to be friends with him; there was never any drama between us. "What's your poison tonight?"

"Hi J, I'll take the usual," I said, giving him a big smile. I felt confident. I was going to forget that Alex was a lying, stupid man-whore. I was going to enjoy flirting and being single and I wasn't going to let a loser like Alex ruin my fun.

"So how's it going?" he asked as he handed me my beer.

"It's going good. How are you? This place is crazy! How are you handling the bar and baseball? I haven't talked to you in a while," I said, pushing closer to the bar so he could hear me.

"I'm constantly running. But things are going great. Josh and I are a pretty good team. And baseball is going great. Spring training is in full swing right now. I'm pitching really well," he said, completely ignoring the guy next to me who jockeyed for Jason's attention. Not only was Jason running the bar, he was also in a minor league baseball team.

"That's great!" I exclaimed.

"Hey, sweet cheeks, if you're not going to order, can you move that fine behind?" said the guy next to me. Though he looked vaguely familiar, I couldn't place him. I rolled my eyes. Black hair, tanned, brown eyes, dressed in a plaid button-down shirt and jeans. I knew him from somewhere. But where?

"Yeah, sure buddy. J, I'll see you in a bit," I said with a grin. I took my drink back to the table and settled in next to Jen. We chatted for a few minutes, but the music called my name. I grabbed her hand and pulled her onto the dance floor.

We danced for what seemed like forever. I danced with the girls and several different guys. They were all cute, but no one had the moves to match mine. There was a saying that what a guy does on the dance floor reflects his bedroom skills. I wasn't looking for a booty call, but it had been a long time.

I started to get hot. The dance floor was becoming too crowded, so I pulled my hair up into a messy knot and yelled to Jen, "I'm getting a drink." I walked toward the main bar, but more people came over as a ballad came on. Finally, I was able to get in front of the crowd and grabbed the attention of the other bartender, Fallon.

"Hey, Megan!" she said, her long black hair hanging loosely over her strapless shirt. She reached across the bar to give me an awkward kiss on the cheek. Fallon was Jen's college roommate and we'd been friends ever since. "I didn't realize you'd be here tonight," she said, passing out drinks.

"Yeah, there's a big group of us. We're with Josh."

"Ah, that's right. Awesome. It's nuts in here tonight. The winter freeze is over and people are getting out."

"Seriously, sweet cheeks, why is it that you're always chatting up the bartenders when a man is trying to get his drink," said a vaguely familiar voice from behind me. It was the guy from before and my brain finally clicked on his name.

I raised an eyebrow. "You're Dominic, right?" I knew I remembered him. He ran with a bad crowd from high school. Apparently, even ten years later, he still hadn't grown up.

"Yeah, baby. I knew you'd remember me at some point. I didn't forget you," he said in a surly tone. He was obviously drunk and tried to run his hand down my arm. I pulled away.

"Yeah. Well, nice talking to you." I turned my back to him and waited for Fallon to get my drink.

"Don't turn away," he said, touching my arm "You're here, I'm here; let's dance for a while and see how well you remember me."

I yanked my arm back. "No thanks. And don't touch me. I'm here with someone, not you."

Dominic grabbed my arm roughly. His brown eyes blazed. I could tell he was not used to hearing the word no. "You don't need to act like that. Come on baby. Let's dance."

I could see Fallon wave to someone, but I couldn't see who. God, I didn't want to cause a scene and cause security to come over. I didn't need anyone to fight my battles, I could fight them myself. I looked down at his sleazy hand on my arm and balled up my fists.

"Listen, asshole, if you don't get your hand off me, I'm going to break it," I warned.

Dominic just laughed and let go. "If you're here with someone, where is he? Huh?"

"Hey, baby, did you miss me?" said a voice behind me. A pair of muscular tattooed arms wrapped around my waist. I knew that voice. Shane. I breathed a sigh of relief. I looked up at him. His beautiful eyes were hard and his jaw was clenched. His body was coiled in anger. Shane was ready to drop this clown to the floor. I played the role and stood up on my toes to kiss his jaw line. I could feel a little quiver in his body as he relaxed his stance slightly.

"Hey, sweetie. Of course I did," I said with a smug smile on my lips.

"What's up, Dominic?" Shane said with a nod, his tone undeniably cold. Shane is a gentle man, but he is also a protector. He never fought unless it was necessary and when he did fight, he rarely lost.

"Shane. Sorry man, I didn't realize she was with you," Dominic said, backing off slightly.

Shane ignored him and loudly whispered, "Let's dance." Taking my hand, he led me to the dance floor. I turned and saw Fallon watching us with anticipation. "Thanks," I mouthed, as Shane pulled me away. She just grinned. She knew how close Shane came to kicking Dominic's ass.

My favorite Usher song came on and Shane pulled me close. With my body tingling from his touch, my hopes soared. But I felt the need to give him an out, just in case. "Thanks for helping me, but I could have handled him. I think you made your point. You don't have to dance with me if you don't want to."

Shane gave me a mischievous grin. "We can't let

Dominic see you dancing alone can we? What, you don't want to dance with me?"

I had to smile. "Oh shut up, you fool."

He put his hands on my hips, and pulled me closer. Shane swayed his body in time with mine, matching me step to step. We fit perfectly. I was captivated by how well our bodies seem to fuse together. I threw my arm around his neck as he held me. We were so close air couldn't have found a space between us. Electric sparks shot straight to my toes and I had to remember to breathe. I looked up at him; his eyes were dark and inviting. I don't know if it was the loneliness of being single or the heat of the moment, but I put my other arm around his neck and tentatively touched my lips to his. *I cannot believe I just did that.* My cheeks flamed with embarrassment.

"Sorry," I stammered.

Shane's response stole what little breath I had left. He crushed his lips hungrily to mine. Those electric sparks were nothing compared to what I felt then. Fire broke out all over my body, the sensation shot right through me to a place that had been idle for far too long—my heart (and some place lower). His tongue gently caressed mine, and I sighed in ecstasy. Shane broke the kiss off first; there was fire in his eyes. "Damn, Megan," he muttered, holding me tight. *Oh my God, what did I do?*

I can't believe we kissed!

"Let's get out of here while we're still standing," he growled, pulling me off the dance floor.

We quickly walked over to the booth. It was practically empty, save for Josh and his wife. They were so busy with each other, they didn't notice when I pulled out my coat and purse. Shane grabbed my hand and led me outside to his Harley. He handed me his spare helmet and put on his. He lifted up the visor on my helmet, looked me in the eyes, and said, "Are you ready?" I nodded. The promise and meaning of his words shot right to my belly, which flipped at the sound of them. My heart slammed against my chest as he helped me climb on. Even though we'd been friends for so long, I'd never had the chance to ride with Shane. Pressing myself against his back with a powerful machine underneath, I was nearly undone. The closer we got to home, the hotter my blood burned. I didn't want to think anymore, I wanted to feel. And by God, I wanted to feel him.

***

Before I knew it, we were pulling up into the driveway. He put the brake down and helped me off.

"I'm just going to put this in the shed," he said, not

looking at me. *Oh God. I've made a complete ass of myself.* I simply nodded and unlocked the door. Penny was fast asleep so I just left my purse and coat on the bench and headed upstairs to my room. Disappointment and sexual frustration rolled off of me. *Did the scene in the club really happen? Did I read too much into his kiss? Oh, forget it.* I couldn't keep it hidden anymore. It was now or never, consequences be damned. I was debating if I should brush my teeth when I heard his footsteps on the stairs.

The butterflies were twisting my stomach. I needed to say something before it got awkward. I hadn't had that much to drink so I couldn't blame the alcohol. Hearing him behind me, I quickly turned around with the words "I'm sorry" on the tip of my tongue. But I never got to say them. Shane put his arms around me and kissed me with such need that I nearly lost my balance.

"Shane, I…" I whispered, pulling back slightly. My body was telling my head to shut up.

"You don't know how long I've wanted to do this," he whispered, his lips against mine. My body melted against his, consumed by need. It was time to live for the moment. His tongue danced with mine as he picked me up and wrapped my legs around him, then placed me on top of my dresser. He lifted my shirt over my head and while his lips suckled and teased the most sensitive spot on my neck, he slowly undid my bra, as if he was torturing me on purpose. My frantic hands fumbled with the buttons on his shirt until I pulled it over his broad shoulders. Shane's lips kissed a trail down my neck and chest, finding my nipple. He gently raised my breast, massaging and kneading while his tongue pulled and fondled the very tip. My body was on fire and his touch intensified it. He picked me up again and laid me on the bed. He pulled off my jeans and my light blue satin boy shorts. The cool breeze from my ceiling fan only fanned the flames that consumed my naked body.

"Megan," he sighed. Pressing his body to mine, I felt his erection through his thin jeans. I wanted—no, I needed—to feel it. I grasped for his belt, but he smiled and slid his body farther down. His lips and tongue navigated every inch of my torso, moving to my core. I cried out with ecstasy as Shane slowly stroked my most sensitive area, first with his finger, then with his tongue. I gasped for breath as I felt myself climbing higher and higher as his stubble grazed my ultrasensitive flesh. I arched my body and tightened my thighs around his neck, begging him for more. With every thrust and every pull, I got closer to the brink. I begged, "Shane. Please." He moaned in agreement. He finally brought his face to mine and I eagerly kissed him, tasting myself on his tongue. Standing up, Shane quickly discarded his jeans and pulled out a condom. I took it out of his hands. Staring straight into his eyes, I placed it over him. Shane growled and crushed his lips to mine as I guided his hard cock inside me.

"Oh dear God," I moaned. That fire on the dance floor applied to the bedroom as well. I had never had a man make me feel so good. It was as if his body was made to fit mine. We moved together, matching each other's movements and needs. My body was a roller coaster, cresting and crashing with each stroke. I felt constant explosions and my body started shaking. I couldn't get enough of him. Shane's teeth nipped the curve of my neck as I dug my nails into his back. I pulled his lips to mine, greedily taking whatever he gave me. We exploded together, groaning loudly. We were both out of breath. My heart was racing. He rolled over on the bed and lay his head on my pillow, pulling me next to him. Panting, I gazed up at his face. I had always imagined what it would be like to make love to Shane. My dreams and fantasies were nothing compared to this. He gently stroked my jawline and kissed my lips softly. I fell asleep as he was stroking my arm, without even worrying about the next day.

CHAPTER 11

I OPENED ONE EYE AND LET my arm reach over to touch him, to see if it had all been real. All I felt was the coolness of the sheets. I closed my eyes, reliving the memories of last night. *Last night was absolutely magical*, I thought, as I stretched my sore muscles. No awkwardness, no hesitation.

I lay there thinking for a while until it was time to face the music. I sniffed the air. Coffee. He made coffee. I sat up and realized I was stark naked. I threw on some clothes and was about to head down the stairs, when my door opened. Shane was shirtless, his sweatpants hanging low on his hips.

"Hi," I said shyly. How was I supposed to act after sleeping with someone who was until very recently totally off limits? I didn't have to wonder long.

"Hey, you." He placed my favorite mug full of coffee on the nightstand and came over to me. He cradled my face in his hands and gave me the most luxurious kiss. My toes curled, my pulse raced, and it took everything I had to keep from throwing him on the bed. When he pulled back, I had to blink to make sure I was in reality.

"Um—," I started tentatively, but his finger on my lips silenced me. He gazed at me with his beautiful brown eyes.

"Last night was amazing. I've wanted to kiss you for the longest time; I just didn't know how you felt. Unless it was just the alcohol talking?" he faltered, raising an eyebrow.

"No. I loved last night. I've been waiting for last night. I just didn't want this to be awkward," I said, deciding that laying it all out in the open would be the best way to approach whatever it was we were doing.

"What would be awkward? It's us, Megan. You and me: two people who are attracted to and care about each other. I've had these feelings for you for so long, but I wasn't sure you felt the same way," he said, gently kissing me again. This was the first time I had truly seen him open himself up to me. My stomach flipped and my heart soared. *He has feelings for me.*

"If only I had known," I whispered. Shane's arms

tightened around me as he pressed his lips to mine. Our kiss deepened as his hands made their way up my shirt and the fire inside me started smoldering again. His cell phone rang.

"Argh," he groaned. "I have to take this."

"Yeah, Adrian," he said, walking out of the room. I wanted to scream, "Come back and finish what you started!" but I refrained. I brought my coffee downstairs and flicked on the TV. I forced myself not to wonder what it all meant. Like Shane said, we were two adults who cared about each other.

I turned on the Morning Show while Shane was upstairs. It was Saturday and I didn't have any other plans but to relax. Apparently, my mother didn't realize my plans when she called.

"Hi sweetie," she said.

"Hi, Mom. What's up?" I didn't pay much attention and choked on my coffee when I heard her say ". . . and the police came to check it out."

"Wait. What did you say, Mom? What about the police?"

"I just told you. Someone broke into the house. But don't worry, nothing was stolen. The police think it was some random teenager prank or something. Apparently there have been a string of break-ins lately," she said, exasperated that her twenty-six-year-old daughter still had the attention span of a child. I quietly processed this. Mom didn't know about the break-in at my house, I hadn't wanted to scare her. I wonder if she had told Kyle.

"Yes, I told your brother," she said, reading my mind like always. "He threw a fit, obviously. Kyle contacted your cousin Jeff, who's coming out tomorrow to install a new security alarm. Apparently the one I have now is too old." She sounded frustrated. I knew my brother. As the man in the family, he took his job of protector extremely serious.

"I'm glad that you're okay. Do you want to stay here until Jeff comes over?" I asked. I didn't want her to be alone if, God forbid, they came back.

"No, that's alright. I was planning on heading out to the beach with your Aunt Nancy anyway. I'm leaving tonight and coming home next week. Just be careful. Okay? Make sure you lock the doors. You have my key and cell phone?"

"I do. Be careful, Mom. Have a good trip." I tried to keep the worry out of my voice. After we hung up, I sat there for a minute. What is going on? First my house, now my mother's? Could the break-ins be related? A sense of foreboding washed over me. As the daughter and sister of law enforcement, there could be any number of people holding a grudge against my family. With Uncle Bob prosecuting the drug cartel case, that number tripled.

"Megs, are you okay?" Shane asked, leaning over behind me to nuzzle my neck. I quickly shrugged. I didn't want him to worry, but I had to tell someone.

"Mom's house was broken into. It just feels odd. It's like we're being targeted or something," I said dryly. I tried to not let the worry creep into my voice but Shane wasn't stupid.

"Is your mom okay?" His eyes were blazing.

"She's fine. She's going with Aunt Nancy to the beach this weekend. It's their annual getaway. This is too much of a coincidence."

Shane circled around the couch and sat down. He pulled me into his arms and said, "I'm sure it's some stupid teen gang trying to assert their dominance. Let the police handle it. I doubt that there isn't any more of a connection than that."

Feeling slightly reassured, I calmed down. I always had an overactive imagination. "You're probably right," I said, gazing into his eyes. Shane always made me feel safe. I briefly recalled how he took care of things when my house was broken into. Well, our house.

"I'm always right," he said with a cocky grin. I leaned into his neck, inhaling his scent of soap and aftershave. He had already showered and was dressed in a long sleeve gray T-shirt, jeans, and work boots. I could see the cut of his muscles through his shirt. "I'm

heading into the shop for a while. I'll see you later."
He pulled me off the couch and lifted my chin. Shane's
enticing eyes darkened. "Your mom is okay. That's the
most important thing. Try not to worry." He lowered
his head and brushed his lips against mine, teasingly
at first, then deepening. I greedily accepted and wanted
more. Shane chuckled as he pulled back. "Bye," he said,
smacking my butt.

I smiled as he walked out the door and the second it
shut, I jumped up and down. I didn't know where our
relationship was headed, but I was determined to enjoy
the ride. I walked upstairs, took a shower, and put on
jeans, a layered pink T-shirt, and a white cotton jacket. I
slid on my sneakers and whistled for Penny.

I clipped on her leash and we headed up the street.
It was a beautiful day. The sun was shining, birds were
chirping, and I was walking on air. My emotions had
been on a roller coaster for the last twenty-four hours.
I didn't think I could be any happier than I was at that
moment. I thought back to Alex and how big of a mistake
I almost made. I fooled myself into thinking that I could
forget Shane. I thought briefly of calling Dr. Collins to
thank him. Without him, I would have never realized
how big of an asshole Alex really was. And I would not
have had the courage to kiss Shane.

CHAPTER 12

WHEN I STARTED CONTEMPLATING what to have for dinner, I froze. Should I assume that Shane and I would have dinner together? I didn't want to be rude and make dinner for just myself. But then again, I didn't want to assume that we were eating together. "Damnit, Megan. Stop overthinking," I told myself as I pulled out some chicken and bell peppers. While the chicken and peppers simmered in fajita seasoning, I decided to just send a quick text. *Nothing committal, just informative*, I told myself as I pressed the send button. *He won't read too much into a quick text that says, "Chicken fajitas for dinner if you're hungry."*. *If he doesn't respond, that's okay. No expectations, no disappointments.*

I was taking the Spanish rice off the burner when I

heard the familiar exhaust of Shane's Harley. Butterflies quickly replaced the hunger in my stomach. I busied myself with slicing up the zucchini and squash for a quick sauté. My back was to him when he came in.

"Something smells good," he said, coming up behind me and hugging me to his chest. The butterflies took off and I could barely keep the glee from coming out in my voice.

"Thanks. It's almost ready," I said as nonchalantly as I could. His lips grazed my jawbone and pulled away. I shuddered at the electric shock and almost sliced my knuckle.

"I could get used to this," he teased. Shane grabbed a beer from the fridge and kissed my cheek. "I'm going to shower. Give me ten minutes."

I just nodded. *I am getting used to this*, I thought as I put the tortillas in the microwave. I replayed his words last night, how he had feelings for me and wanted to kiss me. I wondered how long he had wanted to kiss me and why he hadn't acted. *Does it really matter?* I chastised myself. I knew it didn't matter. I got out the salsa, shredded cheese, and sour cream and had everything ready when Shane came down. I practically drooled at the sight of him. Even dressed in sweat pants and a sleeveless muscle shirt with bare feet, he looked gorgeous.

I pulled out two beers and sat down right as Shane came into the kitchen. "This looks great. I'm starved!" he exclaimed, making himself a wrap.

"I guess Adrian has you working too hard to take a break, huh?" I joked, as I helped myself to the rice and squash.

Shane nodded, his mouth full. He quickly swallowed, took a gulp of beer, and said, "Yeah, we have a bunch of orders. We got behind when I was in Trenton, so now we're playing catch up. I have a feeling we're going to be putting in a bunch of overtime for a while."

We chatted while we ate, like nothing had happened. It was comforting to know that, while our relationship had grown, nothing had changed between the two of us. I didn't feel the shyness or the awkwardness that I felt with Alex. We were still the same two people, just with the added benefits of having mind-blowing sex.

After dinner, Shane helped me put away the food and dry the dishes. I was about to slip on my sneakers to take Penny for a walk when Shane slipped her leash off the mudroom hook. Penny started dancing; she loves her evening walk. "It's starting to rain. Why don't you stay here and get some popcorn ready? I picked up the latest *Transporter* movie. I'll take her out."

I looked at him, surprised. "Sure. That's fine," I said. I made popcorn as the storm raged outside. Ten minutes later, I let out a breath when I heard the mudroom door open. I hurried to the mudroom and grabbed a towel from the basket. I handed one to him and vigorously rubbed Penny dry with another.

"A little wet out there?" I asked. "How far did you walk?"

"Not far. We stopped under the bus stop shelter for a while. The rain picked up more than I expected," Shane said, drying off his face. Penny wiggled out of the towel and raced for her bed upstairs.

"You're soaked. Just put your things in the washer. I'll get you some dry clothes," I said as I turned to go back into the house.

"Oh come here. Where's my hug?" he teased, reaching for my arm.

"No! You're all wet!" I screeched as he enveloped me in his arms. My clothes were getting drenched. I could feel the cold air radiating from his body.

"Well, well, well. Looks like you're wet too. Let's get you out of these clothes," he said huskily. The fire started in the tips of my toes and quickly raged through me. I stared into his brown eyes and saw he was having the same reaction. I gave a smug sigh and we promptly forgot about the movie that was waiting for us.

CHAPTER 13

SHANE AND I FELL INTO A routine, albeit an odd routine of sorts after that first weekend. Shane often worked late and sometimes when he was home, I'd wake up in the night to the sound of his cell phone. But I didn't care; it was enough to be with him. The rest of the time, we were together. We made plans around each other's schedules, ate meals together, went out with our friends together. We were a couple in everyone's eyes, although we never spoke those words to each other. I wasn't seeing anyone else, and I was fairly certain that he wasn't either. Being "together" was amazing, never weird, like a natural progression in our relationship. The way I felt around Shane was nothing like how I felt for Tommy. Tommy was proper and by the books, almost regimented. I felt light and comfortable with Shane. I was so grateful that Tommy and I never got married. Shane is what I had been looking for. I was falling hard for him, harder than I did before. When I thought of the future, he was it.

I was happy. Everyone could tell. At the office, Paul's snarky comments stopped bothering me. I was more motivated and kept the office running like a greased wheel. Even Uncle Bob noticed.

"You're awfully chipper this morning, Megan" he quipped, after I glided in and handed him his coffee after a particularly wonderful and sex-filled evening. I just gave him a serene smile.

"I'm happy, Uncle Bob. I'm in a great place."

"Hrrumph. Does a man have anything to do with this?" he muttered.

"Yes, as a matter of fact, yes," I replied as I walked back to my desk.

It was nice to chat casually with Uncle Bob for a moment. He had been under a lot stress lately. Apparently the case against the cartel was wearing him down. He was crankier than ever. The newer employees walked on eggshells, but for me it was business as usual.

I hummed quietly while I worked on a memo, until I was interrupted by my phone ringing. It was Shane. "Hey, babe." Shane's voice sent shivers down my spine.

"Hi, you," I said, lowering my voice.

"Do we have any plans tonight?" he asked.

"I don't know. Do we?" I replied coyly. I loved how he said "we."

"Well, seeing as how it's Friday night, a bunch of the guys here are thinking about doing a bonfire. We're going to meet up at Eric's house around ten. Is that cool with you?" he responded with a chuckle. Eric Morrison and Shane had been best friends since high school. You'd think they were brothers, they were that close. Eric was a great guy, sweet and caring. Like Shane, he was heavily into mechanics and they worked together at Adrian's shop.

"That sounds like a good time," I replied as Paul walked up to my desk. I gave him the one moment finger and turned back to my conversation. "I'll grab dinner at Mama Lucia's if you're in the mood," I said, naming my favorite Italian restaurant.

"Oh. I'm always in the mood," he joked.

I laughed and my mind flitted back over the past few weeks. Shane and I were always in the mood for each other. While we enjoyed talking, cuddling, and just being together, sex with him was like nothing I'd experienced before. We couldn't keep our hands off each other. I had never felt like this. I felt content, satisfied, and utterly in love. Of course, I hadn't told him that yet.

"I'll be home around six thirty. See you then," I said, and hung up the phone. Sighing, I turned to Paul. "And what can I help you with?"

Paul looked irritated that I had kept him waiting. "Bob and I are expecting some people from the DA's office. They should be here any moment. You need to make sure there is coffee and water in the conference room," he demanded.

The pre-Shane Megan would have huffed and said something snide about Paul's attitude, like a threat to put Metamucil in his coffee or something. But I didn't let him get to me, which, in reality, must have bothered him even more. I went ahead and made the coffee, and set out the nice cups and sugars, smiling the whole time.

The DA rarely came to us for a meeting, so this was a big deal. I made a call to the bakery down the street and placed an express order for my uncle's favorite shortbread cookies. They promised me a delivery within ten minutes. I straightened up my desk and made sure the front area looked presentable. If Paul and Uncle Bob were stressed before, the wide-eyed stares and frantic pace of the office only made it more obvious.

We didn't have to wait long. Right after the shortbread cookies arrived, so did three men and a woman dressed in suits. Eager beaver brown-noser Paul had been waiting at the door for their arrival. I was surprised he didn't pee on the floor; he was that nervous.

"Gentlemen, Madam, this way please," he said, and led them into the conference room. After they shut the doors, I couldn't hear anything more from the group. The fanfare had the interns and new paralegals curious, but I was oblivious. I went ahead with my work and was packing up my files at five thirty when the doors finally opened. Uncle Bob trailed after the group looking positively drained.

"Well, is everything okay?" I asked as I logged off my computer.

"Yes, it is. Of course, I can't talk about it, but there are some bad people out there. Just do me a favor and be safe. Be careful who you associate with. Everyone should," he said absentmindedly. He came over and kissed me on my forehead. "Love you, kiddo. Have a great weekend."

It was late April and the weather had been getting warmer, but I knew it would be chilly at the bonfire. I put on my white cardigan, picked up my messenger bag, and headed out the door.

***

I DROVE THE SHORT distance to Mama Lucia's with the

windows down and Aerosmith blaring on the stereo. I was pulling into the driveway with our dinner at six fifteen when my cell phone rang. Flutters abounded when I saw Shane's number.

"Hey baby. I'm just pulling into the driveway now. Are you on your way home?" I said, as I struggled with getting everything out of the car.

"Hey. Yeah. Something has come up. I can't get out of here anytime soon. Can we meet later at Eric's?" Shane's normally controlled voice sounded strained and distant.

"What's wrong? Is everything okay?" I questioned. It was normal for him to change plans because of part delays or problems at the shop, but his tone sounded different to me. It had me worried.

"Nothing's wrong. Something has come up at the shop with a client's bike. I'll meet you at Eric's house at ten," he rushed. He was trying to get off the phone quickly.

"Um. Okay. I guess I'll see you later then," I said quietly. *I don't like this. I don't like this uneasy, queasy feeling in my stomach.*

"Hey. Everything's fine. Don't worry. I'm just in the middle of something. Would you mind picking up some beer? I have a feeling I'm going to need it tonight." Shane's voice regained some normalcy, which smoothed my nerves slightly.

"Sure. No problem. Do you want your dinner?" I asked, remembering the heavy shopping bag full of pasta and garlic bread.

"Nah, I'll grab it later."

"Okay. I'll see you there then," I replied, disconcerted. Something didn't feel right. I headed into the kitchen, pushing aside Penny as she tried to get at the food bags. I filled her bowl with kibble, but she was determined to get into the dinner bags. I gave her a breadstick to calm her down and put Shane's food in the fridge for later. Knowing him, he would want to eat at four in the morning. I clicked on the evening news and started to eat my dinner.

"And in local news, a rookie Anne Arundel County Police Officer was shot today during a drug deal gone wrong. Here's Amanda Cunningham with the latest."

Any story about a rookie police officer always piqued my interest. I constantly worried about Kyle on the job. A perky blonde came on the screen standing in front of the Edgewater Police Station.

"Yes, Mary. The spokesperson for the Town of Edgewater's police department says that a rookie police officer was shot today while trying to disrupt a drug deal that was taking place underneath the South River Bridge. The name of the officer has not yet been released, however we have been told the officer has been taken to

Anne Arundel Medical Center for treatment. Stay tuned for updates. Reporting from Edgewater, this is Amanda Cunningham."

I froze. My heart dropped to my stomach and I reached for the phone. "Please don't be Kyle. Please don't be Kyle," I muttered, though I knew somewhere inside me that he'd been hurt. I quickly dialed Mom's phone number. Busy. I dialed Kyle's number and it just rang and rang. I hung up the phone and sat there for a minute. Panicked thoughts swirled in my head. I was about to leave and drive over to Mom's house when my cell rang.

"Mom? Kyle?" I blurted out, not bothering to check the caller ID.

"It's Mom. The phone has been ringing off the hook. Did you see the news?" she asked nonchalantly. Hearing her so calm brought my pulse down a bit. *If she's this calm, it can't be serious.*

"Yes, I just heard. Is Kyle okay? Was he the one shot?" I pressed, knowing that she would give me the truth.

"Yes. He was shot. But he will be okay. The bullet went into his shoulder and came out clean. He has already had surgery and will be coming home tomorrow. I'm here now with him," she said, her motherly tone already soothing my worries.

"Whew! I'm glad. I'll change and come right up there," I said as I moved to put my uneaten dinner in the fridge.

"No. Stay there. He's drugged up and won't even know that you're here. I talked to Sarah. She is already on her way down. She took her finals early and was coming home to surprise your brother," she said casually. Like it wasn't a big deal that her baby boy had gotten shot and had to go into surgery. I knew she was worried and scared.

"Mom. Are *you* okay?" I asked gently. A sob escaped her throat and she quickly cleared her voice.

"I am okay. I just wish that he would have chosen a different career path. But no, he had to be like your father," she said, her voice wavering.

"Dad's watching out for him. I fully believe that. Are you sure you don't want me to come to the hospital?" I asked. I didn't care about canceling my plans. Shane would understand.

"No, Megs. Don't worry about it. He's going to be fine," Mom reassured me. "Why don't you and Shane come over for dinner tomorrow night? We can talk wedding stuff with Sarah." Nothing makes my mother happier than planning for an event. Especially weddings.

"Okay. We'll be there around five thirty."

"Good. I love you. Be safe."

I hung up with Mom and chewed on my lower lip. Even though I was deeply worried about my brother, Mom was right. He chose this career path. He knew what he was getting into.

CHAPTER 14

ILEFT THE HOUSE AROUND ten so I'd have enough time to stop for Shane's beer and some s'more fixings. The drive to Eric's house was quick. Four years ago, Eric's grandfather left Eric an old ranch-style home. It was set on the South River, back from the main hustle and bustle of Annapolis. Luckily for Eric, there weren't any neighbors close by, so the house parties were always held there. I made it to Eric's by ten fifteen and already the driveway was lined with cars. Granted, I knew most of the people that Shane and Eric worked with. Most of them grew up in the area. But I felt awkward; it was clearly a boys' night. Luckily, Shane was standing next to his truck when I pulled up.

"There you are," he said as I got out of my car. He

wrapped his arms around me and buried his face in my neck. "You don't know how good it is to see you," he murmured, his lips grazing my collarbone. I shivered, but not from the cold.

"I know. I needed to see you too," I replied quietly. Shane looked up, curious. "Kyle got shot today." Concern filled his face, so I quickly filled him in. "He's fine. He'll be okay. It was a clean shot. He's coming home tomorrow. In fact, Mom wants us over for dinner tomorrow," I said. Relief washed over Shane's face.

"Whew! I'm glad he's okay. Are you okay?" he asked, as he cupped my face in his hands.

"Yeah, I'm fine. I was worried for a while, I heard about it on the news, but I'm better now," I answered. I tugged him closer and raised my lips to meet his. Catcalls were instantaneous from Adrian and Eric, who were standing on the front porch.

Shane broke off the kiss with a growl. "I should throw them into the river," he muttered.

I laughed. "Don't get mad. They're just jealous," I called over my shoulder. Adrian and Eric good-naturedly booed. Shane flung his arm over my shoulder and kissed my cheek with a loud smooch.

"We'll finish this later," he whispered. He took the beer, I grabbed the shopping bag, and we headed up to the front porch. Eric took my bag and gave me a kiss on the cheek and a big hug. I hadn't seen Eric in a while. Shane told me that he had been really busy with the shop and was putting in a lot of overtime. Adrian took the beer from Shane and led everyone out through the house to the large fire pit circled by rocks in the massive backyard. The night was beautiful and clear. The moon was high and reflected off the river. I could see Brian, Eric's brother, setting up the grill. Rachel, Eric's sister, was setting food on the picnic tables.

"Hi, Rachel," I said, walking over to her. Rachel was two years older than I was. We were good friends, although we hadn't talked much lately.

"Hey, Megan!" She reached over and gave me a hug. "I'm glad you're here. I haven't talked to you in forever!" Rachel led me over to the fire pit and sat down on a chaise lawn chair. I chose the one next to her, and for the next twenty minutes we caught up on life until we were joined by Adrian and Shane. Adrian straddled a chair and leaned back, pulling his girlfriend of three years close. Adrian was huge, the type of man you would not want to come across in a dark alley. With Indian and African descent, he was the color of chocolate and extremely muscular. A devout weightlifter, he even competed.

Amid the inside jokes and playful insults, I passed out the s'mores and Adrian went to find some sticks. We moved closer to the fire. Shane leaned back in his chair and I sat between his legs. It was as romantic as it could get with twenty guys milling around and drinking. I leaned back and sighed.

"Having fun?" Shane whispered, his lips tickling my ear. Electric currents shocked my body at his slightest touch. I tilted my head back and met his lips with mine. The kiss deepened until a commotion behind us interrupted it.

"Fuck Shane. I don't care what he said!" I heard Eric shout. Curses and rude comments quickly followed. I turned to look at Shane to ask him what that was all about, but the expression of anger and annoyance on his face stopped me. I raised my eyebrow questioningly.

"I'll be right back," he said quickly and got up before I could say a word. I watched as Shane grabbed Eric by the arm and pulled him into the house. Adrian quickly followed. I could hear muffled shouting from inside, but couldn't decipher what they were saying. I glanced quickly at Rachel; I could tell that she was clueless as well.

A large roar came from the house and Eric and Shane stumbled out, swinging at each other. Rachel and I got to our feet just as Adrian ran over to intervene.

"Hey! Knock it off! Or both of your asses are going into the river!" Adrian shouted. Brothers Ryan and Ben, two friends of ours, ran to hold Eric back. Eric strained against the brothers, trying to get to Shane, who was rubbing his jaw.

"You're like a brother to me! I can't believe you did that! You're such a fucking coward, Shane. You're a motherfucking coward," Eric shouted.

I ran over to Shane and grabbed his arm. "Dammit, Eric! You know I wouldn't do something like that. You *know* I wouldn't. You don't want to do this. Don't listen to Reggie," Shane shouted back, rage filling his voice.

"Get the hell out of here, Shane. I am going to kick your ass if you don't," Eric yelled, his eyes wide. I pulled on Shane's arm.

"Let's go," I said quietly. Shane shook his head in disgust and followed me out. I led him out to his truck. He was fuming; his body was coiled tightly, like a snake ready to strike.

"Do you want to talk about it?" I asked gently. Shane didn't respond, just shook his head. His fists were balled up and I could tell that the slightest thing would set him off. "Let's go home."

"No. I left something at the shop. I'll meet you back at the house," Shane said roughly. I wasn't sure if he needed time alone, or if he was going to go back and beat the snot out of Eric.

"Do you want me to go with you?"

"No. I'm good. Don't worry. I just need to chill out."
He pulled me in for a tight squeeze. "I'll be home later."
Shane kissed me, then got into his truck and pulled out
of the driveway.

I wanted to follow him, make sure he was okay, but I
decided against it and forced myself to leave him alone.
I headed home.

I tried to stay up until Shane got home, but by one
thirty, sleep was calling my name. I set the house alarm,
locked up, and went upstairs. I had to admit that I was
worried about him. I was so used to falling asleep in his
arms that it would be difficult to sleep without him. I
sent him a quick text. "Ready for bed. Wish you were
here. Be careful."

Two minutes later, I got back, "I'll be next to you
soon. Sweet dreams."

With a sigh, I set my cell phone on the nightstand.
Not soon enough, I thought, as I lay there. I slowly
drifted off to sleep, dreaming of his kisses and his touch.

CHAPTER 15

I KNEW SHANE WASN'T IN bed before I even opened my eyes. I didn't feel his body heat, I didn't hear his light snoring. My hand instinctively reached for him, finding only the coolness of the pillow. *He didn't come home.*

Groaning, I opened my eyes and looked at the clock. Only seven thirty? Ugh. I hated waking up early when I didn't have to. The best part of the weekend was sleeping in. I dragged myself out of bed and into the bathroom. No point in being lazy. I didn't have any plans today except dinner at Mom's. I was in the shower washing my face when I heard the door to the bathroom open. Shane walked in.

"Well good morning, sunshine," I called through the clear glass.

"Good morning to you, too. Adrian came back to the shop and I lost track of time. I'm sorry babe," he said. I wasn't going to make this a big deal. He had been upset and I was glad that Adrian was with him.

"It's okay. I was just a little worried. Are you going to join me?" I offered, giving him a sly grin. Shane chuckled as he pulled off his shirt. He opened the glass shower door and got in. The beauty of his body took my breath away. My eyes roved over his now-familiar body. I reached out and gently soaped his sculpted chest, watching the suds fall down his toned thighs. The dragon on his chest took up most of his torso, with the tail ending right below his hipbone. His muscular, sinewy arms covered in two detailed and intricate tattoo sleeves pulled me into his body. Shane's engorged erection pressed into me and the ache between my thighs grew. I gasped and gave him the opening he wanted.

I crushed my lips to his as his tongue plunged into me, exploring every inch of my mouth. Moaning, I arched into him, looking for release. The tension was becoming too much to bear. Shane lifted me up, wrapped my legs around his waist and braced my back against the wall. I took him eagerly, clinching as tightly as I could. With every thrust, my nerve endings screamed. I floated higher until I fell in a dizzying explosion. Shane shuddered against me, pulsating inside me.

Panting, he let me down gently on my quivering legs. Shane kissed my neck, then gently ran the soap over my body. His hands ran down the length of me. It felt like I was being caressed with silk. *Thank God I converted this bathroom into a double steam shower,* I thought. It made moments like these so much more enjoyable.

***

WE GOT OUT OF THE shower thirty minutes later, wrinkled like raisins and out of hot water. Shane moved to the bedroom where he passed out on the bed from sheer exhaustion. I put on denim capris pants and a gray V-neck T-shirt and headed downstairs with Penny following my every move. I let her out the back door and turned to start the coffee. I let out a squeak in surprise. Sitting on the counter, beside the bills and the mail, was a beautiful bouquet of white tulips in a glass vase. What a sweetheart, I thought, inhaling their sweet scent. I started the coffee and poured myself a bowl of cereal. I had just finished my Captain Crunch when my cell phone rang. I was happy to see that it was Sarah.

"Hey, sis. How are you? Are you with Kyle now?" I answered.

"Hey sweetie. Yeah. I'm here with him now. He's incorrigible; he won't stop flirting with the nurses," she said with a laugh.

"That's great news. At least we know he's back to normal," I joked.

"Exactly. We will be going to Mom's shortly. We'll see you at dinner, right? I think Mom's going all out for her baby boy."

"Yeah, we'll be there. I'm sure Mom will cook enough for an army," I said dryly.

"Right. I'll see you later, they are discharging Kyle now. Oh. And I have bridesmaid dresses for you to look at!" With that she hung up the phone. I had to laugh. Sarah was so excited to get a start on planning the wedding. She had already asked Jen, me, and her sister, Erin, to be in the wedding party. I was slightly nervous about what dress she had in mind. Bridesmaids always shared their horror stories of being forced to wear dresses in teal taffeta or sequins. I wasn't a fan of either one, so I hoped Sarah had picked out a great dress.

Hearing that Kyle was doing well made my day. I know my mother was going to be fretting about both of them at dinner, which would hopefully distract her from my own living situation.

My mother equated living together to being practically married, so she had been beating around the bush about our future. I'd had to tell her that I honestly didn't know. As much as I was falling in love with Shane, we had never had that "talk". The whole "where do you think our relationship is going?" talk. I felt that there was something he wasn't telling me, some sort of mystery that he was either hiding or ashamed of. There had been calls late at night or emergencies at the shop that he had to deal with right away. Maybe it was my paranoia, or maybe it was something more. I didn't know.

I lazed about the house for the rest of the day until it was time to go to Mom's. I went upstairs to wake Shane and found him snoring away. I gently shook his arm and quietly said, "Shane. It's time to get up. We've got to go to Mom's for dinner." Shane grumbled and rolled onto his side. I shook harder this time. "Come on, punk. I know Mom's making her famous ziti. I'm going to leave you here and I'm not bringing home leftovers."

"Like hell you won't," he mumbled, rolling over to grab my wrist and pull me underneath of him. "Your mom loves me. She'll make sure I get my ziti." He laughed as he pinned my arms over my head with one hand and tickled me with the other. I shrieked and couldn't contain my laughter. I was extremely ticklish and he always used it to his advantage. I laughed and screamed until I couldn't breathe.

"Okay, okay! Stop!" I cried out, gasping for air. Laughing, Shane stopped and kissed me.

"Let me change my clothes and we can go," he said, getting off the bed. I just lay there, drooling and trying to catch my breath while I watched him change. The muscles of his back were just mesmerizing. I debated on whether or not I had time to attack him, but decided against it. It was already five and Mom wanted us over at five thirty. Shane changed into a gray T-shirt and a white button down shirt that hung loosely over the T-shirt and jeans. He put on his boots and pulled me off the bed.

"How's your brother doing?" he asked, as we walked down the stairs.

"Good. I talked to Sarah earlier and she said that he was flirting with the nurses, so she thinks he's back to normal," I joked. I pulled on my gray hooded sweatshirt and whistled for Penny. I clipped the leash to her collar and let her out of the mudroom door.

***

We arrived at Mom's with a minute to spare. I could see Sarah's Prius sitting in the driveway. We let ourselves in and were welcomed by the wonderful aroma of basil and homemade garlic bread. My mouth watered. I loved my mother's cooking. She never failed to put on a huge spread. In addition to the garlic bread and ziti, she had made chicken with tomatoes and spinach, a salad, and I could see my favorite apple turnovers sitting on the stove top. I was in heaven.

"Hi, baby cakes," Mom said, coming over to Shane and me. She gave us a hug and shooed us into the kitchen. My mother's house was small and didn't have a formal dining room so we all crowded into the kitchen for dinner. The small table had been extended to its maximum capacity. Kyle and Sarah were already seated, apparently waiting for us.

"It's about time you guys got here. I'm starving!" Kyle joked, his good arm slung around Sarah's shoulders.

"I guess we shouldn't keep the invalid starving, should we?" I joked back, coming around to give him a hug. A look of regret flashed over Shane's face as he gave Kyle one of those half hugs before sitting down. It passed quickly, and I brushed it off as a figment of my imagination. We gathered around the table and before long our plates were piled high with food. The conversation was at a minimum while we gorged ourselves.

"So, how are you feeling Kyle?" I asked. He looked awkward with his right arm in a sling. He was having a bit of difficulty using his left hand.

"I'm good. The bullet went straight through and did

minimal damage. Don't think I'll need any additional surgeries or anything." Kyle was calm. He talked about his injury and threat to his life as if he was talking about the weather. I guess it came with the territory, but I would have been a blubbering idiot if I'd been shot. I felt better about Kyle. His spirits were up and he seemed to be doing fine. Sarah had been taking great care of him. I was so thankful that they were together.

We switched topics. Once Kyle's injuries had been acknowledged, we moved on to discussing the wedding. Every girl dreamed of her wedding. Being with Shane made me hope for our future, our potential wedding. Not that it was imminent or assumed, but it was nice to dream. We basically ignored both Shane and Kyle while we talked about the wedding. That was expected, though. What input could they have really had?

***

AFTER DESSERT AND coffee, Kyle looked like he was about to doze off at the table so we said our good-byes. On the drive home, Shane was quiet. In fact, he had been quiet throughout dinner as well. I wondered if all the wedding and marriage talk had scared him.

"Are you okay?" I asked, as I pulled into the driveway. I turned off the car and we sat in silence.

Shane seemed to be lost in thought and when I spoke it startled him.

"Yeah, I'm okay. I'm just tired. I have to meet Adrian shortly," he said vaguely, getting out of the car. I frowned. Adrian was working Shane to the bone. What bike shop was *that* busy that Shane couldn't take a night off?

"Shane, stay home tonight. You need the rest," I suggested as I followed him inside. Penny ran straight to her bed. Poor pup was exhausted.

"That depends," he said, putting his arms around me.

"On what?" I asked, raising my eyebrow.

"On how well you persuade me," Shane replied, giving me an evil grin. I had to laugh because he knew my persuasion skills were unmatched. And needless to say, he didn't go back to the shop that night.

CHAPTER 16

SHANE WAS UP EARLY the next morning. I stretched as I watched him get dressed.

"Can't you go in later?" I mumbled as I burrowed my face in the pillows.

"Babe, I can't. If I don't get over there now Adrian's going to have my ass," Shane said hurriedly, as he pulled on an old gray long sleeve shirt. He bent over, his hair still wet from the shower, and gave me a quick peck on the lips. "I'm not sure when I'll be back, but it will be later today. You will see me later. So stay just like that." He motioned to me, giving my naked body the once over.

I laughed and threw my pillow at him. "Go before I make you stay!" I heard him chuckle as he walked down the stairs. I sighed, content. *It doesn't get any better than this*, I thought. A tiny voice in the back of my head said quietly, *It does if he feels the same way you do.* Stupid insecure brain. I pushed that to the side. If he didn't feel the same way I did, would he still be sticking around? I doubt he was staying just for the sex, regardless of the fact that it was fantastic sex.

I lay in bed for as long as I could until Penny started pacing the floor. "Okay, Penny. You win. Let's go." I pulled on sweats and walked downstairs to let her out.

With the coffee brewing, I made spinach and tomato omelets for Penny and me. She promptly wolfed down her omelet; I doubt she even tasted it. "You're such a piggy," I said as I flipped through the paper. I put the sports and business section aside knowing that Shane would want them later. Browsing the sales ads, I made my shopping list. I figured that shopping would be a good way to start the day. I drained my mug and carried it to the sink. I showered, pulled on a pink scoop neck shirt and jeans, and headed to the store.

***

I WAS SITTING AT THE traffic light when my cell phone rang. "Hello?" I saw a police officer next to me give me the evil eye. Maryland had just passed a law banning cell phones use while driving. Deciding to avoid yet another ticket, I hit the speaker button and put the phone down.

"It's me. Lauren's asking for you and we're about to make some cookies. Do you want to join us?" Jen's voice said. I could hear Lauren in the background singing loudly.

"Sure. I'll be right over."

Putting off grocery shopping to make cookies with my goddaughter was a no-brainer. Fifteen minutes later, I pulled into Jen's driveway. Lauren rushed out to greet me.

"Auntie Megs, come on! The cookies are waiting," she cried as she led me into the house. "Momma, Auntie Megs is here!"

"So I see. Hey, Megs," Jen said. She handed me a glass of wine and whispered, "You will need this to keep up with her." Laughing, I followed them into the kitchen where a cookie workshop had been set up. Cookie dough, sprinkles, and cookie cutters were spread on every available surface. "Matt was called to do a surgery so it's just us girls today."

"Well, what are we waiting for? Let's make some cookies," I said, laughing at Lauren's infectious smile.

While we made the cookies, Jen and I chatted about old times. Our conversation was as general and typical as one would have with a three-year-old in the room until Lauren threw me for a loop.

"Aunt Megs? Where's Uncle Shane?" she asked, as we were making the cookie dough.

"He's at work. He's going to be sad that he didn't get to see you."

"Mommy and Daddy are married. Are you going to get married to Uncle Shane?" Children can ask the most innocent questions that are the hardest to answer. I paused, searching for an answer.

"Um, I'm not sure. It's too soon to tell. I love your Uncle Shane though," I replied cautiously. I obviously was not about to go into detail with a child. She seemed to accept my response and I felt I had dodged a bullet. Once the cookies were in the oven and the kitchen was cleaned up, we put on a Disney movie for her in the playroom. Jen and I thought we were in the clear to talk about more adult topics when she wandered in with another question.

"Auntie Megs, are you going to have babies?"

Where does she come up with these questions? "I hope so. I hope I have a little girl just like you," I hedged.

"You should. So I can play with her," Lauren replied matter-of-factly.

"Oh yeah? Are you going to clean her diapers too?" I asked, tickling her belly.

Giggling, she said, "No! That's what daddies are

for!" I laughed along with her, but now the seed was planted in my mind. I did want kids. I wanted a little girl of my own. Did Shane want kids? Add that to the list of things we needed to eventually discuss. I could see Shane with a baby. He was so good with Lauren. My thoughts wandered to what our potential child would look like. Would she have my hair? His eyes? I was so lost in the fantasy that I didn't hear the oven timer go off.

"Cookies!" All thoughts of new playmates went out the window as Lauren scrambled for the kitchen.

"Her babysitter is having another baby. She's due in a few months. So, of course, Lauren has babies on the brain. She has been demanding a baby brother or sister for the last year," Jen explained. That made sense.

I chuckled. "Yeah, I've been waiting too. So get working!" Jen and Matt were wonderful parents, but hadn't had much luck with having another.

"Next year, hopefully," she replied, taking my hint and laughing along with me. After taking a baggie of cookies, I said my good-byes and headed home.

***

THE RAIN HAD GIVEN way to a sunny day. It was time for Penny to go out so I leashed her up and headed down the street. We were enjoying the walk when my cell phone rang. I didn't recognize the number, but answered it anyway.

"Hello?" I said.

"Megan. It's Tommy," a voice from my past said. My stomach dropped. I had not heard from Tommy in a long while and when I did it was normally via text. This was not like him. *Something's not right.*

"Hi, Tommy. What's up?" I asked wearily.

"I'm in the area and was wondering if I could stop by," he said. My gut dropped. I don't know why, but I felt like it was a bad idea. Call it female intuition or something, but this didn't feel like a social call.

"I thought you were in New York. What are you doing back here?" I asked slowly.

"Oh, I'm working on a case. Are you free this evening? I'd like to stop by and say hi." His cool and calm voice had me suspicious. I immediately thought of the federal case my Uncle Bob was working on. Could Tommy have something to do with it?

"I have a few things to do tonight. Can I take a rain check?" I hedged. The prospect of seeing Tommy wasn't giving me the warm and fuzzies. Not to mention that I knew what Shane's reaction would be when he heard that my ex-fiancé was in town.

"Please, Megs. I promise I won't be there long.

I'll even bring dinner. You still love sushi right?" he pleaded. *Seriously? Dinner with Tommy? This is getting weird.* I didn't know what was going on, but it couldn't be good if Tommy was asking to come over. I reluctantly agreed and gave him my address.

"Great, I'll pick up the sushi on my way over. I'll see you at six," Tommy said cheerfully and hung up. I just stared at my phone. This was crazy. The whole conversation had my guard up. I looked at my watch and realized it was only three thirty. *Great, only two and half more hours to stress.*

I prolonged our walk as much as possible. I tried to enjoy the beautiful weather but Tommy's impending visit was bothering me. The conversation in itself had made me feel uneasy. Eventually we made it back to the house. I puttered around washing the dishes and doing a load of Shane's laundry, all the while not focusing on the task at hand. I was trying to kill time until Tommy arrived. The feeling of dread weighed in my stomach. A visit from an ex-fiancé from out of the blue didn't scream fun times.

I lay on the couch and flicked on the TV. I was barely paying attention to the news when the doorbell rang. I quickly checked my watch. Six o'clock on the dot. Tommy was always on time. I opened the front door.

"Hi. Come on in," I said, standing aside. He looked

the same, maybe leaner. Tommy was very tall and lanky with green eyes and short light blond hair. He must have come straight from work, as he was wearing standard federal agent uniform: a black coat and pants with a gray button-down shirt.

"You look great, as always," he said, leaning in for a kiss. He aimed for my lips, but I quickly turned my face so he got my cheek instead. I feigned a cough and gestured him in. He chuckled hollowly at the lack of warmth in my reception.

"So, what brings you here?" I asked, leading him into the kitchen. Lucky for him, Penny was outside. Tommy was highly allergic to dogs. I debated on keeping Penny in, just so he would leave sooner, but decided I did not want to be a bitch.

He set down the food and took off his jacket. "I was in the area and wanted to see how you're doing. This is okay, right?" he asked, raising his eyebrows.

"No, it's fine. Just not like you," I replied as I took plates and chopsticks out of the cabinet. I set them down. "Beer or soda?"

"I'll take a soda. I'm going back to the office after this," he said, settling into a seat. I brought over two cans of soda and sat down. I selected a tuna roll and added soy sauce. The whole situation was strained and awkward. I didn't know much about his new life in New York. In fact, I couldn't recall much of his life in general. *Huh. It's amazing what a great relationship and mind-blowing sex can make you forget.*

"Oh, Emily and Samantha give their regards. Samantha got accepted to William and Mary. Emily is about to graduate from Juilliard this spring. Folks are good. How are you?"

This formality crap is getting old, I thought. "Mom and Kyle are good." We sat in silence for a while, each of us testing the waters with mindless questions. I finally got fed up with it and bluntly asked, "Really, Tommy. Why are you here?"

"What? Can't two friends get together for dinner?" he asked innocently. I rolled my eyes. I dated him for three years. I knew when he was full of crap.

"Yes. Two friends can get together for dinner. But we're talking about us, and it's not like we're close friends. This is not normal," I shot back.

"I'm just worried about you. I haven't heard from you in a while. I wanted to make sure you were alright." He busied himself with the soy sauce.

"So you came all the way out here? We rarely talk as it is, don't you think a text message or a call would have been better? I don't mean to sound like a bitch, but be real with me. What's going on?" I insisted.

Tommy sighed. "I am helping Annapolis PD and the

DEA on a big case, Megs. I figured that since I was in the area, I'd just stop by. Honestly, nothing is going on. I am worried about you though. You may not think so, but I do care about you. I just want to make sure you're good," he said sincerely. The moment he said "big case," my interest piqued. What big case was he talking about? Uncle Bob's federal case? Or something else?

"Tommy. I appreciate your concern. But really, I'm fine. Things are going well. I really don't need you to check on me," I replied, picking up a piece of eel.

"If you don't need me to check on you, then whose bike is out front?" he demanded.

Bingo. I knew this would come up. I rolled my eyes. "Shane Turner's. He moved in a few months ago." I mentally dared him to react.

"Shane Turner. Huh. Are you two together?" Tommy inquired, his eyes widening innocently. That irritated me. It none of his business who I was dating.

"Why do you ask?" I asked, my eyes narrowing.

Tommy leaned back in his seat and put his hands behind his head. "I'm just curious and a little surprised. I ran across his name recently. He's not doing so well for himself. He's bad news, Megs. You should really pick your friends better."

I immediately became defensive. "And how do you know this, Tommy? Are you checking up on all my friends too?" I asked. I could feel my blood start to boil.

Tommy leaned toward me in his chair. "I'm not checking up on your friends, I'm watching out for you. Did you know that Shane has a record a mile long? Possession of cocaine and marijuana, intent to distribute, breaking and entering, grand theft auto? Did you know that he is on the DEA's radar? You shouldn't be hanging out with him, Megan. He's going to drag you down with him," Tommy said, seemingly annoyed that I questioned his motives.

"What the hell are you talking about, Tommy? Shane did that crap years ago. He's been out of jail for a long time now. What is the point of bringing it up now?" I asked, standing up to look him in the eye.

"It wasn't a long time ago, Megan. The last time he was arrested was almost a year ago. If you don't believe me, have Kyle look it up. You don't know your boyfriend as well as you think you do," Tommy pleaded, as he tried to hold my hands.

I jerked my hands away. "How dare you! You have no reason and no excuse to be meddling in my life. None. It's none of your damn business who I see or who my friends are," I yelled.

"I'm making it my business, Megan. Did you know that your man is hanging out with Reggie Cruz, a murderer and third in line to one of the biggest drug cartels in the world? Did he tell you that he deals for the same cartel? Is this something you really want to get involved with? What would your Dad say if he knew you were living with a drug dealer? How would your mom feel if her baby girl was thrown in jail because she was living with a known dealer? Guilt by association and facilitating a drug deal are real offenses, Megs. Are you going to throw away your life for him? For nothing?" Tommy yelled back. His face was turning bright red and veins were popping out of his head.

"You stay the hell out of my business. Get the hell out of my house, Tommy!" I yelled, my hands clinched in fists.

CHAPTER 17

"Hey! What's going on in here?" yelled a voice behind me. Shane had walked in, obviously from the shop. He had grease marks on his jeans and shirt and looked exhausted. "What the hell are you doing here, Tommy?" he asked. He clenched his jaw and fists and looked as if he was going to throw Tommy out.

"I'm leaving. Think about what I said, Megan." Tommy picked up his jacket and brushed past Shane. Shane glared at him as he walked out, then came over to me and put his arms around my waist.

"What was that about?" he asked, searching my eyes. I couldn't speak. I was too furious so I just shook my head.

"Megan, tell me. What's wrong? What did he do?" he

lifted my chin up with his finger so I could look at him. I needed something, anything, to dissolve the doubt that was growing. I pulled his face to mine and kissed him hungrily. Taken aback at my aggressiveness, he eagerly responded. I ran my hands under his shirt, feeling his muscles ripple with excitement. He gently pulled away.

"Not that I don't love this reception, but tell me something. What is going on? What did he say to you?" he asked, his voice husky.

I had to verify the truth. That was the only way I could handle it. "Tommy said that you were arrested almost a year ago on distribution charges. Is that true?" I asked.

Shane sighed. "More like last year. It happened before you moved back. I guess I never told you. I was with this guy, Monroe, and he had about seven grams of coke on him. It was more like guilt by association. I'm not doing that now. I've left that life." He tightened his grip around my waist.

I believed him. God help me, I believed him despite the nagging feeling in my gut planted there by Tommy. "I'm just making sure. He told me that you were still dealing. That you're on the DEA radar and he's worried that you'll drag me down with you," I said quietly.

Shane's steel gaze hardened. "Tommy needs to shut his damn mouth. It's not a big deal. I got arrested and made a deal with the prosecutors. I served my time, did community service, and now I'm free. Adrian gave me a job and I have been straight ever since. I would never put you in that sort of danger. Tommy needs to keep out of our business."

I nodded, relieved. Tommy was trying to cause unnecessary drama. I wasn't going to believe him. But the feeling that Shane was lying wouldn't go away. I shook it off and let Penny inside. Shane stood there, brooding.

"Hey, look at me," I said, as I walked over and put my arms around his waist. "Tommy's just causing trouble. I believe you. I know you've done better for yourself. You have me now, so of course you're better," I half-joked.

Shane's eyes softened. He put his arms around my neck and kissed my forehead. "You're right about that, babe." He let out a heavy sigh and dropped his arms. "I'm going to jump into the shower. Do you have plans for the night?"

"Nope. Let's go rent a movie. I'll wait for you to change and we can go together and pick something out," I replied, brushing the hair out of my eyes.

Shane nodded. "It will be good to relax for a night," he said, almost more to himself than to me.

I finished the dishes and pulled towels out of the dryer. I was in the process of folding them when Shane's phone rang. I was determined not to be that type of girl that checks her boyfriend's phone. I ignored the phone until mine rang a minute later. Someone was trying to get a hold of Shane. I checked the caller ID. It was a number I did not recognize and hesitated before answering.

"Hello?" I asked cautiously.

"Megan! Where's Shane?" Adrian's frantic voice came over the phone.

"Shane's in the shower. What's wrong, Adrian? What happened?" I asked, worried. Adrian was usually so calm and cool. Hearing him like this was not a good sign.

"Megs, it's Eric. He's been shot," Adrian said in a low voice. My heart stopped for a beat and then a rush of fear went through my stomach.

"What the hell happened? How did he get shot? Is he okay?" I demanded.

"Just get Shane and tell him to meet me at the hospital in Annapolis," he cried and hung up the phone. Dread came over me and I was scared. Eric is practically a brother to Shane. I dropped the phone on the table and ran upstairs. Shane was still in the shower. I opened up the door and stood in the doorway, contemplating how I was going to tell him.

"Babe, you waited too long to join me. I'm just getting out," he called over the sound of the water. I closed my eyes. The thought of telling him this news made my stomach feel like lead. Shane got out and wrapped a thick navy blue towel around his waist.

"Megan? What's wrong?" he said, coming over to me and grabbing my arms. Tears streamed down my face.

"Shane. Adrian just called. He said that Eric's been shot."

Shane's eyes went hard and his body turned rigid. Without a sound, he dashed into the bedroom. I followed him and watched him throw on jeans and a graphic T-shirt. "Where are my shoes?" he called, looking under the bed for them. I found them near the door and silently handed them to him. He grabbed his watch and wallet and thundered down the stairs. Wordlessly, I followed him. I grabbed my coat and purse and quickly locked up. He was waiting for me in the truck. Shane was stoic, his body tight with emotion, but nothing showed on his face. I could see that his hands were softly shaking.

"Hey. He's a tough guy. He'll be okay," I said softly, putting my hand on his arm. Shane just nodded mutely. We quickly navigated the back roads to the hospital. The highways were faster, but I wanted to avoid ending up stuck in traffic and getting a speeding ticket.

As we pulled up to the hospital, I could tell he was about to jump out of his skin. "I'll park the truck; just go. I'll find you," I insisted. He got out and I slid over. When I finally found everyone, Adrian was comforting Rachel. Tears streamed down her face and her body was shaking with sobs. I could feel my throat closing up and I looked desperately around for Shane. He was sitting in a chair, with his head in his hands. I hurried over to him and threw my arms around his body. He gazed at me, tears in his eyes. I didn't have to ask, I already knew. "Oh God, Shane," I said softly as I began crying for him.

We sat there, amid the hustle and bustle of the emergency room. A few minutes later, I heard an unmistakable wail of agony. We both looked up. Eric's father and Adrian were holding up Eric's mom, Marie. Shane rushed over to help. "Why, Shane? Why my son?" she screamed, holding onto Shane for dear life. Then she suddenly smacked Shane across the face. He didn't even flinch.

"You brought him into that life, Shane. He was trying to get his life straight. He was doing so well! Then you go and bring him back into a life of dealing and drugs. This is your fault!"

Shane looked sadly at Marie, tears running down his face. "I'm so sorry. I tried to talk Eric out of it. I didn't want to get him involved. This was not supposed to happen."

"Get out of here, Shane. You do not deserve to say

goodbye to him!" she screeched, her short round body balled up tight. I could tell she was going to strike again, so I rushed over to pull Shane out of the line of fire.

As we walked away, Rachel grabbed Shane by the arm and threw her arms around him in a bear hug. "Don't worry, Shane. Mama loves you," she choked out. Shane whispered something in her ear, which made her break down in sobs. He kissed her on her forehead and shook Adrian's hand. He put his arm around my waist and we walked out of the emergency room and into the setting sun.

We walked to the truck in silence. Rage and pain radiated off his body. I wanted him to know that I was here for him. As we got in, I looked at him and said, "I'm sorry Shane. If you want to talk..."

"I'm fine," he interrupted, the sadness replaced by determination. I didn't respond, just watched his face as we sped down the highway. He was being reckless, almost daring the police to pull him over.

***

WE MADE IT HOME without incident and he walked upstairs and slammed our bedroom door shut. My heart was breaking for him. I felt helpless and unsure of what to do. I knew that just being here would help, but

I wished I could do something more. I placed an order of flowers for Eric's parents and sat at the kitchen table. My thoughts wandered to the exchange Eric's mother had with Shane. Since when did Eric deal drugs? Did Shane ever try to get him out of it? I wondered, as I made some tea. I quietly carried the tea up the stairs and knocked on the door.

"Yeah?" he demanded as he flung open the door. The anger in his eyes and face was set in stone; he looked different. Shane did not look like the same man that I had slept with last night. He had changed clothes into a black oversized hooded sweatshirt, and was clearly about ready to leave. Taken aback by his change in demeanor, I struggled to find my voice.

"Can I do anything for you? I'm here if you need me," I said timidly. He seemed on the brink of losing it.

"No," he said roughly, as he brushed past me, duffle bag in hand. I quickly glanced at our room. Drawers were pulled out, the closet door was wide open with clothes hanging haphazardly. I quickly set the tea down on the dresser and rushed down the stairs.

"Wait. Where are you going, Shane?" I asked in panic. I didn't want him to do anything stupid, like try to find whoever killed Eric. Shane ignored me and headed out the door. I raced after him.

"Shane!" I shouted, "Goddammit! Will you just stop

for a second?"

"I have to leave, Megan," he said, throwing his bag in the front seat of the truck and turning to me. The pain in his face was the only emotion I saw. Shane tried to get into the truck but I pulled his arm back.

"No. Stay here. Talk to me," I pleaded. *I don't want him to leave. He can't leave. I won't let him.*

Shane sighed with impatience. "Megan, I have to."

"The hell you do. Why? Where are you going?" I demanded. *I don't care if I look crazy, I'm not letting Shane leave.*

"I just have to get out of here," he growled, turning back to his truck.

I pulled back hard on his arm. "Please don't leave me like this," I whispered.

He pulled me into his arms and crushed his lips to mine. As if he were trying to memorize the way my lips felt, the way they tasted. I kissed him back with the same passion. Then he abruptly pulled back.

"Be good," he whispered as he got into his truck. The engine roared and he peeled out of the driveway. I watched him until he disappeared around the corner, not knowing when or if he was coming back.

CHAPTER 18

DAYS PASSED WITH NO word from Shane. I tried to help Rachel and Marie make the funeral arrangements but felt in the way. I stumbled through the week, going through the motions at work. My heart mourned the loss of Eric, but my deepest ache came from missing Shane. I felt empty inside. By Thursday, I was an absolute mess. I couldn't stand not knowing where he was, if he was okay. Despite my determination not to, I had fallen for him hook, line, and sinker. I was in love with him. I had gotten used to having him in the house, having him around all the time. It felt like something was missing.

Eric's funeral was on Friday so I took the day off. I took Penny for a rare morning jog, hoping to clear my head. It was a beautiful May morning with a slight breeze and clear skies. I had been keeping in touch with Rachel about the arrangements, but she never mentioned if she had contacted Shane. I sent him a text message with all the information and got no response. I wasn't sure if he would show. As I dressed, I kept a watchful eye on my phone for a call, a text, for any sign that he was coming.

I was walking out of the mudroom door when I saw Shane come up the driveway. As always, he looked absolutely gorgeous. Dressed in a gray linen suit, a black button down shirt, and a black tie, he looked like he was a model posing for a secret service ad. I gave him a small smile and hoped he couldn't hear my heart trying to pound out of my chest.

"I guess you got my message?" I asked tentatively when he got close. I could smell his cologne and it took all I had not to leap into his arms. I wanted to ask him where he had been, if he was okay, if he missed me. But it wasn't the right time.

"Yeah, I did. I'm sorry that I didn't call you back. Are you ready to go?" he asked quietly, taking my hand. His touch sent my heart reeling. He led me down to the truck and opened the door for me. He climbed into the driver's seat, leaned over to me, and gently kissed my lips. I let my eyes close briefly and sighed. I'd missed that. I'd missed him.

The drive was quiet. There were so many questions

running through my head, but I waited. I didn't want to get him anymore upset than he already was. We drove the short distance to the church and arrived with ten minutes to spare. Rachel, Marie, and Adrian were waiting outside, greeting their guests. Marie greeted Shane with open arms.

"Oh, Shane. I am so sorry. Please forgive me. I know it's not your fault," she cried, throwing her arms around his neck. Shane squeezed her back, his eyes closing in grief. He said something softly to her, causing her to nod. I was curious as to what he said. I only heard the words "Doing what I had to do." What did he mean by that?

I didn't have time to ask, as Marie gestured us into the church. We sat in the second row behind Eric's family. The whole town had turned out to pay their respects. The service was beautiful, with the traditional hymns and verses. Shane was stoic, silent throughout the service, emotion barely registering on his face. When it came time for the pallbearers to come forward, Shane stood with our friends Ryan, Ben, and Adrian, men who were practically brothers at the funeral for one of their own. Bob Dylan's, "Forever Young", normally out of place in a church, filled the air as they carried Eric's casket down the aisle. Eric was laid to rest underneath a large oak tree next to a soccer field. Memories of him playing soccer with the boys caused me to choke back a sob.

After the service, Eric's family was hosting a reception at their home, and I asked Shane if we were going to attend.

"No. I need to get back to the house," he muttered as he led me away. He seemed to be in a hurry because we left the cemetery in a rush. Something else was going on. Something more than his best friend dying and it was time I knew.

***

I TURNED TO HIM and said, "I know you're going through a lot, Shane. Please. Please talk to me. Maybe I can help. If anything, it will feel good to get it off your chest."

Ignoring me, Shane turned the radio up. Heavy metal music filled the cabin of the truck. Fine, he didn't want to talk. We would have to talk at some point soon. We would have to deal with this together.

We arrived back at the house and he charged inside. I followed him up to the bedroom, where he started changing his clothes. Another duffel bag was sitting on the bed, opened.

"You're leaving again? Why? What the hell is going on Shane?" I demanded. I was flabbergasted that he would leave so quickly. I understood that he needed to come to grips with Eric's death, but I needed him at home.

"I can't stay here, Megan. I can't do this anymore," he muttered, throwing balls of socks and underwear into the bag.

"What do you mean 'you can't do this anymore'? Do what exactly? Talk to me, Shane!" I cried, pulling his clothes out of the bag. He grabbed my hands and threw them aside.

"People have gotten hurt because of me. It's my fault Eric's dead. I don't want to be responsible for your death too," he said angrily. Shane threw a sweatshirt and a pair of shoes into the bag. He walked into the bathroom and slammed the door behind him. I flung open the door. He was standing at the sink, getting his things from the medicine cabinet.

"Shane. Wait. I don't understand. What's going on? How is Eric's death your fault?" I asked. I was so confused. Why did Shane think that he was responsible? Shane pushed past me and into the bedroom. I trailed behind him, impatient for answers. He dumped his shaving cream, razor, and toothbrush into his bag.

"Eric died in a deal gone bad," Shane said impatiently. "Last year, he got into a bad situation and needed some cash. He knew I was working for Reggie then so Eric started dealing. I tried to stop him, but he wouldn't listen. He was my partner of sorts. We would be each other's back up. So when I got out, he took over my list. I didn't want him to; he insisted, saying that he needed the money," he said defeated.

"When was the last time you saw him?" I asked.

"At the bonfire. That's what we were arguing about. I didn't like the way he was handling Reggie. Reggie has these connections to the Cruz cartel in Jersey, Florida, and Mexico. You don't want to cross Reggie. He doesn't play around. He has no issues with putting a bullet in someone's head. This whole organization is huge, with Reggie's cousin Christian running the Jersey end. Reggie is terrifying, but Christian, he puts the fear of the devil in me. I've only met him once, but that's all it took. I tried to warn Eric. I begged and pleaded with him to lay low and keep to the background. Eric didn't listen. He started making waves about how much of the money Reggie was taking and started talking trash about the whole organization." Shane sat on the bed and shrugged sadly. "I tried everything I could for him. I didn't know what else to do."

I came over to the bed and sat next to him. "This is not your fault," I said quietly. Shane jumped off the bed.

"The hell it isn't. Megan, I led him into this world. I got him hooked up with Reggie. And now he's dead!

How is that not my fault?" he shouted, smacking the chair behind him.

Unfazed, I stood up and got in his face. "Eric was an adult, Shane. Not a child and not stupid. I'm sure he knew the dangers of dealing. You can't take responsibility for his behavior. I won't let you beat yourself up over this," I shouted back.

Shane reared up and punched a hole in the wall. "You have no fucking clue what you're talking about, Megan. No fucking clue. He thought that I went to your brother and got the cops on his ass. Eric was my best friend and he died thinking I narc'd him out."

I wrapped my arms around his waist. Shane tried to move away but I held on. I grabbed his face and stared him in the eyes. "It is not your fault. Eric knew that. He loved you like a brother. He knew deep down that you would never do that to him. You're not leaving because of this. I won't let you," I said passionately. I could not lose him. My heart couldn't take it. A panic was building inside my chest. Could he really leave, could he not see how I felt about him?

"I just can't deal with the possibility of you getting hurt," he whispered, cupping my face in his hands. *How will I get hurt?* I pushed the question out of my mind. All that mattered was making Shane stay.

"Shane. You just came into my life. I don't want to

lose you. Please," I whispered, hoping he would see how much he meant to me. Shane let out a growl and kissed me with such force that I almost fell over. He caught me with one hand around my waist and the other on the back of my neck. With lips locked, we tumbled onto the bed. The only way I could convey how I felt, was to show him. I rolled him onto his back and pulled his zipper down. He shuddered and uttered a groan. I smiled. It was bittersweet. I took him in my mouth. I would do anything to get him to stay, but I knew if he did, it would only be temporary. Shane was stubborn and if he had his mind set leaving, he was leaving.

"Come here," he whispered roughly. His voice was thick with emotion. He sat up, threw off his shirt, and reached for me. I eagerly got out of my dress and complied, settling myself on his pelvis. I gasped with pleasure at the first thrust, riding the wave of ecstasy. It was bittersweet, knowing how much he was hurting and how much I wanted to make him feel better. Sex was one thing, but there had to be a way to get him to open up to me, to talk to me. To stay with me. Sex was just sex, until love was involved. Knowing how I felt for him made this truly exquisite.

I was completely lost in the feeling of our bodies together. I almost didn't hear Penny growl outside the bedroom. Penny never growled, and hearing it for the first time startled me. I glanced over my shoulder and stopped moving. Penny was in the hallway, her shoulders tensed and hackles raised. Shane's body hardened beneath me.

"Was that Penny?" he asked. He tightened his grip on my arms. I nodded, meeting his stare.

"Penny? What's up girl?" I asked. Just then, a loud crash came from downstairs. Shane picked me up and got off the bed in one swift motion. Thunderous footsteps came up the stairs and all of a sudden, our bedroom was filled with gun-pointing men wearing black flak jackets. I screamed and reached for Shane's T-shirt, pulling it on quickly. Shane was busy pulling up his jeans and shouted, "What the fuck?" He pulled me behind his back and pressed me up against the wall, shielding me from their view. I struggled as I pulled on a pair of sweatpants. What the hell was going on? I looked up at Shane and could see the fury on his face.

"FBI! Everyone stay where you are! Shane Turner, you are under arrest for possession of narcotics, distribution, bank fraud, and extortion. You have the right to remain silent. Anything you say, can and will be used against you in a court of law," a familiar voice bellowed. *I know that voice.* I glanced over Shane's shoulder and was dumbfounded to see Tommy in the doorway, dressed like the other gun wielding solders in all black and a bulletproof vest.

"Tommy, what the fuck is going on?" I shouted angrily. Mad as hell, I no longer feared these idiots for breaking into my house. I tried to go over to Tommy, but one of his cronies stopped me in my tracks.

Shane pulled me back. "Stop. Don't Megs. It's not worth it. I'm not worth it. It's over. I'm sorry," Shane said quietly, his lips against my ear. His voice filled with sadness. I looked up at him, confused as hell. What was over? Why did he think he wasn't worth it? Why was he sorry? Questions were on my lips but before I could voice them, Shane was roughly pulled away from me.

"Shane. No. Stop! Let him go!" I shouted, grabbing at the officer's arms. Tommy rushed over and wrapped his arms around my waist, locking my arms behind my back. I struggled against him, kicking him and anyone else who got close.

"Calm the fuck down, Megs. I warned you this was going to happen. You wouldn't listen would you," he said low enough for only me to hear. I got a fist loose, whirled around and punched him in the jaw. Instantly my hand screamed with pain, but I didn't care. It felt good to finally punch that asshole. Then an ominous sound of guns locking filled the room.

"It's okay. Lower your weapons," Tommy grumbled, rubbing his jaw. "Good thing you hit like a girl." I looked over to see Shane in handcuffs, being pushed out the door.

"Shane. Don't say a single word! I'll call my uncle and we'll meet you down there!" I shouted. I turned and grabbed a pair of socks from the drawer.

"Megs. He won't be at the station. He's in FBI custody. We're taking him to our office for questioning," Tommy said.

"Why are you doing this, Tommy? Really? What's the point?" I demanded, shoving my feet into my sneakers.

"I told you he was bad news. You didn't listen," he replied rudely.

I rolled my eyes. "Get the hell out of here." I rummaged through the clothes that were on the floor and threw on a hooded sweatshirt.

"Can't do it, Peaches. You're in my custody now. I need to bring you in for questioning as well. You can call your Uncle Bob on your way to the office," he answered. Freaking jerk had a response to everything.

I could hear Penny whining underneath the bed. She was scared to death. As soon as she had seen the men, she ran and hid.

"Guard dog you ain't," I muttered, kneeling to see her. I gently tugged on her collar and pulled her out from underneath the bed. She whimpered and lay her head against my shoulder.

"Megs, I'm giving you the courtesy of waiting for you. But we need to get going," Tommy said from the door.

I narrowed my eyes. "Bullshit. What courtesy? You didn't give me any courtesy by breaking down my door. Go to hell, Tommy. And get out of my house."

"Dammit, Megan. You don't get it. And you know what? Now you're going down with him." He roughly grabbed my arm and yanked me up. He pushed me up against the wall and put my hands behind my back.

"Seriously? You're putting me in freaking cuffs? You fucking asshole. You know I haven't done anything wrong," I seethed.

Tommy gave a slight chuckle. "Maybe I wanted an excuse to pat you down."

"Touch me one more time, and I'll break your hand," I threatened. He snorted and pulled me out the door.

The scene outside was out of a movie. Police cars and black Suburbans were parked haphazardly on the street. Curious neighbors milled around, gossiping. Dogs held by uniformed officers were sniffing around my car. I quickly turned to Tommy.

"Look. If you are making me do this, at least let me call Mom to get Penny. She's going to freak out," I reasoned, hoping to God that Tommy had some compassion left in him. Tommy heard the worry in my voice and decided to be a decent guy.

"Yeah, I'll call your mom."

He pushed my head down and put me in the back of a black sedan, then walked away. I was finally able to catch a breath, being alone in the car. My mind raced. What the hell had Shane gotten himself into? Was this related to Eric's death? What were all those charges about? I was so confused; I couldn't keep my thoughts straight. The door suddenly opened and Tommy got in the front seat.

"Seriously, Tommy, why am I under arrest?" I demanded, trying to get a straight answer. Of course, he decided to be vague.

"You're not under arrest Megan. I could have you charged with assault on a federal officer, but I'm going to be a nice guy. We just have some questions for you," he replied vaguely.

"Questions about what exactly?" I implored. Tommy just pressed his lips together and ignored my plea for information. *Fine. Whatever.* I sat back in a huff, just imagining what my mother would say when she found out that I had been taken in.

***

WE TRAVELED IN silence for twenty minutes, finally coming to a stop in front of a nondescript high-rise office building. Tommy pulled me out of the car and led me to a seventh-floor office. He finally took the cuffs off and left me alone. I winced and rubbed my wrists where they'd bitten into my skin. *Well, now I know I won't be bringing* those *into my bedroom any time soon.* I did a mental head slap. *You're in an FBI building for questioning, Megan. Focus!*

The room was as big as my bathroom at home, with dull paint, no windows, and the requisite brown table and chairs. A security camera loomed over me from a corner in the ceiling. I gave it the finger. I didn't care how immature I looked, I was being held here for no reason other than plain spitefulness. I sat for an hour in the most uncomfortable chair. My back ached. And it never failed that as soon as I was held up somewhere—in traffic, in line, or locked in a briefing room—I always ended up needing to pee.

I pounded on the door in hopes that someone was listening. Thankfully, Tommy poked his head in. "What?"

"Tommy. I have to use the bathroom."

"Tough. Hold it. We're about ready to come in."

"Honestly, Tommy, you break into my house, interrupt me and my boyfriend, scare the crap out of my dog, and drag me down here. You make me wait here for an hour and now you're going to make me pee in my pants? Since when did you become such an asshole?" I demanded.

Tommy sighed, then opened the door wider. "Fine. I'm not going to cuff you. I'm going to walk you down, so behave yourself." I rolled my eyes and stuck my tongue out at him. *He always brings out my immature side*, I thought as he led me down a narrow hallway. He pushed open the ladies' room door and held it open for me. "Be quick. It's your turn," he muttered.

I walked in and quickly used the facilities. I washed my hands and face. The harsh fluorescent lights made the bags under my eyes appear much darker. My hands shook. I was worried about Shane. I wanted to see him, to hold him again, to make sure everything was going to be okay. I wanted answers. From him. Not from anyone else.

I walked slowly out of the bathroom and Tommy hurried me along back to the tiny room.

"Have a seat," Tommy said briskly with no emotion on his face. He was FBI Agent Tommy, not the man I was going to marry not so long ago.

I sat down in a chair, crossed my arms, and stared at him. Tommy sat across from me and pulled a couple of manila files from his bag.

"I'm here to ask you some questions regarding Shane Turner," he started formally, opening up one of the files.

"I'm not answering any questions until I see him. I need to see him," I replied quietly. Tommy ignored me.

"Tell me, what do you know about Ricardo Cruz, a.k.a Reggie?" he asked, not looking at me.

Damn it, look at me Tommy. Do not do this to me, I silently pleaded.

Tommy finally looked at me, and with a grave voice said, "Megan, he's leaving. He's going in front of the magistrate." Panic filled my stomach. Shane was in trouble and there was nothing I could do to stop it.

"Did he call his lawyer?" I demanded. He couldn't go down to the magistrate alone. That would be crazy.

"Your Uncle Bob is here." Tommy replied slowly. "He'll be back shortly. He just needs to be formally charged."

I leaned back in my chair and glared at Tommy with narrow eyes. "I demand a phone call. I get one phone call, right?"

Tommy sighed with exasperation. "Megan, I'm just asking you some questions. Help me out here. Please."

"Tommy, I'm sorry. But honestly, I don't think I can answer any of your questions," I replied truthfully.

"Let me bring you up to speed on your boyfriend. Shane has been arrested and will be charged with intent to distribute narcotics, possession of marijuana, and assault with a deadly weapon. Megan, these charges aren't stemming from a year ago. We've been watching the drug ring he is *still* involved with for months now. Eric was in this ring as well. Megan, he's been lying to you," Tommy replied angrily. As if my disbelief was not enough, I was getting angrier by the second.

"What the hell are you talking about? What ring?" I demanded.

"The Cruz Cartel. Does the name Reggie mean anything to you?" Tommy asked, looking through his file.

"Shane just said that he's a bad guy, with connections in Jersey, Florida, and Mexico. Eric was dealing with him. That's all I know," I answered quietly, feeling like the wind had been knocked out of me. *Shane lied to me.* He had been dealing this entire time. Why would he lie? There had to be more to the story. Tommy kept going through his files. I could tell that he was holding something back, that he was hesitating.

"What aren't you telling me, Tommy?" I asked as a heavy dread filled my stomach.

He sighed and closed his folder. "We have reason to believe that Shane was the one who shot your brother. Now, we don't have any firm evidence on it and, trust me, we're looking into it. But from what I was told by a trusted informant, Shane was the one to pull the trigger."

Dizziness and nausea overwhelmed me. Tommy was full of crap. Shane would never shoot Kyle. Never. I started shaking my head no. Tommy took my hand and looked me dead in the eyes.

"Megan. I'm sorry. I'm really sorry. I know Shane means a lot to you. I know that. But he's just bad news."

Flashes of the last couple of months played through my mind: having dinner at my mom's, spending time together, making love practically every night. How could the man I loved be the person that Tommy described? I wanted to refuse to believe Tommy's lies, but the doubt that had been in the back of my mind crept forward. The late night phone calls, the long work hours—it never made sense. Shane's words came back to haunt me, "People have gotten hurt because of me." *Is Shane really this person?* I felt like I didn't know Shane at all. "I want to see him. Now," I managed to blurt out.

Tommy nodded. "I have to go talk to my boss, but as soon as Shane gets back, I'll allow five minutes."

I just nodded, my body turning numb. Tommy left me in the room, alone with my thoughts and worst fears. I had to hear the truth from Shane before I jumped to any conclusions. *Did Shane really shoot my brother? Why?* And if was lying about the drugs, what else was he lying about? I didn't know what to think and my emotions were all over the place.

About forty minutes later, Tommy brought Shane to the door, looking tired and defeated. I wanted to give him the benefit of the doubt; I didn't want to believe Tommy's crazy story. But when I saw Shane, it was obvious he had changed; sadness filled his eyes.

"Shane!" I ran over to him and wrapped my arms around him. Tommy stood in the doorway.

"Megan, you have five minutes," he said as he walked out.

"Please, Shane. Please tell me that everything Tommy said is a lie," I begged as tears started falling. Shane just looked away.

"NO DAMMIT!" I snapped at him. "Look at me, Shane! Tell me the truth. Tell me that Tommy is lying and that you aren't dealing. Tell me that you didn't shoot Kyle!"

"I can't," he uttered gruffly.

"What do you mean 'you can't'?" I asked, shocked. I grabbed his face and forcibly turned it toward mine.

"Megan. I can't tell you that Tommy was lying. I can't. It is what it is," he said, his voice turning hard as steel.

"Is Tommy right? Did you shoot Kyle?"

Shane hung his head like he was ashamed. I took that as confirmation and anger flowed through me. I shoved him with both hands, but my fury was no match for his size. He barely moved.

"You shot my brother? You son of a bitch. Why? He's my family and practically your brother! How could you? I guess that means you're still dealing too." I shoved him again, with as much power as I had. He finally stumbled back, hitting the wall. I backed away and shook my head in disbelief. "You lying bastard. You told me that you stopped. You are better than that! Why would you put yourself through this web of lies? Why drag us into this?" I yelled.

Shane's eyes narrowed and his body tensed. "It wasn't supposed to end up like this."

"What the hell are you talking about?" I demanded. "What wasn't supposed to end up like this? Were you not supposed to shoot my brother? Did you not mean to lie to me for the last four months? Did you not mean to make me fall in love with you?" I screamed the last sentence. All that time, emotion, pleasure—it had all been a lie. I felt my heart breaking like glass, showering down like confetti. I was devastated and felt used.

"I didn't mean to hurt you," he said quietly, finally looking me in my eyes. It hurt too much to look at him anymore. I turned away.

"Well, it's too fucking late for that. I thought you were feeling the same. But I guess that was all part of the act too," I whispered. I roughly wiped away the tears.

"Dammit, Megan. Do you think I want to be here? Do you think I really meant to hurt you? I didn't. I'm sorry this shit happened, but I can't help it. I didn't want to get you or your family involved!" he shouted back at me. "This was just supposed to be a quick thing, not some long drawn-out drama."

Not thinking, I pulled back and punched him. Tears flowed but I didn't care anymore. That bastard didn't care at all about me or what he had done.

"Meg, I'm sorry. I didn't mean it like that..." he stuttered, holding his jaw in shock. I put up my hand to silence him. I couldn't let him finish. I couldn't let him have the last word.

"Fuck you, Shane. You really deserve what's coming to you," I said coldly. I walked over to the door and knocked, knowing that Tommy stood just outside. I knew he had heard every word, but at this point, I didn't care. When he opened the door, he looked at me with sadness in his eyes, then he put his arm around my shoulder and led me out.

Crying freely now, I sat down on a bench along the wall and broke down. Everything that I thought was good had gone horribly wrong. My chest heaved with crushing sobs. Questions floated in my head, questions I didn't dare voice. *Had everything been a lie? Our nights together, were those all part of the act? How could he do this to me? To my family?* My heart felt broken, destroyed. I didn't notice that Uncle Bob had put his arm around me until he spoke.

"Megan, let me take you home. Your mom is waiting for you," he said gently, as he handed me a tissue. Nodding, I blew my nose and stood up. I headed into the ladies' room and washed my face. He used and betrayed me. *Holy shit, I need to throw up.* I resisted the urge, walked out of the bathroom, and let Uncle Bob take me outside. It had gotten cloudy, threatening rain. It suited my mood.

***

WE DROVE BACK TO my house in silence. My mom was there when we arrived and she rushed out to greet us. "Megs! What happened?" she asked, drawing me into a hug. "Are you okay?"

I nodded and walked into the house without saying a word. I saw the glance that my uncle shot her. I could hear their muted conversation as I closed the door. *Let Uncle Bob explain that my heart was broken, that Shane had led everyone on.* I walked upstairs and lay on the bed. Penny whimpered and jumped up next to me. She put her paws on my arm and gently licked my hand.

"Oh God, Penny. What am I going to do?" I whispered as the sobs racked my body.

CHAPTER 19

W<small>HEN</small> I <small>OPENED</small> <small>MY</small> eyes, it was dark outside. Penny followed me as I went downstairs. I felt sick. My nose was all stuffy and my eyes were swollen. Mom was puttering around in the kitchen when I walked in. Immediately, she pulled me into her arms.

"Oh, baby doll. I'm so sorry that you're hurting," she murmured. I could feel myself growing weak as tears started to form. I pulled back and wiped my eyes with my sleeve.

"Don't, Mom," I muttered, as I sat down at the table. Mom set about making me a cup of tea with honey, my comfort drink from childhood. I was grateful that she was here, but at the same time I wanted to do nothing more than wallow in my sadness and self-pity. I sniffed.

Dinner. And by the smell of it, roast chicken and sweet potatoes. My mom's comforting tactics. "It smells good, Mom," I said, sipping the hot tea.

"Dinner will be ready in half an hour. Why don't you go take a hot shower? It will make you feel better." I just shrugged. It would be worthless to argue with her. Even with the tea, I still felt like garbage. I was exhausted and I had the beginnings of a migraine. I took my tea with me into the bathroom and started the shower. I grimaced at the zombie staring back at me from the mirror. Dark shadows circled my red, dry eyes. I was pale and sickly looking. I climbed in and stood underneath the spray. Visions of Shane tortured my battered mind. His haunted look, the guilt on his face, the ease with which he pushed away any sort of attachment that we shared. My emotions were on a roller coaster. I was so angry with Shane. He lied to me. The betrayal and the lies and the dealing had crushed my heart. I tried to push past the fact that he wasn't in love with me, but I couldn't. I felt like the most stupid girl in the world, a fool. I had been used. I broke down, feeling like I was going to break open.

When the water started to cool, I got out slowly. I walked into the bedroom in just my towel and was shocked at the scene. I hadn't notice it before, but the room was trashed. There were clothes everywhere, books and trinkets were knocked over, drawers were out of my dresser and lying on the floor. The detectives must have searched for evidence. A flash of nausea hit me. Like a movie, the entire scene of the officers breaking into my room played over in my mind. Rage overcame me and I quickly got dressed, pulling on the first items that I could find. I flew into the guest room, pulled out a large box of books from the closet, and dumped them on the floor. I darted back into the bedroom and started throwing Shane's clothes and shoes into the box. I swore loudly, cursing every article of clothing, blaming inanimate objects for my despair. His favorite cologne, the boxers, the shirts, the Stephen King novel he was reading, the extra pair of glasses. Everything went into the box. I went into the closet and took out all the hooded sweatshirts and jeans. A woman on a mission, I was determined to get rid of everything that reminded me of him.

I had just reached for a T-shirt when a picture on the dresser stopped me in mid-reach. I picked up the picture and sat back. It was my favorite picture of us. I remembered the day; Jen and Matt had come by to play some games and I had just beaten Shane at Scrabble. He picked me up and threw me on the couch in objection to my winning word. Our faces were flushed, and you could tell that we were laughing hard. I was leaning back against his chest, his head on my shoulder. The laughter was still in our eyes, and we both had a huge smile. Seeing this picture, my heart crumbled into a million pieces and my rage deflated.

The false bravado that had been building up in me came crashing down in a fresh wave of sadness. *I can't do this. I can't just get rid of him. I will never be able to get rid of him out of my heart and thoughts as quickly as he left my life.* I picked up the box filled with the remnants of Shane and shoved it in the corner of the closet. I quickly cleaned up the rest of the room. I wanted to erase any traces of what had transpired, but I knew that was stupid. The memories were burned into my mind for the rest of my life.

I headed back downstairs. Mom had kept dinner warm for me. She wordlessly pulled out a plate from the microwave. I sat down and poked through my food. It was my favorite, but I couldn't eat. The mere thought of eating made me feel sick.

"Mom, I'm sorry. This is really good. I guess I don't have much of an appetite," I said, finally pushing away my plate.

"It's okay, baby. I understand." She got up and put my plate in the sink then came around to my chair. She sat next to me and took my hands into hers. She still wore the anniversary band that my father had given her a month before he died. They celebrated their twenty-fifth wedding anniversary with a huge party in St. Michaels, Maryland. It was a fantastic night with our closest friends and family. Shane had been there. *Ugh.* I pushed the memory of him in a suit out of my head. *When will everything stop reminding me of him?*

"Megs. Uncle Bob told me what happened. I'm shocked that it's true. It doesn't sound like Shane."

"Well, he was good at fooling people, wasn't he?" I grumbled. I toyed with her ring and then pulled my hands away. "I really don't want to get into it Mom. I really don't. He lied to everyone. He shot Kyle. He broke my heart. What's done is done," I muttered.

I took a bottle of water out of the fridge and headed upstairs. I knew I wasn't being very hospitable, but Mom wouldn't take it personally. She had a key and would lock up when she left. I crawled back into bed and watched the clock move. I was physically exhausted but my mind wouldn't shut down. I couldn't stop thinking about what Shane had said about his intent. What had been his actual plan? Why did he move in with me? Was it just for the sex? Did he truly have feelings for me or was it just a plan to hide from the police? My thoughts were interrupted by the cell phone ringing. I picked it up, not bothering to look at the ID.

"Yeah." Rude, yes, but I was in no mood for

pleasantries.

"It's me. Why was Shane on the news?" Jen's voice came on the line. I should have called her. I sighed and then went into the whole story. Jen was speechless. As close as she and Shane were, she had no clue what had been going on.

"Holy shit! How are you doing? How are you handling it?" she asked gently. I could feel the tears start again and I angrily wiped my face.

"Jen, I am incredibly furious at him and feel so betrayed at the same time. I made the stupid mistake of opening myself up to him, trusting him. Falling in love with him. I guess I was wrong. He lied to everyone. It makes me wonder who Shane really is."

"Oh, Megan."

I didn't want to hear her sympathy. I didn't want to hear the pity in her voice. "I gotta go. I'm exhausted and I think I'm getting sick." We ended the phone call and I turned off my cell phone. I didn't want to hear from anyone else. I just wanted to go to sleep. I threw the covers on and closed my eyes, allowing the exhaustion I felt to finally take over.

CHAPTER 20

I WOKE UP THE NEXT MORNING feeling just as tired as when I went to bed. I forced myself to get up and put on a pair of cotton capris and a gray long sleeve shirt. I turned my cell phone back on and realized I had ten urgent text messages. Among them, Rachel, Kyle, and Sarah. They all probably wanting to talk about Shane, I surmised. I deleted them, not bothering to read them. I didn't want to rehash the whole story to every single person. I was sure my mother would fill in Sarah and Kyle. I went downstairs to make some coffee. I needed something to get rid of the fog in my head.

Mom had gone home sometime the night before and left a note. I had to smile. She made jokes about my cooking and said that just because Shane was gone didn't mean that I shouldn't still eat regularly. She left the chicken and sweet potatoes in the fridge. I made coffee, took it into the living room, and began mindlessly flicking through the TV channels, only stopping when I turned on the news channel.

"Former hockey prodigy Shane Turner was arrested by federal agents in a drug sting yesterday. Investigators allege that Mr. Turner was part of the Cruz Cartel, a drug ring located here in Crofton that stretches across the country. It is thought that his friend, the recently deceased Eric Morrison, was also part of that ring. Turner will appear before the U.S. federal court today to be indicted on charges of extortion, possession, and intent to distribute in addition to other charges. Turner is also being questioned in the shooting of Edgewater police officer, Kyle Connors. This is Melvin Booms. Back to you."

It didn't mention if anyone else had been taken into custody. I wondered which one of his friends was going down with him. I sent a quick text to Rachel thinking she might know. Adrian was Shane's closest friend and had to know more than I did. She sent a response immediately. "Adrian and Ben were questioned but not taken in. Adrian was just as surprised about this as we are. We're thinking of you, Megan. Please call us if we can do anything for you."

Well, shoot. There was nothing anything anyone could do; there was nothing I could do. My life had taken an unanticipated turn. I had nothing more to do than pick up the pieces. I had to live, but at the same time, I couldn't bring myself to even fathom what tomorrow would bring. I had a hard time believing that Adrian was unaware. Shane told Adrian everything. If Adrian didn't know, then Shane must have been in over his head.

I turned off the TV and whistled for Penny. I took her for a long walk. It was a beautiful day. I tried to keep my thoughts to a minimum, but Shane kept creeping back to the forefront. I recalled every conversation and every interaction we had with his friends. There were so many signs that I ignored, the hushed conversations, the late night work hours, and the missed phone calls. I felt so stupid. I had turned a blind eye because I wanted to be with him. Just like with Alex, I ignored the obvious. How desperate of a woman was I, to be that oblivious? The answer was disturbing.

We walked the entire length of the neighborhood. The sun felt good on my face. I hoped I was getting some color, as the pasty complexion look I had going on was too Goth for my taste. I didn't pay much attention to my surroundings and was startled when I heard a truck roar past me. It took me a minute to realize that it looked like the same SUV I saw back in February, right before someone broke into my house.

It was entirely possible that there was a new person with the same SUV in the community, but it seemed out of place. Maybe they were lost? I wasn't sure, but I quickened my pace and kept Penny close. I hurried inside and locked the door. I looked at Penny and told her, "You will protect this place, right?" She cocked her head to the side in the classic dog expression of "Huh?"

"Right. You'll attack the intruder and lick him to death."

I spent the rest of the weekend and the following week hanging around the house. I cut the grass in the backyard and plucked out the weeds that were invading my front garden. I stayed away from the news shows and only took calls from Jen or my mom. I didn't want to talk to anyone else or have to answer the inane question of "how are you coping?". I coped by working. Working in my house, working in the garden, catching up on all the work I had missed at the office the previous week. I stayed busy. Uncle Bob understood and didn't object when I called in. The busier I was, the less I dwelled on the heartbreak that was crushing my chest.

I did end up getting a lot accomplished. Everything was cleaned, straightened, or thrown out. I reorganized my pantry. I went through my closet and took out everything I had no intention of wearing again. I went shopping for new curtains. Eventually, I ran out of things to do. I couldn't avoid the real world any longer. It was time to pull on my big girl undies and be an adult.

***

AFTER A WEEK OF hiding from my everyday life, I went back to my normal routine, the routine I had before Shane came into my life. On Monday I woke up at my normal time and blasted the music while I was in the shower. I dressed in a brown and white polka-dotted wrap dress, a pair of kitten heels, and added some color with a topaz necklace. I looked normal on the outside, even though I felt sick as a dog on the inside.

I walked into the office as if nothing was wrong. I smiled at the paralegals and interns, and brought my computer up as the coffee was being made. I was pouring myself another cup when Uncle Bob coughed behind me.

"Megan, I wasn't sure if you would be in today. How are you doing?" he asked gently. A lump formed in my throat and I swallowed before answering.

"Just fine, Uncle Bob," I replied. The cheerfulness in my voice was fake and Uncle Bob knew it.

"I'm meeting Shane today. Is there anything you'd

like me to tell him?" Uncle Bob asked, putting a hand on my shoulder.

"Nope. I have nothing to say to that lying jerk. In fact, I'd appreciate it if you didn't tell me anything about the trial. It's bad enough that it will be dominating the news. But honestly, I don't care anymore," I answered, lifting my head to show him the steely gaze in my eyes. I told myself the same thing—that I didn't care. I was done worrying about him, regardless that my heart was dying for any shred of information, which I knew Uncle Bob had. I knew that I shouldn't hang on to anything related to Shane. It would kill me to know any more. I didn't want to know if he was still thinking about me, if he was doing okay in jail. I had to go on. Like it never happened.

Uncle Bob accepted my resolute answer and gave me a quick peck on the cheek. "I understand. I hope I see you next week for the barbecue." Every year my aunt and uncle went all out for their annual barbecue. Colleagues, family, and friends all got together at my uncle's house on the Chesapeake Bay. There were games and a moon bounce for the kids, swimming in the bay, and face painters.

I nodded. "We'll be there. I'm sure Mom is already making trays of brownies and cookies." He gave my hand a squeeze and headed out the door, his briefcase in hand.

The rest of the day wore on slowly. No one really talked to me and I was grateful, but at the same time, their glances of pity and hushed whispers had really started to grate on my nerves. It took a while before I got through my inbox. I had barely made a dent in my workload. Uncle Bob was back from seeing Shane, and it took all I had to keep from asking any questions. He understood though, and told me to go home. I was in no shape to be at work.

***

I FINALLY WALKED OUT of the office at six thirty, knowing that I really should have gone home earlier. My eyes felt like they had a mind of their own and I struggled to keep them open. I had a horrible headache and an upset stomach. I was able to keep the vomiting down to a minimum, but anytime I even glanced at a piece of food, my stomach churned. *I must be coming down with a bug.* I made my way to the car, not paying any attention to the beautiful afternoon. I just wanted to go home and sleep. I was fumbling with my keys when I felt a hard stab to my head and a low voice. "Do not scream. Turn around now, you stupid bitch."

My heart raced and my hands started shaking.

I slowly turned around. He was dressed in all black with a black mask over his face, showing nothing but a menacing tattoo under his dark eyes. I had never seen him before but the threat in his voice was all it took to make me comply. I didn't want to show that I was afraid, but I couldn't stop quaking. I stared at the man who held a pistol to my head. "Here. Here's my purse and my keys. Take them," I stuttered. I winced when I heard the fear in my voice.

He took his free hand and gave me a hard shove against my car. My head hit the roof and I bit my lip to keep from crying out in pain. I didn't want him to hear how terrified I was. He threw my purse and keys to the ground. I could hear my phone clatter and break.

"I don't want your fucking purse, bitch. I want Shane. Where the fuck is Shane?" he growled.

"Shane was arrested last week. I don't know where he is," I said desperately. I held out my hands in surrender. Panic and adrenaline were rapidly coursing through my veins. I tried desperately to remember the self-defense techniques that my brother taught me, but I was helpless.

"Shane was arrested, but he was released on bail. Where the fuck is he?" the stranger demanded, pressing the gun to my temple. I didn't even consider what he said, that Shane had been released. Apparently, I didn't answer quickly enough; he wheeled back and sent the butt of the gun flying across my face. I fell to the side, pain screaming down my jaw.

"I don't know where he is!" I cried, holding my face. Tears stung my eyes as I tried to hold it together. He grabbed me up and shoved me against the car again. His hand closed around my throat as he held me there. I struggled against him, smacking at his hands and kicking his shins, desperate to get free. I was terrified at what might come next. I grappled against his bulky jacket. I scratched and clawed at his hands, frantically trying to free myself. My vision started getting cloudy and I was struggling to breathe. I could see black dots and I frantically tried to do anything I could.

"Wrong answer. We've been to your house. His shit is gone. I know he's been there." He threw me back down. I was wheezing for air, trying to breathe, when the first kick came, right against my side. I screamed, I felt such heat and burning in my side. The second kick was harder. The sharp pain took away what little breath I had.

"I don't...know...where he is," I struggled to say. "Please," I begged helplessly. I grasped for anything I could throw: rocks, keys, anything. I could see the jagged edge of my phone and I scrambled toward it. The monster saw what I was doing and pulled me back.

"No. You won't be calling anyone but Shane. Give him a message. We're looking for him and this is the least of what we're going to do," he threatened as he pulled back his fist. I braced for the impact and held up my hands in a weak shield, but I was unable to stop the crack of my cheek as he put his entire weight behind the punch. I could feel myself falling to the ground. I closed my eyes, waiting for more.

CHAPTER 21

I SLOWLY OPENED MY eyes, my vision blurred. My heart raced and I tried to look around, to see where my attacker was. Thankfully, he was gone. I pushed myself up with trembling arms. It was so painful to breathe and I couldn't see out of my right eye. My entire face felt like it was on fire. I made my way slowly back to the office. It was late, but I knew that Uncle Bob was still in the building. He was always the first one in and the last to leave. I got to the front door just as he was walking out. The horrified look that came across his face gave me an inkling of how bad I really looked. "Uncle Bob," I said weakly. I didn't want to cry, but I couldn't help it. The pain was too much. Sobs broke through as he rushed over to me.

"Jesus Christ! What the hell happened? Get inside right now." He helped me into the office and locked the door behind us. He sat me down in the reception area and rushed to get an ice pack from the fridge. I cautiously held the pack to my face, wincing at the sting of the cold. I managed to relay the attacker's message. The furious look on Uncle Bob's face shocked me. His face turned purple and the veins in his head bulged and pulsated. He ran to the phone and dialed 911. I didn't want to ride in an ambulance. I could have had someone pick me up, but he ignored my protests. He stayed by my side, going through the horrific episode with me again, trying to pull together as many details as he could.

Ten minutes later there was a sharp rap at the door. Uncle Bob rushed over to let in the EMTs and police. Luckily, we were in another jurisdiction so my brother wasn't there. *I'm sure he'll find out sooner or later.* I answered the police questions as best I could. I described the creep's tattoo. I didn't remember seeing a vehicle so I was no help there. As I was answering their questions and being lifted onto the stretcher, I heard my uncle's furious tone. He was yelling at someone and even though his office door was closed, I could clearly hear him.

"Dammit. You said she would be protected! That is the main reason why I agreed to this. You said you would protect her! Where was her protection detail? Why didn't anyone see anything? I demand answers! So help me God, if anything more happens to her, I'm pulling my support from this case. Do you hear me?"

Who the heck was he talking to? What was he talking about? What protection? I was so confused. My head was pounding, my body was crying in pain. I couldn't move my arm anymore and it tortured me when the EMTs strapped me onto the gurney. I could hear Bob moving behind me, calling out, "I'll be right behind you, Meg! I'm going to call your mom."

Good lord. Not my mom. First, Kyle was shot, now I was banged up. She didn't need this. Guilt and dread kept me occupied while I was in the ambulance. The medics worked over me, checking my vitals and examining the bruises on my face. They asked me inane questions, like What is your name? and What day is it? I understood that they had to follow protocol, but I didn't want to talk to them. I just wanted to close my eyes and forget what happened.

***

ONCE WE ARRIVED AT the hospital, they wheeled me into the ER and I heard my mother's voice in the waiting room. "That's her! That's my daughter. Please let me go back there!"

I glanced wearily at the nurse who was checking my chart. "If you don't let her back here, she's going to tear this place apart," I warned, only half joking. Mom is a force to be reckoned with when it comes to her kids. As the nurse retook my vitals, she smiled and said, "I understand, but I want the doctor to take a look at you first. We'll let her come over in a minute."

An older doctor came around the curtain and asked me the same questions the EMTs did. His hands were freezing and shaking, but his eyes were sharp. He examined my face and side. His fingers were light to the touch, which was needed. The pain was excruciating. The nurse hooked me up to an IV. I took a quick peek and saw that my ribcage was already turning colors.

The doctor noticed my glance. "It looks like your ribs may be fractured. We're going to take an X-ray just to be sure. Your jaw line is severely bruised, and it looks like your cheekbone is bruised as well, but nothing looks broken. I'm going to send in an ophthalmologist to check your vision after the CT scan. I also want get some bloodwork done so I can see if you're anemic."

After he gave the nurse the orders, he turned around and walked out. Apparently, his bedside manners were in need of a booster shot. The nurse began asking me questions and I answered automatically, but she stopped me in my tracks when she asked when my last period was. I thought back. I knew it was before Eric's bonfire. Had there been one after that? I answered her as truthfully as I could.

"Could you be pregnant?" she asked, her eyes darting down to my ring finger.

"No. It's just stress. I've been dealing with a lot of crap," I muttered. I could feel the blush creeping up. My sex life wasn't the issue here. My ribs were killing me and my face looked like I had been whacked with a hammer. Luckily, I started to feel numb thanks to the nifty little painkiller button they had installed next to me.

"I'm letting your mother in for just a quick second. We need to get going to radiology," the nurse quipped, pulling back the curtain and gesturing to my mom. She rushed over to me and I could feel my eyes welling up with tears. I could see the anguish in her eyes.

"Oh, Megs. You poor thing. I told you not to wear those heels," my mom gently chastised, sniffling through her smile. *What the hell is she talking about?* I looked at her, confused, until Uncle Bob came up behind her.

"Megs, I'm sorry. I had to tell your mom. We are quite concerned, especially with you hitting your face on the sink." His voice was gentle, but the look on his face was anything but. His eyes were urging and he nodded slightly. I took a deep breath. He was right. Keeping the truth from my mom was probably the best thing to do.

"Yeah, I know Mom. You know how gravity and I don't get along. Add a pair of heels to the equation and you have a recipe for disaster," I replied. Thankfully, the nurse hustled in at that exact moment and ended the conversation.

"She'll be back in an hour or so. Why don't you take a seat in the waiting room?" The nurse ushered my mom out of the way so that the orderly could wheel me down the hall. Mom squeezed my hand and kissed my cheek before she let go. I felt so bad for lying, but the truth would be too much.

I got through the CT scan and the X-ray without too much poking and prodding. Five hours later, I was back in my little curtain-enclosed room with my mother hovering. The doctor came in and barely acknowledged her. "Amazingly, young lady, you're not as bad off as you look. Your ribs are severely bruised but not enough to be seriously worried. Your lung function is fine. Your cheekbone is also pretty bruised but not broken. Your jaw will be sore, but nothing is shattered. It will hurt to chew, so I'm recommending a soft diet. When you sneeze, hold a pillow to your chest. I want you to stay home and rest for the next week. You'll be in pain. I'm writing you a pain prescription, a medication that's safe to take during pregnancy, ready to be filled. This IV drip is fine for now and will not hurt the fetus. If at any point you feel worse, get dizzy, or have weakness in your legs, please let me know as soon as possible. If it becomes hard to breathe, contact emergency services immediately. I've signed the discharge papers so the nurse will come and get you shortly," he said curtly and started to walk around the curtain. As an afterthought, he paused. "Do you have any questions?"

My mind was in a haze. He must have put me on some good drugs because I hadn't heard a single thing after he mentioned the word fetus. Fetus? Did that mean I was pregnant? No. No way. Huh? I shook my head, then instantly regretted it when I yelped in pain.

"Um…Wait. What? Did you say fetus?" I asked. I glanced at my mom, who was staring at the doctor like he had grown a second head. Bewildered and disoriented, I slowly turned back to the doctor. "There has to be a mistake."

I must have been messing up his late-night dinner plans because the doctor sighed with exasperation. "Yes. You're pregnant. About six weeks along. You'll need to make an appointment with your OB/GYN. Prenatal vitamins can be picked up at the pharmacy along with your prescription. The nurse will be in shortly." With that, the curmudgeon of a doctor turned on his heels and walked away.

Dumbfounded. I was absolutely dumbfounded. I was pregnant. I couldn't wrap my head around it. I had been on the pill, but then there were those couple days when I had forgotten to take it. *Oh, crap.* I remembered my mother was sitting next to me, and I slowly turned and checked her reaction. She was just as stunned as I was.

"Momma?" I ventured. "Mom? Are you okay?"

She shook her head. "Did he just say what I think he said?"

I shrugged. "I think he said I was pregnant." I couldn't say any more than that. I was speechless. Thoughts flew through my head in a drug-filled haze. Me? A mom? How in the hell was I going to make this work? I wasn't married. I wasn't with Shane anymore. Was I really going to end up a single mother? I rubbed my eyes with my hand, grimacing as the slight movement hurt.

"Well. Let's not think about this now. We'll get you home and into bed. I have Penny at my place already," Mom said briskly, gathering up my things. "Sarah brought over some clothes for you. She stopped by while you were getting X-rayed. She had a bridal dress fitting or she would have stayed. I'm going to run and get the car while the nurse discharges you. I'll be right back." She hurried out of the room. The wedding was in

October, and Sarah had already picked out form-fitting dresses for her bridesmaids to wear. *I'm not going to fit in my dress!* I momentarily panicked, then gave myself a mental slap. *Really?* Why was I freaking out about this now? I needed to think straight and worry about what was happening, not about fitting into some dress.

I felt flustered, only this time I knew it wasn't the drugs. I lay back onto the pillows and tried to rationalize my way through what I'd just been told. This was the twenty-first century. A woman had options. But no options came to mind when I pictured Shane's baby, a baby boy with his mischievous grin and hazel eyes; my father's dimples.

Shane. A stark realization hit me. Shane didn't know. How could I get a hold of him to let him know? He had left his cell phone at the house and, from my understanding, hadn't touched base with anyone. *He would make an excellent father.* I could just imagine the conversation. "Oh, I know you lied to my family and me. You shot my brother and dealt drugs. I also heard that you bailed yourself out of jail and didn't even bother to let me know. By the way, I'm having your baby." No. That wasn't going to happen. My baby deserved better than that. My head felt so heavy and confused; thoughts kept bashing into each other. It was too much to think about.

The nurse came bustling in at that moment and I was grateful for her interruption. "Now, Megan, here's your prescription for your pain reliever. Take it twice a day for the next couple of days. Then you'll decrease it over time. Make sure you follow up with your primary physician and your OB. You should refrain from driving for the next week and lifting anything heavy for the next six weeks. Here you go, just sign here," she said with a perky smile. I dutifully signed the release forms and she helped me stand up. "I believe your mom is on her way back in. I can help you get dressed if you want."

"That's fine," I muttered. She helped me pull on the yoga capris and T-shirt that Sarah had brought over. I felt like a child when she pulled on my socks and sneakers. The nurse sat me in the wheelchair and rolled me out into the lobby. It was close to midnight. I could see Mom's blue sedan at the front entrance. With the nurse's help, I managed to slide into the passenger seat without hurting too much.

"Did anyone get my car?" I asked as I realized that my car was still in the firm's parking lot. As much as I loved having my mom take care of me, there was a limit to the amount of coddling I could take. I would need the ability to escape.

"Bob and Tommy brought it back to my house," she replied vaguely. I slowly turned to look at her.

"Tommy? As in Tommy Greene? Like my ex-fiancé Tommy? Why is he still around? I thought that after he busted Shane he'd be living it up back in New York with his FBI buddies," I replied. I watched her expression to see if she was hiding anything from me.

"Yes, that Tommy. He stopped by the hospital as well. He's concerned about you, Megs. He feels horrible about what happened. And honestly, I have to say that I'm glad he did what he did. I could kill Shane myself. He shot your brother. He brought drug dealers into your home. I don't think I can ever forgive him."

I stayed silent. I knew she was right. I knew that what Shane did was unforgivable. But at the same time, the pain of losing him only deepened with the knowledge that he was going to be a father. That he would never know about his child, the one that I was now carrying. I turned and stared out the window as the highway gave way to the huge houses and big lots that made up my hometown. We turned down my mother's street and a wave of nostalgia hit me. I remembered riding my bike down those streets, playing kickball and hide-and-seek. Things were so much simpler then. What I wouldn't give to have that innocence back, to not know the dangers of a broken heart, to not feel the pain of betrayal.

Mom helped me inside and into my old room. My mom had never changed my bedroom. It still had the peach walls, blue carpeting, and white furniture of my childhood. But gone were the rock posters, which had been replaced with family photos. She settled me into bed and Penny jumped up to join me.

"Go to sleep, sweetie. You need to rest," she said gently, as she tucked my hair behind my ear and kissed my forehead. Just like when I was a kid. I choked back the tears.

"Mom, thanks for everything. I love you," I whispered. She smiled.

"I love you too. You'll know soon enough. There isn't anything you won't do for your children." And with that, she headed out of the bedroom.

I rubbed Penny's ears and thought about what she said. She never failed to insert words of wisdom when I least expected it.

"So, Penny, are you ready to have a baby in the house?" I whispered. Penny just gazed at me with her brown eyes and thumped her tail, then gave a wide yawn and closed her eyes. I followed suit.

***

I SLEPT HORRIBLY THAT night and woke the next morning feeling mangled. The drugs had knocked me out. I felt so stiff and sore. My right side was throbbing and pulsing.

I needed to get out of bed, but every move I tried, made me want to scream out in agony. I cursed the bastard who did this to me and wished I could shoot hot irons under his fingernails. Helpless, I gave in. This wasn't going to work. I wasn't going to be able to do this alone.

"Mom! I need to pee! Can you please help me?" I wailed pitifully. Our walls were thin so I could hear her rattling in the kitchen. Footsteps came down the hall and I was so glad to hear the door open. However, I wasn't so glad to see the face that poked in.

"What are you doing here?" I grumbled. I really didn't want Tommy's help going to the bathroom. It would be so awkward. "Where's my mom?" I demanded, as I struggled to get up. Apparently, the flailing of my arms and legs amused him, because he busted out with laughter.

"You look like a fish out of water!" he said, masking his laugh with a cough. "Here. Let me help you." He managed to pull me out of bed with the least amount of pain possible. I suffered through the embarrassment long enough; I gave him my evil glare.

"Thanks. I think I can manage fine now," I muttered as I shuffled my way to the bathroom.

"Are you sure? I can come in and help you," he called out. I gave him the middle finger over my shoulder and closed the bathroom door. *This freaking sucks.* I glanced in the mirror and groaned. I looked like I had gone ten rounds in a boxing ring. My face was a rainbow of colors. My eye was swollen with shades of purple and red, with my cheek and jaw line a psychedelic swirl of yellows and greens. I looked like a monster. I used the bathroom and debated about jumping into the shower but decided against it. I didn't have any clothes with me and I would be damned if I was going to let Tommy see me naked. I opened the door and shuffled to the kitchen. Tommy was pouring a cup of coffee when I walked in. I sat down at the table and he handed it to me.

"I already added your creamer. There's your juice. You're due for another round of pain meds," he said cheerfully. He brought my pain pills over and sat down across from me. I swallowed them with the juice then picked up my mug.

"Thanks," I said dryly. "Where's my mom?"

"She went to the grocery store. I offered to babysit while she was gone."

"Yeah, well, I'm up now. I don't need a sitter," I mumbled. I didn't want him to have the satisfaction of me having to depend on him.

"Well, I did have an ulterior motive. I wanted to talk to you," Tommy said softly.

"I really don't think I want to talk to you right now, Tommy. I don't think you have anything to say that I want to hear," I replied wearily.

"Look. I get it. You're pissed. And you have every right to be. But you have to understand what's going on," he replied tersely.

"Fine. What is so important that you had to come over here?" I retorted, meeting his gaze.

"I'm sorry for busting Shane like that. But you have to know the truth. You're in danger, Megan."

I scoffed. "Really? What gave you that idea? Because some asshole beat the shit out of me? All because he was looking for Shane? Who, by the way, is out on bail. Did you know that?"

"No. He's not out on bail," Tommy replied slowly.

"Well, that guy thinks he is. And I want to know why I wasn't told. Why didn't anyone tell me? Why didn't he call me?" I said as angry tears welled up. *Crap.* I didn't want to cry in front of Tommy.

"Shane isn't out on bail. He was moved to a safe house."

"Uh. Okay. Why?" I was confused. I knew a little bit about the prison system because of my uncle and father. I knew it was not normal procedure for felons to be transported to a safe house unless they were going to rat someone out. "Is he going to talk and cop a plea?"

"Well, yeah. He works for us," he said softly.

me. The words hit me like a ton of bricks. I was thrilled that he felt the same way I did, but mortified at my own behavior. I grasped at the threads, trying to piece together the very fabric of our torn relationship. *I can salvage this,* I thought. Everything that had gone wrong could be made right again. If only I could talk to him, tell him how much I love him. *We can still work. We can be a family.*

"I need to see him, Tommy. I need to tell him I'm sorry," I said firmly as I furiously brushed away the tears.

Tommy sighed with regret. "I'm sorry, Megan. You can't. I don't know where he is. The federal marshals have that information and I'm not privy to it. He's in protective custody now and will be for a very long time."

Any hope that I had of seeing him again quickly deflated. "Why is he in protective custody?"

"He is now a wanted man by the rest of Reggie's crew. Reggie managed to get himself out on bail, and as we now know, some of his thugs are still out there."

I sat there and tried to absorb it all. This was so much to take in. "So you mean to tell me that I will never see him again? I won't be able to talk to him?"

Tommy hesitated and then said, "Honestly, Megs, I'm not sure. We still have the rest of the gang to pick up. It will be at least until Reggie goes to trial. And we both know how long that could take."

"Well that's fucking lovely," I muttered. I pushed away my bowl and coffee. "I'm done with this. I need to get dressed. I need to go home."

Anger flicked in his eyes. "Yeah. About that. We're assuming it was Reggie's crew that went through your house yesterday. They didn't destroy anything, but your home alarm went off at four thirty yesterday afternoon. The alarm company contacted your mother when they couldn't get a hold of you."

Suddenly feeling exhausted, I leaned back and rubbed my eyes. "The jerk that attacked me said that they had come through and that's how they figured Shane had left. No one could find his things because I went through it all last week and put it in storage. Shit. What are we telling my mom? She doesn't know what happened yesterday."

"The truth," he said simply. I stared at him in disbelief. Was he serious?

"The truth? Why would you say that? I mean, I know honesty is the best policy, but really? In this situation? She is already going through the roof that Shane shot Kyle. That he lied to everyone else. She is going to freak out and be paranoid that someone is out to get me. She'll go nuts trying to protect me!" I sputtered as I tried to paint the only possible scenario.

Tommy just shook his head. "Your mom isn't stupid. She's put two and two together. She's not buying the story your uncle gave her and truth be told, she's pretty pissed that he lied to her. But aside from that, you're not getting the point. These people are dangerous. You were lucky last night. It could have been much worse. Reggie's crew is out to get you. They are at least going to be watching to see if you have any contact with Shane. They are going to try to draw him out. It isn't going to be safe for you here. You and your mom need to go away for a while. We can set you up in a nice house, take the dogs with you—"

"Hell NO!" I glared at him. "I'm not letting these crazy-ass fools think they can drive me away. This is my house. My life. They already screwed up Shane's. This isn't going to happen to me again. I refuse to leave my family, my friends, and my life because some street-urchin thug is looking for Shane. I'm not going to run scared every time I turn the corner or see a stranger. I'm not going to do it," I seethed.

I was wiped. My little rant had taken a lot out of me. Either that or the pain meds were finally kicking in. I stood up despite the protest from my knocking knees. "I think I need to lie down," I whispered. Tommy rushed to my side and supported my weight as he helped me down the hallway and into my bed. I gingerly rolled onto my side and he sat on the floor next to my bed.

"We're going to talk about this later. You and the baby need your sleep," he said softly.

My eyes had been slowly closing but shot open at his remark.

"You know?" I whispered.

"Yeah, I know." He leaned over and gently tucked a strand of hair behind my ear.

"Are you okay with it?" I wasn't sure why I asked that. It just slipped out. It wasn't like he had any choice about it. It wasn't going to affect him either way. My speech was beginning to slur. I started to sound like a drunk. *All of the side effects and none of the fun.*

"I'm okay. I can't help but wish that it was under different circumstances. I mean, what baby wants a convict for a daddy?" He gave me an impish grin that told me he was kidding. I rolled my eyes. "Seriously, Megs. I'm going to protect that baby. I'm going to protect both of you." He leaned over again and kissed my forehead. "Take a nap. I'll be here later."

***

I WOKE UP THREE HOURS later. The pills had really knocked me out. I hated feeling woozy all the time. Even though the doctor said that they were safe for the baby, I decided I wouldn't risk it. I gingerly rolled out of bed, cradling my right side. I heard voices down the hall and I followed them. My mom, Uncle Bob, and Tommy were sitting in the living room talking. They stopped and looked up when I walked into the room.

"Did I interrupt something?" I joked, feeling uneasy. It was clear that I did.

Uncle Bob stood up. "Megs. I am so glad you're doing better." He kissed my forehead and led me to the couch. As soon as I sat down, my mother draped the afghan over my legs.

"Mom, I'm not sick. I'm fine," I protested. Her look hushed me and I sat back while she fussed over me.

"I was telling your mother what sort of situation we're in," Tommy said gravely. I groaned and rolled my eyes. *Great, just one more thing that she needs to stress about,* I thought as I gazed at the worry etched on her face.

"I think we should do what Tommy suggests and leave for a while."

I disagreed. "He's right. You need to get out of here. But I'm not going anywhere. They know Shane is gone and they think that he'll come back for me. If I leave here with you, they will come after the both of us. There is no way I'm putting you in danger, Mom."

"Megan Louise Connors! You listen to me and you listen well, dammit. I am not letting you or my grandchild stay here and wait for a potential bloodbath. Do you honestly believe that you're safe here? You're going to end up being their target!" my mother cried out.

I turned my face and brushed away the tears that had started falling. She was right, obviously. I had to think about my child now and protecting it at all costs.

Tommy coughed and said, "I think we're too late for that. We've been noticing an increase in vehicle traffic in the neighborhood. Now, without putting Reggie's crew on notice that we're here, we can't stop every single car and ask for identification. It isn't safe for either one of you here right now. I've made arrangements for you to go with a member from my unit. They will take you to an undisclosed location for the time being."

My mom held my hand while we listened to Tommy lay out the plan. My heart sunk even lower. The situation that we were in seemed a lot more dangerous than I had led myself to believe. He described the tactics that Reggie's crew used and it scared the crap out of me. Tommy was right. We needed to leave.

"I'll go pack a bag right now," my mother said quickly. Her lips were pressed into a tight line and I could see the pain she was in. She was terrified, but putting up a brave front.

"I don't have anything here, besides the clothes I

wore yesterday. What am I going to do?" I asked quietly. I didn't want to become a bigger pain in the ass than I already was.

"The plan right now is to take you separately. Your mom was already planning on a vacation to the beach with your Aunt Nancy. We're going to stick to that. You were planning on leaving tomorrow, right?" Tommy looked at my mother for confirmation, who nodded.

"Yes we were, but I canceled. I told her that I was going to stay home and take care of Megan," my mother replied nervously.

"Good. Pack your bags like you're still going. You'll load up your car and head out tomorrow morning. If Nancy calls, just tell her that you and Megan had to be alone for a while to help her recover. Megs, you're going to go home and wait. A fellow agent, Kate Parks, will meet you there. You're going to pack up your things and act like Kate is your friend. Tell Jen or whoever that you're going away for a while. Make up an excuse that you're going away for some R&R. Bob, you'll tell the office the same thing. Tomorrow Kate will take you to the rendezvous point where you'll meet up with Rick's team. At no point will you have any contact with anyone else," Tommy said. I was seeing the side of him that I rarely saw when we dated. I was impressed with his demeanor and his calmness amidst the chaos that was taking place.

"You'll take the dogs with you. I want you to pack away as many items as you can. Anything that can't be replaced, I want you to give to Bob. We're going to keep watch on the house as best as we can, but our resources will be needed elsewhere."

I was processing all this new information, taking it all to heart. There were so many things I needed to do and so many questions to ask. I wasn't sure where to start. I turned to my uncle.

"You knew. This entire time," I stated.

Uncle Bob nodded. "After Shane was arrested, he immediately called the office. He wanted to talk and let it out. I was there when Shane signed the plea agreement. He wanted a better life for himself and for you. He loves you so much that when he agreed to talk, he demanded that you be protected. Even though you weren't in danger initially, Shane knew that you would be the only one Reggie's crew could use against him. Part of his plea agreement was that you were assigned a protection detail. Agents have been monitoring your movements. I wasn't taking any chances and neither was Shane."

Tears rolled down my cheeks as I hugged my uncle. "Thank you," I whispered.

Tommy checked his phone and glanced quickly at

his watch. He looked uncomfortable at breaking up our moment but said, "Megs, I'm going to take you home. You'll pack up what you need and be ready to go tomorrow morning."

I stood up awkwardly with my mother's help. "I guess this is for real, huh?"

CHAPTER 23

"I'M STARVING. DO WE HAVE time to eat?" I asked as my stomach reminded me of the time. Tommy busily darted his eyes back and forth and quickly hustled me into his SUV. He got in on the driver's side and we headed out of the neighborhood.

"Yeah, we'll pick up something on the way to your place. I'm sure Penny won't mind a cheeseburger for dinner," he said, giving me a quick grin. I guess my reaction didn't suffice, because he quickly grabbed my hand. "Hey. I didn't mean to scare you back there. I really didn't."

"I know. It's…It's just that so much has happened in the last few weeks. I'm having a hard time processing it," I said slowly. I felt so overwhelmed. If anything more happened, I'd probably have a nervous breakdown.

We grabbed burgers and soup for dinner and made it back to the house. Penny happily followed the scent of beef into the house and had no issues settling into her spot under the kitchen table. I left my dinner on the counter and walked through the house. Tommy was right; the bastards didn't touch anything. The only thing that was messed up was my front door. A man was already replacing the frame when we got there. I looked at Tommy, who was by my side. He answered the question on my face.

"Mr. Stevens is with us. He's part of our cleanup crew. We have people in place at Mr. Gentry's house down the street. He's visiting his kids for the summer and we talked him into letting us rent it for the month. We have every aspect of the street covered with cameras and surveillance teams. There won't be a cat that we don't see. You're safe now. Come and eat dinner, Megs," he said gently, pulling my hand and leading me into the kitchen.

"If you have so much surveillance, why do I have to leave? Why can't I stay?" I asked. Selfish as it seemed, I really didn't want to leave.

"If you stayed here you would essentially be a prisoner in your own home," Tommy replied bluntly. There was a curtness in his tone that didn't leave much room for argument. "There would be no work, no dinner and drinks with Jen or Sarah, no jogs with Penny. You would be in this house 24/7. Do you really want that?"

"I guess I understand," I said, feeling chastised like a child.

"Hey. I'm sorry. I just want you to take it seriously. I know it's not easy, but I am trying to make this as painless as possible. I—" Tommy's phone rang and cut him off. "Hang on." He put the phone to his ear. "This is Thomas Greene," he said as he got up and walked out of the room.

I ate my vegetable soup without really tasting it. My appetite had diminished since I had gotten home and it just hurt to eat. I was putting off the inevitable packing that would take up most of the night. I sighed and poured the last of my soup into Penny's bowl just as Tommy walked back in.

"That was Kate. She is on her way from Baltimore and will be here in about thirty minutes or so. I'm assuming you may need a few things so write them down and let me know. I'll have her grab them on the way here."

I quickly went through the list of my toiletries. I had gone to the store last week and was pretty well stocked on everything. "A pregnancy book," I blurted out. *Real smooth.* I mentally rolled my eyes and tried to keep the blush from spreading. "I just found out yesterday. I haven't had time to get a book or vitamins or clothes or anything."

Tommy looked slightly embarrassed. "That's it?" I nodded. I wasn't sure why he was embarrassed. He sent a quick text to Kate. "Okay. Right now I want you to call Jen. Tell her that you're joining your mom and your aunt on their vacation. Play it cool. Keep it simple. Don't overact or be too casual. Jen knows you too well. Be yourself."

I picked up the phone and dialed her number. "Hi, Jen," I said quickly.

"Hey, I was going to call you. How are you?" she asked warmly. My eyes started to burn and I blinked furiously to stop the tears.

"Um. I'm good. I'm actually calling to cancel our plans for the weekend. With everything that's happened, I need a break. I'm going to the beach with Mom and Aunt Nancy."

"Oh good. Yeah, you need to get away from all this drama. How are you feeling?" Jen inquired.

"I'm...I'm okay. I do have some news," I said, putting the fake smile back into my voice.

"Oh yeah? What's—wait. Hang on. Lauren Amanda Walsh! You better get your naked behind back in that bathtub right now or you're going to be in so much trouble!" Jen said distractedly as she yelled at her precocious three-year-old. I heard giggles in the background and busted out laughing. I hadn't laughed in ages and I felt the weight of all the bad news and stress lift off my chest. It felt so good, but it hurt my ribs terribly.

"Oh God, that hurts!" I gasped, as I tried to hold my sides and breathe calmly.

"Just wait until you have kids. Then we'll see who's laughing," she replied smugly.

What a perfect lead-in.

"Oh, I'm sure. I'll let you know how it is in about eight months," I replied cautiously. I eased myself onto the chaise lounge in my study. That left the normally talkative Jen absolutely speechless for a full minute.

"Are you—? Did you just say—?" she stuttered.

I giggled then said calmly, "Yep."

The shriek that came out of my phone was so loud it could have been heard in Florida. "Dammit. I am coming over. Give me an hour to get Matt home, then I'll be there. Is it Shane's?" she demanded.

What the hell kind of girl did she think I was? "Of course it's Shane's, you dingdong," I scoffed. "But you can't come over. I'm exhausted. I need to pack and by the time you get here, the pain meds would have kicked in. I'll call you when I get back. Okay?" I said. "But hey,

I wanted you to be the first to know. Well, besides Mom, but still. I love you, Jen," I said quietly.

Jen chuckled. "Those hormones are already getting to you, huh? We will talk about this tomorrow. Call me when you get to the beach. I want to know everything."

We said our goodbyes and hung up. I stared at the phone, feeling slightly disconnected. I wasn't sure if or when I would be able to call her back. It frightened me to not know the ins and outs of the plan. I hated feeling this way.

I headed upstairs with my empty suitcase in tow. I grabbed all the yoga pants and gym shorts I could find. I wasn't sure how long I should pack for. I had a horrible over-packing issue as it was. I simply took everything that had an elastic waistline and that I thought I could wear for a month or two. I left my beautiful heels at the bottom of my closet, settling for the more practical flats, sandals, and sneakers. As an afterthought, I grabbed the picture of Shane and me and wrapped it in Shane's favorite sweatshirt. I had just managed to get the suitcase zipped when Tommy knocked on my door.

"Come in," I called.

"Hey. Kate is here. I wanted to introduce you guys," Tommy said. The person who walked in shocked me. With beautiful pale skin and bright blue eyes, she looked like the Allison that Shane had dated, but Kate's hair was a light brown instead of the raven black. My mouth dropped; I was flabbergasted.

"Allison?"

"Well, my name is actually Kate. I work with Tommy," she said and gave me a huge smile.

"Um, wow! You look completely different. Great, of course, but different," I stammered, startled by her transformation. She was still beautiful, but somewhat less intimidating.

"Thanks. I switched back to my normal color after Shane and I 'broke up'," she replied, using air quotes. She was quite blasé about the whole thing, which confused me even more. But then again, when wasn't I confused lately.

"You sound so casual about it. Does that mean…? You guys weren't really dating?" I questioned, feeling slightly relieved. A girl never wants to compare herself to her boyfriend's ex, but sometimes it's hard not to. In Allison—or Kate's case, it had been extremely hard not to be critical of myself.

"Shane and I were never dating. It was all part of the story. We were working together. I was his handler. Having me here was a good way to keep an eye and ear on the situation," Kate replied nonchalantly. "Besides, I don't think any girl could handle her boyfriend mooning over some other woman the way Shane swooned over you. He may not say much about his feelings, but his feelings were quite evident whenever your name came up."

I was floored. I couldn't believe it. Was I so blind that I couldn't see what was clearly obvious to everyone else? I didn't know what to say. Luckily for me, Kate handed me a shopping bag as she sat down.

"I stopped by Target and picked up a few things for you. Some prenatal vitamins, the bible of all pregnancy books, and a couple of magazines. We have a long drive ahead of us in the morning."

"Yeah, speaking of that. Where are we going?" I asked as I shoved the items into my tote.

"I'm not sure. I know we're meeting up with Rick's team and heading up north. I'll know tomorrow. Are you packed?" she asked, flicking her head at my overflowing suitcase.

I grimaced. "I guess so. I still have to get Penny's stuff together. I'll grab enough of her food to last a week. We'll have to go shopping at some point." Kate nodded.

"If you need anything, let me know. We can always send out for it. Unfortunately, we don't have an exact time line. Your uncle is trying to talk the prosecutors into a quick trial. But Reggie's defense may try to push it back. In the meantime, you're going to get a break from all the drama that's unfolding. You'll be able to chill out and rest. You and your baby certainly need it." The idea made me uncomfortable. I hated feeling that someone evil was pulling my strings like I was a marionette.

"How's Shane?" I asked quietly. I had known better than to ask Tommy about Shane. I didn't feel that he could handle any more questions from me, and surely not about Shane.

Kate thought for a minute. "He's safe. He is going to testify against Reggie. They know that he's mysteriously out on bail and they are going to make it a point to make sure he stays quiet. They are going to go for his weakest point. That's you. That's the main reason why we're leaving here tomorrow. Well, for two, actually. Shane is worried sick about you. We've been telling him that you're fine, and we're keeping what happened to you last night under wraps for now. But if Shane finds out that you were assaulted, he'll run from that safe house and come find you. He would end up taking matters into his own hands. That is all great and romantic but that would damage the case. Shane could get hurt or worse. Without Shane, our case is finished. And while the world wouldn't necessarily grieve if Reggie Cruz was taken out, we need him alive so we can grab whomever is supplying him. So with Reggie looking for you, you're toast. We're doing this to save both of you, and to save our investigation."

Kate's brutal and honest assessment of the situation gave me pause. The thought of Shane dying felt like a punch in my gut. I pushed down the scream that was desperately trying to come out and asked, "Say this whole thing blows over. Reggie's in jail, no more threats. What is going to happen to Shane once this is all over with? Will he be able to return?" *And stay with us as a family*, I silently added. Kate's face looked remorseful.

"Megan, I'm not sure. As part of the deal that he has with the prosecutors, he tells us what we want to know about Reggie and then we cut him loose. His record gets expunged. But will he be able to live a normal life? I'm not sure. His life before you was not great. He dealt drugs and was involved in a bunch of shady activities. Granted, he was working toward a normal life and getting everything straight. That's a good thing. But the dark side has a way of seducing even the strongest men. He'll have a hard time adjusting, but anyone can change if they really want to."

I took what she said to heart. Shane had gone down a wrong path and now he was setting himself straight. I'm sure he could escape the confines of dealing and gangs, but would he want to? Yes, I resolved. But I wasn't going to sit around and make assumptions about the future. We would talk after the trial. *We'll make amends and we'll be a family.* I ignored the nagging feeling in the pit of my stomach. I refused to think the worst.

I showed Kate where she could sleep, in the barely used guest room, and set out fresh linens. She took my suitcase and I followed her back down into the living room where Tommy and his partner, Rick Sims, were pouring over some papers. Rick, a six-foot-five-inch-tall man with short brown hair and brown eyes, had a presence that commanded respect. Tommy made the introductions and said that Rick would be going over to mom's soon and then continued the conversation. They were talking tactics and weapons. It was all gibberish and I felt so stupid listening because I didn't understand any of it. I set about packing Penny's belongings. In a canvas bag went her leash, a large plastic bag of dog food, her Kong and favorite treats, and, finally, her woobie. I set the bag, along with my suitcase, next to the front door.

I felt like I was in the way. I decided that fixing dinner would be the best thing to do. My anxiety was getting the best of me and I needed to keep busy. When I was stressed, I ate, and since I couldn't eat much, I cooked instead. I made chicken, broccoli, and cheese casserole; macaroni and cheese for the trip; and steak fajitas. I took out the frozen ground turkey and ground beef. We could take most of the food with us.

More agents stopped by as the night wore on. They

came through the back door. The vehicular traffic had died down considerably, but Tommy didn't want to take a chance of them being seen. To the unknowing, I was leaving on a vacation and would be coming home to an ultraclean house. They wouldn't realize that I had stowed my most precious family treasures in the bottom of my suitcase. That I had packed up most of my albums and genealogy documents in a bag that Kate would give to my uncle. I could feel the panic and fear choking me as I gazed around my home. Yes, items could always be replaced, but home is where you live, where you love, and where your family is. In a short time, I had built a life, a home, and at one point, I thought, a future.

Tommy came over and gave me a hug. His arms didn't feel comforting, but I didn't want to be rude. "Get some sleep, Megs. We'll be leaving at 4 a.m." Tommy patted my shoulder and then headed into the kitchen. By then it was close to midnight and there were two other agents in the house. With the lights dimmed, they took their positions in the living room. Tommy sat in the kitchen going over paperwork and, with Kate upstairs with me, I should have felt secure. But I knew that if Reggie wanted me dead, this thin blanket of security wouldn't stop him.

CHAPTER 24

I HAD BARELY CLOSED MY eyes when Kate shook me awake. "Megan, it's three thirty. We need to get going." My eyes flew open. I rolled out of bed as carefully as I could. With adrenaline as my caffeine, I dressed quickly in the dark and headed down the stairs with Penny in tow. Tommy threw my bags in the trunk of a blackened SUV and put Penny in the back seat. He came back to the mudroom and hustled me out to the SUV and into the backseat as well. He locked up the house and jumped into the passenger seat, all in under five seconds.

We headed toward the main highway and made it to Baltimore in twenty minutes, an unusual feat regardless of the time of day. Then we veered west toward the mountains. The sun was rising as we crossed the Allegheny Mountains. I knew immediately we were going to Deep Creek Lake, a beautiful vacation spot in the mountains of Western Maryland. I hadn't been there since I was a little kid.

"I figured you were due for a little vacation. Since your mom was originally going to Ocean City, I figured the mountains were a safer alternative," Tommy said as he glanced at me in the rearview mirror. We stopped off at McDonalds for breakfast then drove another five minutes, turning down Crows Point Road to a secluded lake front area. We pulled into the driveway of a typical A-frame mountain home with a spectacular view of the lake from the backyard. I held Penny's leash while she sniffed around. The cool air filled my lungs and cleared my mind. With a two-story back porch, beautiful patio, fire pit, and expansive windows, I was in love. I could see myself enjoying a vacation here, if it weren't for the minor fact that some bad guys were looking for me and all. Tommy came up beside me and smiled.

"Isn't this amazing?" Tommy said as he took a deep breath. "I love coming up here."

I chuckled. "What, do you bring all your troubled ex-girlfriends up here? I'm amazed the FBI has such a nice place. I would have thought more along the lines of the rundown homes that you see in the movies."

Tommy scoffed. "The FBI can't afford this. This is

my place. And, no, I don't bring all my troubled ex-girlfriends up here. You're the first," he replied with a smile.

"Your place? I didn't realize the bureau paid this well," I replied as he led me around the front and into the two-story foyer. The main level was beautifully decorated with walnut floors and leather furniture. I followed him into the kitchen where he set down the cooler. The cabinets matched the floors with beautiful black granite countertops and stainless steel appliances. The look that crossed his face was slightly uneasy. I guess finances were still a sore subject with him. Tommy's family was very wealthy and very pretentious and not at all happy with Tommy's career path.

"Yeah, it doesn't. I was lucky enough to have some investments pay off. Plus, with the economy the way it is, people are practically giving away houses," he muttered as he put away the food. In an attempt to change the subject, he took me on a tour of the house. Not only was the house immaculately furnished, but it also had a top-of-the-line security system in place. Monitors, a weapons case, and computers and communication equipment took up the entire basement level. When I commented on the excess of it all, Tommy just shrugged. "Yeah, when it comes to the FBI, we don't mess around."

On the second floor Tommy showed me the four bedrooms, each equipped with a spa bathroom. He set my bags in the master bedroom. I protested, but he wouldn't take no for an answer. The beautiful room was decorated in rich, warm tones with a four-poster, king-size bed. There was even a plush dog bed.

"Have you always had this here?" I asked, curious. Knowing that Tommy was allergic to dogs, I was confused. Sheepishly, he shook his head.

"I had it brought here last night. We have a liaison of sorts, someone who runs our errands and sees to our needs. I want you, your mom, and Penny to be comfortable. With the situation as tense as it is, there is no reason why you can't try to relax in the meantime."

I was touched. Through everything that had happened, Tommy had been there for us. It meant a lot. I turned and threw my arms around him.

"Thank you, Tommy. For keeping us safe, for allowing us the use of your home, and for making us feel comfortable," I whispered.

"Megan, regardless of what happened between us, I still care a lot about you. I wouldn't let anything happen to you," he murmured. Feeling somewhat awkward, I moved away and changed the subject.

"Speaking of Mom, do we know when she'll get here?" I asked as I stared out the window. The lake view was absolutely breathtaking. I couldn't wait to go and dip my toes in the water. Penny was going to love it too. Then I realized I didn't bring a bathing suit. I guess it didn't matter, considering I was almost two months pregnant. I doubted I'd be able to fit into my bikini much longer.

"They are about an hour out. They were able to leave when the sun came up. Apparently, your mother pitched a fit about having to wake up at three thirty. She threatened bodily harm and lack of apple turnovers if someone so much as nudged her that early."

"Yep. That's my momma," I chuckled, then yawned loudly. Despite the plush interior of the SUV, I didn't fall asleep during the ride. I turned to Tommy and he laughed.

"Yeah, you're beat. Take a nap. You'll be fine." Tommy walked toward the door, then turned. "I'll wake you up when she gets here." He shut the door gently behind him.

I sighed. I could try to fool myself into thinking that this was just an impromptu vacation, but it wouldn't work. There were too many factors. Too many uncontrollable entities at play. *I wish Shane were here with me.* I climbed under the luxurious down comforter. I melted and the weariness of my body eased. Through my lashes, I saw Penny settle into her new luxurious dog bed. It wasn't long until I followed suit.

CHAPTER 25

I WOKE UP FOUR HOURS later and, honestly, if I hadn't had the urge to puke, I would have kept sleeping. After I brushed my teeth and rinsed my mouth, I slowly headed down the stairs. I needed something to settle my stomach. Mom was in the kitchen, her safe haven. She sat at the massive island, lost in thought. She didn't hear me coming and I startled her.

"Mom," I said as I held her tightly. "Why didn't you wake me?"

"You were exhausted and you're pregnant. You need your rest more than you think. How are you feeling?" she said with a small smile.

I sat down next to her on the tall barstool. "I feel like crap. I'm in pain. I'm nauseated, exhausted, and hungry all at the same time. I can't stop thinking about Shane. I'm worried to death about you and whoever is looking for us. I can't wrap my head around this baby. I'm…just overwhelmed," I said grimly. I felt like a four-year-old child, whining to her mommy about things she couldn't control. I heaved a sigh.

My mom had the audacity to chuckle. "Well, the nausea and the exhaustion are typical pregnancy symptoms. It's going to wipe you out for a while. We should have picked up a pregnancy book for you."

"Oh! That's right. I had Kate pick one up for me. It's in my bag. I'll grab it later. I need something to settle my stomach," I said as I laid my head on the island. My stomach was rolling and it was all I could do to hold it together.

Again, she seemed to find it hilarious that I was feeling like crap. "Oh honey. You gave me the worst morning sickness. I was throwing up day and night with you until I passed the second trimester. This is just payback." My mom got up and rummaged through the fridge. She found a can of cola and handed it to me. "The cola syrup will help with the nausea. You'll have to read your book. I'm sure you're going to be limited on what you can eat and drink."

I stifled a groan as I recalled Jen's pregnancy. She couldn't drink, or eat sushi or soft cheeses. And there were times that I'd thought she'd kill me for a cup of coffee. "Yeah, I know. Speaking of pregnancy, I'll need to talk to Tommy. I haven't seen an OB yet, and I'm not sure if I should wait until we're back home."

Hearing his name, Tommy came up from the basement.

"There is a clinic up the road that we can use. We've already done a background check on the doctor. Your appointment is for next week. I'll be escorting you myself."

I raised my eyebrow in disbelief. "Why you? Why can't Mom go with me?"

Tommy chuckled as he reached in the fridge for a soda. "Because, dingdong, you're being hunted. The first thing Reggie is going to look for is an unwed single mother going into a backwoods clinic by herself. I'll be joining you as your loving husband."

The irony of the whole situation was laughable. Tommy, who really could have been my loving husband, was now pretending to be that guy. The loving husband who puts his wife and family in front of his own wants and needs. I nodded. I didn't want him to think that I was ungrateful for his help. He was doing everything he could to keep me and my mom safe.

Mom got up and started puttering around in the kitchen. She pulled out the casseroles and put them in the oven for heating. It was past lunchtime.

"Tell your coworkers that lunch will be ready in twenty minutes," she told Tommy with a no-nonsense tone in her voice. Tommy understood that he couldn't say no to Mom. Even though he was in charge of this operation, she was in charge of the kitchen, and while she was here, no one would be left hungry.

"Yes ma'am. There won't be many here for long. We're getting everything set up then we'll be heading out."

I was surprised. I thought for sure he was going to stick around and watch over us. My face must have shown my reaction, because Tommy continued. "Kate and Rick are going to stick around here with you. I need to keep in touch with headquarters and keep an eye on Reggie. I can't do that out here in the sticks. Don't worry. I'll be back for your appointment."

He made sense. Reggie was dangerous and there was no telling what could happen if he was left unattended.

Twenty minutes later the large dining room table was full of FBI agents digging into the lunch buffet mom had created. Mom handed me a plate, but I shook my head. My stomach hadn't fully recovered and the mere smell of the chicken and cheese made my stomach churn. I nibbled on some crackers and sipped my cola. The general consensus of the room was that Tommy and most of his group would head back to Annapolis and regroup. Tommy was looking into who Reggie worked for, but the man was as elusive as smoke. No one knew his name or what he looked like. They hoped that by following Reggie he would eventually lead the agents to his boss.

***

AFTER THEY LOADED up their SUVs and were about to head out, I stood outside with Tommy. Night was falling and the sunset was beautiful, almost romantic. As always, the thought of Shane went from the back burner of my mind to the forefront. My heart ached and loneliness lodged in the pit of my stomach. *I miss him so much.* Regardless of his stupid acts and shady past, I knew in the bottom of my heart that I needed him. *Even more so now with the baby on the way.*

"Thanks, Tommy. For everything," I said softly. I hugged myself tighter against the chill. Tommy noticed and rubbed my arms.

"Megs, it's fine. You're completely welcome. Enjoy your stay here. Relax. Rest. You've had a hell of a couple of weeks and you really need to get your strength up. Try not to worry too much about Reggie. Now that you're up here, we can focus all our attention on him."

I nodded. "Just make sure you get what you need quickly. I want everything to get back to normal as soon as possible." *Whatever that is*, I thought.

Tommy read my mind. "There is no such thing as normal now, Megs. Your life has changed for the better and the worse. The best thing that has changed is that you're going to be a momma. That's an honor right there. By the time that baby is here, you'll be home safe and sound. Things will get back to normal then. But until then, just hang tight. Okay?" he said gently, then pulled me into a tight hug. "I'll take care of you, Megs. I promise."

I closed my eyes and took that moment to believe him. And wished that it was Shane who was saying those words to me.

CHAPTER 26

As THE DAYS AND WEEKS went on, I barely heard from Tommy. His team was following lead after lead, and he never made it back to the lake house. Despite Tommy's claim that a single woman at the clinic would have raised flags, the appointment went perfectly fine. There wasn't a man in the entire office aside from the elderly doctor. After performing an ultrasound and some blood work, he concluded that I was eight weeks pregnant, with a due date of Valentine's Day. It hit home then, the pain of the unknown. Not knowing if Shane would be able to come back to us, not knowing if he still loved me, not knowing if he would be happy if he knew that he was going to be a father.

I pushed the unknown aside and focused on the now.

At first it was awkward living in the house. We walked on eggshells around each other and were constantly looking out the window to see if we'd been found out. Eventually, tensions eased. We slowly started to laugh, to enjoy the lake, and generally tried to relax our vigilance. Mom and I hunkered down, only going out of the neighborhood with Rick and Kate as escorts. Mainly we stayed outside on the porch. Mom passed the time by teaching me new recipes and experimenting with making baby food. In exchange, my pants and shorts started to get snug. When I would complain about how much weight I was putting on, she would laugh at me. "Oh shush. You're pregnant; you're supposed to gain weight," she'd tsk as she put a chicken into the oven to roast.

The open windows let in the warm breezes. Even close to dinnertime the sun was as bright as if it were noon. The peace and quiet of the lake soothed me. We were secluded from the rest of the vacationers and only encountered other people when we went into town. We had the beach area behind the house all to ourselves. We spent the evenings in front of the fire pit reminiscing and learning more about each other. She told me stories about how my father courted her, stories of when she was younger, and stories of Kyle and me when we were children. I enjoyed it. It was mesmerizing to see her face light up as she recounted her memories. I laid my hands on my somewhat protruding stomach. I couldn't wait to build on and add to my own memories.

The stillness and the quiet did nothing to hamper my thoughts of Shane. I desperately wanted to talk to him. Kate always refused. I could write a letter to be hand-carried to Shane via a series of agents and officers, but I didn't want that. I didn't want the first time I told him that he was going to be a daddy to be via messengers. I wanted to be there to see his face, his expression, his reaction when I told him the news. I wanted to hold him, to make sure he was safe and sound. I wanted to make sure he knew I loved him.

With rarely any updates from Tommy, we had resorted to keeping up with things on the internet. The case was barely making the local blogs and there wasn't a blip from the national media coverage. Kyle, Sarah, and the rest of our family and friends suspected that Mom and I had jumped ship. They weren't stupid. Of course, knowing the possible ramifications of contacting them, we simply left well enough alone. Our sole contact was my uncle, who had been a part of this process since the beginning. He kept us updated on all the happenings in the world that we had left behind. His letters, typed on the computer, seemed sterile, like he was holding back. There was never any mention of

Shane or updates about the case. Just that things were coming along slowly. Perhaps he was afraid of the letter getting into the wrong hands. Kate did the best she could with the limited resources she had. Most of her information seemed secondhand, and I could tell she was frustrated. She was used to being in the field, not acting as a babysitter. I tried not to bug her. It was nice to have her around. The more I got to know her, the less intimidating she seemed.

CHAPTER 27

Days turned into weeks, and soon it was the Fourth
of July. I was twelve weeks along and definitely
showing. Mom, Kate, and I headed into town to do a
little shopping. We needed groceries and I needed more
shorts with elastic waistbands. Rick, the ever-imposing
agent, acted as our personal chauffeur. I hadn't gleaned
much information about him. Aside from his formidable
stance and his obsession with the Washington Redskins,
I didn't know much.

We were loading our shopping bags into the back of
the SUV when Rick got a call. He rushed over, his eyes
hidden behind aviator sunglasses and his lips set in a
grim line.

"Just got a call from Tommy. They've lost Reggie

and have no clue as to where he is. There was a sighting of him heading down I-95 toward Virginia. But we can't confirm it," he said quickly as he loaded the rest of the groceries into the back of the SUV. Kate went into high alert mode and ushered me into the backseat, all the while scanning the area.

"Tommy and a couple other agents are on their way up here just as a precaution," Rick said as he jumped into the driver's seat. Mom passed me a worried look and I tried to squelch the panic that was building inside me. Kate was in the passenger seat, scrolling through her bureau-issued Blackberry.

"When was the last sighting?" Kate asked, peering out the window.

"Six hours ago," Rick said bitterly.

Six hours? What the hell? Kate's voice echoed my thoughts perfectly. "What the hell do you mean six hours? Why didn't we hear about this earlier? Who fucked up?" she spat out, anger rolling off her in waves. Rick gave her a knowing look and Kate just looked away, shaking her head. That look meant something, something that they weren't telling me.

"What? What aren't you telling us?" I demanded, but they didn't answer. We pulled up to the house. Rick got out with his gun drawn and motioned for us to stay put. Five minutes later, he returned and opened the passenger doors.

"It's good. Let's get you inside." He held onto my mother's arm and quickly ushered her into the foyer. Kate did the same with me. Penny came running toward us and did the happy dance of joy with her woobie in her mouth. I absentmindedly threw it into the next room while I waited for Rick and Kate to bring in our purchases. Mom and I unpacked everything and set about making dinner. Rick and Kate stayed in the command center down in the basement. All the alarms were activated. We were only allowed to have the sliding glass door open. Mom stared Rick down when he tried to close it. The air was tense. I needed answers, so I headed to the basement. Kate and Rick were huddled in front of a monitor, and barely glanced at me when I entered the room.

"What is going on? Why do I feel like you're holding something back?" I asked cautiously. I wanted to know the truth.

Kate turned around and sighed. "I'm sorry, Megan. We don't want to worry you and honestly, we're not sure ourselves."

"But…" I led, encouraging her to finish.

She gave a funny look to Rick, then turned back to me. "We can't figure out why we were told six hours later that Reggie had gone off the radar. That's not standard protocol. Our counterparts in Maryland should have told us right away, but we didn't get any sort of message or phone call. And there have been some other issues too. A witness who saw Reggie and his brother Christian doing a drug deal has been murdered, and we didn't know about that until a few hours ago. We are being kept in the dark. We should be one of the first people they call, especially since we're supposed to be protecting you. We're limited regarding who we can trust and who we can't."

"So what are you saying exactly?" I asked slowly, trying to wrap my mind around this wave of information. My stomach suddenly soured as I saw the coldness in her blue eyes.

"We think there is a leak. Someone is trying to cover Reggie's ass and make sure no one talks. The bigger issue is that we don't know who," Rick piped in, his eyes still glued to the monitor.

My mouth dropped open and I looked at Kate in terror. "Okay. What about my mom? What about Shane? Who do we need to talk to in order to get him more protection?"

"We haven't heard from Shane's location; we're not in constant contact. I'm sure more agents were added to his detail, and more agents are coming here with Tommy. Your family is going to be okay. We just have to be more vigilant. And it could be nothing more than a miscommunication or an alert that didn't get sent out. It could be nothing," Kate said in a rush. It was a lackluster attempt to calm my fears. I appreciated that, but it did nothing for me. I gave her a worried look then headed upstairs. Mom was putting the finishing touches on the potato salad when I walked in.

"You missed it, Megs. I added my secret ingredient. Wait. What's wrong?" she said, as she hurried over to me with worry etched on her face.

I didn't want to worry her. There would be no point in that. Kate said more agents were on their way. Tommy would be here soon and Reggie was last seen in Virginia. There was no reason to panic.

"Nothing. I just had a mild hormone attack. These flashes come on quickly," I lied as I grabbed a bottle of water out of the fridge. She patted my arm and gave me a small smile. She brushed a tendril of hair out of my eyes.

"Baby cakes, you're handling this so well. I'm proud of you. And Shane would be too," she said softly. Mom pulled me to her in a tight hug. I buried my head in her shoulder and inhaled her perfume. Having her here kept me from falling off the brink of sanity. I wiped away the tears that threatened to spill over and smiled.

"Are the hormones always this bad?" I joked, forking

a bite of her potato salad.

Mom chuckled as she pulled the apple pie from the oven. The intoxicating smell of Americana—cinnamon, apples, and sugar—swept through the house. "It gets worse. Soon you'll be crying over toilet paper commercials."

"Great," I replied dryly. I was antsy. I hated not being honest with my mom, but at the same time it wouldn't do any good to get her or myself all worked up. I plucked a cherry tomato out of the salad bowl and popped it in my mouth. I really wanted to take a walk, but not until Tommy arrived. It was an unspoken rule that we were to stay indoors. I made my way back to the bedroom and lay on the bed. I was on edge. I hated being in the dark and not knowing what was next.

I didn't have to wait long. I heard Rick bound up the stairs and run to the front door. The ringing of the alarm startled me out of bed. I hurried down the stairs to see Tommy talking with Rick. Our eyes met and he hurried over to me and took me aside.

"Tommy? What's going on?" I demanded. He rubbed his face and paced in front of me.

"Megan. I'm sorry. I'm so sorry. Shane's safe house was blown up last night," he whispered, holding me tightly. It was a good thing that he grabbed my waist, because my legs gave out. I stopped breathing. Tommy's face said it all.

"Oh God, Tommy. Please don't tell me that Shane..." I couldn't finish. I couldn't say the very words that would destroy me.

Tommy shrugged helplessly. "I don't know, Megs. Bodies were found but we haven't identified them yet. There is no way anyone got out of that place alive. There was an accelerant and what looked like several homemade explosives. They are going through the crime scene now. But we need to get out of here. We need to leave now."

I stood stock-still. I couldn't move. I couldn't fathom the very notion that Shane could be dead. My heart dropped to the bottom of my stomach as I fought back tears.

"Megan, we gotta go. Norah! We're leaving. Grab the dogs! We're rolling out!" he bellowed as he ran to the basement. My fight or flight instincts kicked in and I ran upstairs. I would deal with this later. I would grieve as I deserved to. But now my child's life was at stake. My mother's life was at stake. My mother was already on her way up the stairs to grab her things. I followed her lead and threw some clothes and a few personal items into my duffle bag. The rest of the clothes and books could wait. I grabbed Penny's woobie and whistled for her to follow me downstairs. I met Tommy at the bottom where he grabbed my bag and threw it to Kate who carried it outside. Rick and Tommy were speaking in code, talking of mileage, weapons, and such. Kate rushed back in and took the dogs out to the car.

"Will someone please tell me what the hell is going on?" my mother yelled. Her face was flushed from running around, and she was missing a shoe. Tommy and Rick gazed at her with an openmouthed stare, as if they had forgotten that we were standing there. Rick quickly shook his head and gestured for my mother to follow him.

"Shane's safe house was destroyed and we just received word that Reggie is twenty miles out. We need to get you guys to safety," Rick said as he ushered my mother into the back of a waiting black Suburban.

"I thought there were more agents coming with you?" I questioned as Tommy led me outside.

"They are more than thirty minutes out. We can't wait for them. We have to leave now. They'll catch up with us once we get on the highway."

I quickly shook out the cobwebs that had been nesting in my head. I grabbed his arm and demanded, "What about Mom? Who's going to protect her?"

"We're separating you. It's for the best. You're his primary target, not your mom. The further we get her away from here the better," Tommy muttered to me. I stared at him in grim horror. After what had happened to Shane, I fully accepted it now. We were in incredible danger. We both knew I might not make it home. I could see the pain in his green eyes; he hated that we were in this position. A passing thought went through my head. Tommy actually thought that this would work. That we would be safe and that he could protect me. He had never meant for this to happen, neither had Shane. But it would never end. Reggie would keep coming after me, whether Shane was around or not. I understood. I would face my demons and accept my fate. I took Tommy's hand and gave it a squeeze and a nod. Then I ran over to my mom. She was fighting against Rick, who was trying to shove her into the back seat.

"*No, No No*! You're coming with me. You get in this car right now. I'm not leaving without you," she screamed, tears streaming down her face. I choked back a sob and threw my arms around her.

"Mom, I'm going to be with Tommy and Kate. I'll be well protected, I promise. Nothing is going to happen to me. I swear, Momma. I'll be fine. Just, please, go with Rick. Take care of Penny for me until we get back. And when this baby is born, you can spoil him or her rotten," I whispered. I wanted her to believe that everything was going to be okay even though I knew deep down that it would probably end badly. I smiled at her through my tears and kissed her cheek.

"You're damn right I'm going to spoil my grandchild. And your behind better be home soon. You come home. Do you hear me? You come home," she cried. I tried to pull away, and with assistance from Rick was able to step back. Kate and Tommy hurried me over to the other SUV as my mother yelled behind us, "Tommy! If you don't bring her back to me I'm hunting you down myself!"

Kate and I clambered into the back seat while Tommy got into the driver's seat. "Megan, remind me when we get through this never to piss off your mom. She scares me."

I gave an uneasy grin and wiped away the remaining tears. "Everyone is scared of my mom."

Kate helped me into a Kevlar vest and told me to keep my head down and body slouched. We pulled out in front of Rick's car, gravel from the driveway flying behind us. Unfortunately for us, the town's Fourth of July festival was going on, and most of the major thoroughfares were full of families and stargazers intent on seeing a spectacular fireworks display. Little did they know, the fireworks were just about to start—in more ways than one.

CHAPTER 28

K ATE CLIMBED INTO THE front passenger seat to use the FBI computer and communications equipment. She was reporting our location to someone who I assumed was at FBI headquarters. Tommy told Kate what to relay to headquarters while trying to navigate the traffic and the street crowds. He let out a stream of curse words once we hit the open road. We were on the outskirts of town trying to meet up with the rest of the caravan that would take us to our next destination, our new home away from home.

"Fucking traffic. Reggie really planned this well. He knew full well that we'd have trouble getting out of town," Tommy grumbled as he picked up his phone. "Mac. It's Tommy. I need some help—"

Tommy never finished the call. We were crossing over an intersection at full speed in an industrial part of town when I saw a red blur coming from the right of our SUV. Suddenly we were thrown sideways, the car rolling over three complete times before coming to a stop. My head was thrown against the window. All I heard were the tires screeching, the groaning of metal bending, and screams. My screams, maybe Kate's. I couldn't tell. Glass and plastic showered down. A groan escaped me as I fumbled for the seat belt. My head screamed in pain, my body ached. It hurt to move and there was blood blocking my vision. I struggled to get up when the door I was leaning against was thrown open. Kate's face swam into my vision, looking like an angel with her bright blue eyes.

"We've gotta run. We have to get you out of here," she urged. I could see the fear on her face. With her help, I managed to get out of the SUV. My leg buckled and I saw a large gash in my knee. Tommy was screaming into his cell phone for backup. Kate led me away from the SUV when I heard the *rat tat tat tat* of gunfire. She pulled me alongside a boarded up storefront, looking for a way in. Kate found a wooden back door and shot out the lock. She pushed me inside. "Get in, get down, and stay out of sight. I'll be right here," she reassured me. I believed her. The courage in her eyes was quite clear.

My heart was trying to burst out of my chest. I could barely breathe, let alone take in anything that was happening. I didn't think, I just reacted. I hurried over to the small counter and crept down. Kate was hunkered down by the back door, waiting. I wanted to ask her about Tommy, if he was okay. If my mother and Rick had gotten away in time, but fear silenced my voice. I glanced to my right and, through a small sliver of open glass, could see the carnage of the crash. More cars were on the scene and the sound of gunfire echoed the sound of fireworks. I wanted to close my eyes and wish it was all a dream, but I couldn't tear myself away.

Suddenly, the storefront was blown open. Automatically, I threw myself down and covered my head. Wood particles and flames flew across the room. As if in slow motion, I could see Kate dive to get to me. At the same time that she leaped into the air, bright red circles appeared on her T-shirt. She landed two feet away from me, her face twisted in pain. Horrified, I struggled toward her. She had been shot in the neck, back, and stomach.

"Megan, run," she managed to shout out before moaning in pain. A strangled scream came out of my mouth as I crawled over to her. I couldn't let her die. I couldn't. I groped her neck for a pulse. Kate shuddered a breath. Spasms took over her body and then she went limp. I was panic-struck.

"Dammit, Kate, no! You stay with me!" I screamed. Adrenaline surged through me and my heart pounded. I needed to save her, to save myself. I had to fight. I started CPR when I heard voice. A voice I will never in my lifetime forget.

"You have been the biggest pain in the ass I have ever dealt with." The voice. Menacing and dark, my attacker had returned. I quickly scooted backwards, slicing my hands on broken glass, only to stop once I hit the counter. Recognition finally dawned on me. The high school creep who never grew up, the same one that Shane was going to beat down in the club. Dominic. Holy shit. Everything was coming together. Dominic didn't fight with Shane because Shane was supposed to be part of his crew. Dominic worked for Reggie.

"Dominic. Why are you doing this?" I asked, my voice coming out hoarse and meek. Desperation filled me and I could feel the hysteria building. The opportunity to run was quickly fading. The only light in the store came from the busted window and it filled the room with shadows. I lightly ran my hands across the floor around me, hoping to find something I could throw at him; I needed a distraction or a weapon. Either one would do. My hand brushed against the cold, hard steel of Kate's Glock. I slowly pulled it underneath my knee, hiding it from Dominic's already obstructed view.

"Why? Your boy is the reason why. At first, I thought he was alright. Dude was chill. But after that night in the club, I didn't like him. Once he ran off, without you, we knew something was up. We found out that Shane talked to the feds and we weren't having that. We needed to get a message to him. Unfortunately for you, the message was sent. Shane's dead, and now you're our only loose end," Dominic said, walking slowly toward me. Any hope of Shane being alive sank to the pit of my stomach. He was truly dead, and if I didn't act soon my baby and I wouldn't live either. But I was backed up against the counter. I had nowhere to go.

"Dammit, Dominic. Just shoot the bitch and go," demanded another voice. A large man, heavy set and the size of Andre the Giant came into view. With a shaved head, black menacing eyes, and a huge tattoo covering his face, the man had a horrifying presence. With Dominic, I was scared. This man brought a whole new level of terror. Panic filled every fiber of my being. Scared beyond belief, I struggled to stay focused.

"Look. I don't know who you are. I really don't. Just please leave me alone. I won't talk to the cops…I won't…" I stammered. Bile was rising from my stomach and burning my throat, and the overwhelming need to puke put me in a frenzy.

"Shut the hell up, bitch. Don't worry, Reggie. I'll take care of her," Dominic said, an evil grin spreading on his fat, ugly face.

"Like hell you will." *Rat tat tat tat.*

Dominic's facial expression didn't change as he collapsed, like it was frozen in ice. He dropped listlessly to the floor. The only thing that changed was the three perfectly round holes in the side of his head.

As soon as the shots rang out, Reggie whipped out his gun and pointed it toward the deadly shadow where the shots came from. I didn't think. I reacted. Before I could even fathom the thought, Kate's gun was in my hand. I pointed the gun at Reggie and fired. The recoil pushed me back, but I barely noticed. I couldn't stop firing. This needed to be over. I needed it over. Screams filled the room.

"Megan! Megan! STOP! He's dead. It's okay. Stop!" someone shouted. I could barely hear over the ringing in my ears and the screams that were still echoing in the room. My screams. I turned my gaze to the voice. Tommy stood beside me with his hands out, reaching for the gun. My hands quaked, and my body started to heave. Tommy bent down to me. Terror and fear filled his face.

"Tommy?" I asked helplessly. The chaos that had

erupted after Reggie went down was beyond deafening. Tommy gathered me in his arms and carried me outside. Once I was placed on the ledge of the ambulance, I broke down. My body shook violently. I didn't know what to feel. Relief, shock, fear, guilt all washed over me. I couldn't form a coherent sentence. I just listened to him whisper to me that everything was going to be okay.

"Where's Mom?" I cried out frantically as I wrestled my way out of his arms.

His arms tightened around me and softly said, "She's fine. Rick has her safe and they are waiting for us at the hospital."

I nodded, then tears formed in my eyes when I thought of the bloody mess inside. "Kate. Oh my God! Kate! Is she okay?"

Tommy shook his head sadly. "I don't know. She's in really bad shape, Megs." My heart broke and the tears became sobs. Kate, a woman that I had despised based simply on my own insecurities and ignorance, had become a good friend. A friend who saved my life, whose own now hung in the balance. *I will never be able to thank her properly.*

Tommy put me in the ambulance and sent me on my way. He had to stay behind to write up the report and go over evidence, but he promised to stop by. Although I knew the threat was gone, I wished that he had come with me. I didn't know how to process everything that had happened.

***

MY KEVLAR VEST CAME off in the ambulance. When I arrived at the county hospital Mom rushed over and grabbed my hand, tears streaming down her face. "Thank the Lord that you're okay! We saw the accident and Rick turned us around and we went another way. I wanted to come back to you," she said frantically, her hands running over my face and arms.

"Mom, I'm okay," I whispered. She hurried alongside the gurney as they pushed me into the emergency room. A gentle-looking elderly nurse was waiting for me, a clipboard in hand. Another nurse ushered my mother beyond the curtain, stating that they needed to check me out and that she had forms to fill out. The nurse helped me out of my bloodstained clothes and into a thin gown.

A fetal heart rate monitor immediately went around my waist. The galloping thump of the baby's heart raised my spirits. Aside from a bruised rib and cuts in my hand from the glass, I was alright. I was safe. My baby was safe. My family was safe. *The only thing missing is Shane.* As much as my heart was broken, I couldn't cry. I wasn't ready. My head told me he was dead, but my heart wouldn't let me believe it. *When I see his body, when I see him laid out in the casket, that is when I will believe it. But until then, I will hold on to the mere sliver of hope that he made it.* I had too much to process. I needed to separate everything that had happened. I needed to deal with the profound emotion of putting a bullet in someone's body, of killing someone. I needed to deal with the insanity that had encompassed my life for the last month. I needed to heal.

My mom came back in, sliding the curtain behind her. "How are you doing, baby cakes?" she asked gently, pushing back a lock of my hair.

I gave a plaintive cry. "Mom, I want to go home. Take me home."

EPILOGUE

OCTOBER IS MY FAVORITE time of the year. The sting of the summer heat makes way for cooler temperatures. The leaves change color. Apples are plentiful and pumpkin spice flavored pastries and drinks make their way into the stores.

After leaving the hospital with a clean bill of health back in July, Rick drove the dogs, my mother, and me back to her house where we were met by Uncle Bob and Aunt Karen. The cartel had been losing its footing in the drug trade for a while and the death of Reggie sparked a drug war between them. The possibility of someone coming after me was slim and the threat had diminished enough that our protection detail was no longer required. But that didn't stop Kyle, Adrian,

Ryan, and the rest of the guys from watching over us. It stayed that way for about two weeks, when Mom pushed everyone out. I stayed with her for a month as I tried to mentally heal. But staying with my mother, as much as I love her, was stifling. I felt constricted, so Penny and I moved back home. The first thing I did was open the windows. The house had been closed up for two months and it was time to do some airing out.

Letting everything air out also meant filling in Adrian and the rest of the guys on the truth of Eric's and Shane's deaths. The shock was mine when Adrian pulled me aside and told me what he knew.

"Megs. I was the only one who knew what was going on. I helped Tommy out by giving the feds permission to wiretap the garage, where a lot of deals went down. I was trying to help Shane and Eric. I knew Shane wanted to straighten his life out, and I hoped that if Eric got busted, it would scare him straight. But it didn't end the way we wanted it to," Adrian said sadly. I could see this giant monster of a man starting to crumble.

I threw my arms around him and whispered. "I don't blame you. Does Rachel understand?"

"No. She left me as soon as I told her. I doubt she'll ever forgive me." Another casualty of this mess, the repercussions of which will go on for a long time.

I didn't go back to work until mid-September. I

needed time to mentally prepare myself. I didn't deal with things very well in the beginning. A lot of sleepless nights, nightmares and paranoia. My roller-coaster emotions exploded against the unpredictability of my pregnancy hormones and I was a mess. At the advice of my mom and Kyle, I started seeing a therapist, someone I could vent to without hurting anyone's feelings. Someone who could help me work through and explain the wide range of emotions that I felt. Someone who would listen without judgment.

I slowly came back. I felt more and more like a normal person as time went on. My mom went with me to doctor appointments and shopped with me for the nursery. She was there when the sonogram technician said, "You're having a girl." Her name is Katie Louise Turner. No doubt about that.

Nights were the hardest. As the baby grew and she began keeping me up at night with the kicking and the dancing on my bladder, I thought of Shane. I thought of him missing this. He didn't get to feel her first kick. He wasn't there when we got the sonogram. He wasn't there to help pick out the perfect lavender and pink for her bedroom. But I knew that he was with us in spirit.

Kate's condition improved gradually. After a month at the Shock Trauma Center in Baltimore, she transferred to a hospital closer to her home base in Florida. Kate eventually recovered enough to go back to work, albeit in a desk job position. She hated not being in the thick of the madness and was eager to be medically cleared for field duty. We kept in contact through Facebook and Skype. She was a great help to me and my state of mind. I confided in her and she understood the issues and turmoil the situation caused.

Tommy stuck around and helped me heal as well. After all, this was part of his job. I could never understand how he dealt with such things on a regular basis. When I asked him about it, he said dryly, "Meg, this is not an everyday occurrence. I'm mostly doing wiretaps and surveillance. Gun fights? Not as often as you might think."

After everything settled down, he took some time off. He helped me put together the nursery and paint the walls. Tommy was there for me, more than any other time in our relationship. It felt good to have someone know and understand what I was going through. But then, Tommy took it a step too far. One night, we were sitting on the couch watching an old movie when I felt Katie kick for the first time. Elated, I grabbed Tommy's hand. I held it over my stomach as the little bump kicked again. He looked at me with such amazement.

"Megs…I know I'm not her father, but I could be her daddy. You don't have to do this alone. I could make you both so happy," Tommy whispered. I barely heard him over the loud beating of my heart. I knew what it took for him to utter those words. However, my feelings for Shane were still too strong. Shane was her daddy; I couldn't allow anyone else to fill that role.

"Tommy, as much as I appreciate everything you have done, and as close as we have become, I have to say no. You're a part of her family, of our family. We wouldn't be here without you. But, I can't admit that Shane's gone. I even refused to have a memorial service because I can't grasp it. Shane's her Daddy and I never want to take that away from her," I said, as gently as I could.

The sadness in his eyes pained me, but I couldn't let him go any further. Soon after that, he stopped coming around as often. The bureau had him going back and forth between Florida and New York. We still talk everyday, but our conversations are strained. I turned to other family members for support. I started talking to people more. I joined Jen for dinner and played with Lauren. She was tickled that I was having a baby. Although in her little three-year-old mind, she was confused about Shane not being there. Jen explained it to her, but Lauren still brought it up from time to time.

Kyle and Sarah's wedding was held on a beautiful Saturday at a historic mill located in Savage Mill,

Maryland. The ceremony and reception were amazing. No detail had been left out. Sarah was as excited as I was about my pregnancy, and she picked out a new beautiful cranberry gown with an empire waist that obliged my protruding belly. I was so excited for her. The love that radiated between Kyle and Sarah was infectious, but soul crushing at the same time. I missed Shane so much. The pain of losing him crashed down on me at the reception, and so I begged off early and went home.

At two in the morning, the dancing queen in my belly decided that my bladder was her favorite dance spot. After several trips to the bathroom, she was still wiggling, as if trying to get comfortable. I couldn't sleep. My thoughts kept drifting to Shane. A truck's engine downshifted to just an idle in front of the house. Because of the previous events, I peeked outside as my paranoia took hold. A black SUV idled in front of my neighbor's house as a man got out. I assumed that it was my neighbor's husband just getting home from a night out. I climbed back into bed.

With my belly, it was difficult to find a comfortable sleeping position. Suddenly, I heard a noise downstairs. Penny, the useful guard dog that she is, started barking excitedly.

BANG BANG BANG.

What the hell? A familiar grip of fear clenched my stomach, but I forced myself to relax. There hadn't been any sign of Reggie's crew lately, and with Halloween in two weeks I was sure it was just teenagers acting stupid. I threw my cotton bathrobe over my T-shirt and shorts, grabbed my brother's baseball bat and, as stealthily as I could for a woman who was six months pregnant, crept down the stairs. I peered through the kitchen window and didn't see anything, only rain. Curiosity burned through me. I knew it was stupid, but I opened the door to check outside. Nothing. Trembling, I walked down the driveway just as the squeal of tires on wet pavement pierced the night. Tears mixed with rain as disappointment engulfed me. I had hoped—no, prayed—that Shane would be waiting for me.

But he wasn't, and now I was soaking wet, watching brake lights fade in the distance. I hung my head and walked up the driveway. A shadow emerged from the carport. I could barely see through the rain, but the light from the carport was enough to shine on those beautiful hazel eyes.

My stomach flew into knots and my heart swelled. I let out the breath I had been holding for God only knew how long and whispered the name I'd been dying to say. "Shane."

ACKNOWLEDGEMENTS

I couldn't have done this without the support of my family and friends.

Brian—you were at the end of my broken road. Thank you for your love, your support, and your encouragement. I am so lucky to have found such an understanding and loving husband. I love you so much.

To my team – Carla, Cassy and Emma - Thank you!! Thank you for your patience, your hard work, your humor. You're amazing. You're freaking rock stars. xoxo

Fallon and J—this book wouldn't have happened without the two of you pushing me. Your suggestions and your input were always right on point. Thank you for reading all my rough drafts, the odd ball plot outlines, and helping me with my writer's block. I am so grateful to have you helping me. This story would not have gotten this far without you both. Thank you from the bottom of my heart.

William and James – Thank you SO much for letting me use that badass image and for supporting me! It was great working with you both. Next time I'm in AZ, drinks are on me.

To all my family, friends, M&M mommas, co-workers and strangers who let me drone on and on and on about the book—thank you for listening and being interested (or at least pretending to care!!!). I love you all.

And finally—to all my readers. Thank you for your love, your support, your enthusiasm! This is all for you!

ABOUT THE AUTHOR

Melissa grew up in Maryland by the Chesapeake Bay, where her favorite memories took place near the water. Now she lives near Washington, D.C. with her family, dog, and a lot of fish. In between the chaos of laundry, chasing after her three children and trying not to burn dinner, Melissa continues to find her escape by feeding her addiction of reading and writing about love, suspense, and humor.

Melissa loves to hear from readers! She can be contacted at:

Email — melissa@melissahuie.com
Website — www.melissahuie.com
Twitter — www.twitter.com/melissahuie
Facebook — www.facebook.com/melissadhuie
Goodreads — www.goodreads.com/melissa_huie

94249779R00183